# A Queen's Fate

## BOOK 2 OF THE CROWNING SERIES

### Nattie Kate Mason

Cover illustration and design by Beth Gilbert
Interior illustrations by Creativeqube Design Studio

Copy editor: Chloe Hodge
Series: The Crowning, Book 2

To my precious daughter Lily,
I love you more than all the stars in the sky.
You inspire me every day.
Never be afraid to follow your dreams.
Anything is possible if you just believe in yourself.

To my husband Joel,
Thank you for always being there for me.
A life without you is unimaginable.
You are my person, my fate.

Hattie Kate Mason

# A Brief Overview of the Realm

Summarized by Sir Quinton Thompson,
Member of the Alearian Scholar Brotherhood

Alearia:

Alearia is a mountainous alpine Kingdom blanketed in snow six months of the year. The city proper is among the tall old oak trees. The noble's homes are situated around the city centre and leading up to the castle which is on the peak of Mount Alearia. On the other side of the castle is a thick mountainous forest.

On the castle grounds, a hedge maze surrounds a century-old rose garden, gazebo and water fountain. Surrounding the entire grounds is a stone wall. The royal family crypt is situated on the far side of the castle just before the wall and gate leading to the oak forest. The castle is made of sandstone and has multiple high towers, suite balconies and elaborate archways. There is a stable behind the castle, alongside a large training arena that is open to the public only on special occasions such as the Crowning Ceremonies.

On the outskirts of the city proper are the peasants' farms and cottages, nestled among the mountain range. The cemetery is on the lower outskirts of the city proper below the river, which acts as the city's main water supply. There are watchtowers surrounding the Alearian mountain ranges; a day's travel from the edge of the city proper, and about half a day's travel between posts.

Farming communities are scattered throughout the Alearian plains to the east of the mountain ranges extending to the border of Quillencia.

Watchtowers are situated at regular intervals along the northern border between Alearia and Shadows Peak, and to the south along the border between Alearia and Stanthorpe.

Quillencia:

      In Quillencia, scattered around the countryside are various towns and villages. Lavender Grove, Blackberry Hill, and Two Peaks are situated near the Alearian and Quillencian border. The Black Lands River runs through these towns with several water channels flowing into this river. Half a day's travel on foot from Lavender Grove is the Quillencian Falls, and surrounding the falls and nearby villages are the Rosewater Forrest Mountains.

      Upon the peak of Mount Galicia, on the border of Alearia and Quillencia, north of the Quillencian Falls, is the Home Temple of the Goddess. A sacred spring rises from the mountain's peak where the Priestesses collect all their water to complete their anointings.

      The Quillencian City proper, is a peaceful city, where the notion of class was eradicated approximately fifty years ago. This modern way of thinking, however, has not yet reached the regional towns where nobles still oversee the smaller towns and villages. This Kingdom has prided itself on its united people, who each have a vital, valued role to play in their communities.

      Castle Caston is located within the Quillencian City proper. The Quillencian City proper is a beautiful city, with the Turpentine River flowing through it and out to the sea. The Quillencian royals have a love of luxury, but compared to other castles, they appear quite modest. Their giftings are mostly of the mind: i.e. sage wisdom/mind conquerors.

Shadows Peak:

Shadows Peak is situated to the north of Alearia. The residences of Shadows Peak city are built into the mountains with a castle on the highest peak also built into the mountainside. The terrain consists of tall, closely gathered mountain ranges, leaving the Kingdom perpetually shrouded in shadow, cloud and darkness, hence the Kingdom's name, Shadows Peak.

The Kingdom's inner workings are mysterious, their people are mostly gifted shadow walkers or wind whisperers. This Kingdom closely guards its secrets and extraordinarily little is known by outsiders of its history due to its tight security and isolation.

Stanthorpe:

Stanthorpe is situated to the south of Alearia. Mostly consisting of fire-wielders, the residents are a very practical, no-fuss, primal people. They place great value on their lands and the development of a strong, physical Legion force.

The terrain consists of grassy plains with expansive training camps and farms scattered throughout. The Stanthorpe Legion is land based with mandatory male conscription into the Legion at the age of sixteen, except for apprentice farmers, blacksmiths, and carpenters.

All females are conscripted into the care services attending to the Legion's cooking, cleaning, laundry and apothecary treatments. Their castle and Stanthorpe city proper could be best described as a strong, impenetrable fort.

# A Queen's Fate

Isle of Treseme:

A small island Kingdom to the south-east of Alearia. The Isle of Treseme has the most impressive naval fleet anyone has ever seen. Their people are mostly gifted water mages and wind whisperers.

The Kingdom climate is perpetually tropical, their terrain rather flat. No walls surround the city proper or the open planned, colosseum-like palace. The people of the Isle of Treseme view their remote location and surrounding oceans as protection enough.

The people of the Isle are harmonious; their lifestyle much more relaxed than the other Kingdoms of the realm. The royal house of Ocea has ruled over their Kingdom for over three centuries — the longest period in recorded history.

# Day Seven of the Crowning Ceremony

## Princess Anastasia

Soft falling snow blanketed the Alearian castle grounds beautifully. Icicles hung suspended from the castle archways and ornate balcony railings like a scene out of a fairy tale. The sun rose over the mountainous Kingdom of Alearia, bringing with its gorgeous light a promise of a new Heir to be crowned, and a fresh start for the Kingdom. After so much devastation in the previous year, the royal family hoped that a new crowned Heir would help to restore hope and direction for the Kingdom's people.

Anastasia awoke that morning with new resolve in her heart. After a restless night's sleep, the Princess knew deep within her soul what she must do to set things right.

With the help of her Lady's Maid, she dressed in her preferred lavender day dress for family breakfast; her hair arranged in a simple bun atop her head. Anastasia insisted to her family, that she take a walk after breakfast to calm her nerves before today's main event. She assured her Lady's Maid that she would return afterwards to formerly dress and be groomed for the Crowning Ceremony.

The Princess chose a pair of simple rabbit fur-lined boots to wear beneath her gown, which she knew would allow her to walk silently around the castle without drawing attention to herself.

After attending family breakfast, Anastasia thanked her parents for the wonderful meal and bid them farewell, as she would not see them again until the ceremony was underway. She meandered through the castle corridors, heading for the family's private temple, under the guise that she wanted to beseech the Goddess for blessings upon the day.

*'Keep calm, keep smiling, or else they will suspect me. It's a simple plan, all I need to do is follow it. Breathe. I can do this. I must do this. I have already lost one sibling and a grandfather. Agnes and I have never been close but it's not right that she should be sentenced to death because her powers seduced and corrupted her. If I never see her again, it will mean I have succeeded in saving her life. I must stay calm.*

*'Thank the Goddess for Annie's soothing tea. Without it there is no way I would have the confidence right now to carry out my plan…*

*'But what if I am caught? What if the King and Queen discover it was me? They have sentenced one child to death, they could just as easily do the same to me. No one is above the law,'* Anastasia thought as she tried to work through her mixed emotions.

*'Anastasia, focus! Almost there... Just a couple more corners...'*

Anastasia rounded the final corridor corner, slowing her pace as she approached the entrance to the Goddess's temple and calmly opened the hand-crafted wooden doors. Various images of the Goddess were carved elegantly into the centuries-old oak. Anastasia approached the temple dais reverently, and dropped to her knees atop one of the silk cushions to pray.

*'Please Goddess, I beseech you for protection this morning. If it is your will that Agnes is freed today, let everything go smoothly. Let no one get in my way.'*

After a few deep breaths, Anastasia rose. Certain she was alone, she crept on silent feet in the dimly lit temple and knocked on the concealed door to the priestess's quarters on the far side of the chapel. To Anastasia's surprise, the door slid open to reveal one of the priestesses-in-training, Helena.

Anastasia masked her shock with a serenely painted smile across her face. Helena was not the brightest of the priestesses, but if she suspected anything amiss, the Princess feared she would be judged accordingly.

"I am sorry to bother you Priestess Helena; I came to the temple to beseech the Holy Goddess for blessing upon today's Crowning Ceremony. Whilst I was in prayer, a tremendous idea occurred to me. Could you please visit each of my sisters this morning to bestow upon them a blessing? I am sure it would help alleviate any anxiety they are feeling towards today's announcement," Anastasia requested sweetly.

The Princess knew it would be considered improper of the low-ranking priestess to refuse or question her request.

"Certainly, Princess Anastasia," Helena responded keenly with a shallow curtsy, "it would be my honor. I must get going right away or else I will not have enough time to visit each of the Princesses before the ceremony begins."

"That would be greatly appreciated, thank you Helena. I will remain here for a little longer to pray. But please go right ahead. I would hate to hold you up from such an important task," Anastasia offered sweetly.

The priestess-in-training appeared slightly more flustered by the Princess's request. "I'm afraid that's not proper Princess. I have always been told that a Priestess must remain in the temple at all times whilst a royal is in attendance."

"Oh, I am sorry, I wasn't aware of that rule. I am sure it will not be a problem. Our relationship with the Goddess should always come first, is that not correct? Go ahead and attend to my sisters. I promise I will leave in a few minutes, and if it worries you that much, it will be our little secret. Also, Helena, I would hate to embarrass my sisters, so please don't tell them it was my idea for you to visit them," Anastasia concluded sincerely.

"As you wish Princess," Helen replied uncertainly before bowing to the Princess and leaving out the main entrance of the small private temple.

As soon as the temple door closed behind Helena, Anastasia quickly opened the concealed door handle to the Priestess's quarters and walked inside, shutting the door behind her.

The quarters were small; an office of sorts, designed to accommodate one to two priestesses at a time whilst they were rostered on duty. Anastasia was glad that only one priestess was currently on duty in the temple. The other Priestesses would likely be assisting High Priestess Elizabeth with the Crowning Ceremony preparations.

Inside the quaint room was a heavy mahogany desk with two matching chairs. A small chamber pot was hidden in the corner behind the two cots set up for the priestesses during the night shift, to use when their services were not required. Just as Anastasia suspected, the room contained an old oak wardrobe filled with freshly laundered Priestess robes.

Anastasia quickly hitched up the skirt of her day dress and tucked it underneath the bottom of her bone corset, so that the length of the dress would not show beneath the robe that she then donned. After pulling the hood of the robe low over her face, the Princess rapidly chose another long gown, pulled it over the top of her already worn robe, securing it firmly around the front.

*'If I keep my head bowed, hopefully no one will suspect it's me with my hair concealed under the hood.'*

Taking a deep breath and peering in the small mirror on the desk to ensure her appearance was concealed, Anastasia re-opened the door, revealing herself to the Goddess's temple, and instantly froze.

"Hello Anastasia..." Princess Alecia purred, stepping out of the shadows to stand in front of her sister. "You have been busy this morning. What are you up to, playing dress-up? Black really isn't your color, don't you know? You are much more suited to that gorgeous lavender you prefer. It brings out the blue in your eyes," Alecia taunted.

"I'm afraid you are mistaken Princess, I am a new Priestess," Anastasia lied weakly, dropping into a curtsy before attempting to walk around her sister towards the entrance to the temple. Anastasia had never had a skill for deception.

"Don't be so stupid Anastasia!" Alecia growled, pulling the hoods off Anastasia's head, revealing her face. "Do not mistake me for a fool. Surely you are not going to do what I think you are? You will get yourself killed! Why waste your life on someone who doesn't deserve your compassion! Besides... you don't have it in you to carry out such a plan," Alecia fumed.

*'Of all the people in the castle... Seriously Goddess!'*

"I am only doing what is right sister!" Anastasia replied through gritted teeth. "Agnes may be horrible, but she is still our sister! She does not deserve to die. Now lower your voice before you give me away."

"For Goddess's sake Anastasia, see reason! She tried to kill me, she threatened to kill all of us and yet you want to save her? Wake up to yourself Anastasia! Agnes is a dead weight that needs to be severed from our family before she brings our good name any more shame," Alecia fumed.

"Be that as it may, I could not live with myself if I did not try to help her. I promise, once I have set her free, she is on her own. I will wipe my hands clean of her. But I need to do this, or I will regret it for the rest of my life. Alecia, please don't get in my way," Anastasia begged.

"For Goddess's sake, if you are determined to carry on with this idiotic plan then I will join you. I cannot stand to see that traitor set free, but I could not live with myself if you were caught. You are the closest family I have in this damned castle," Alecia begrudgingly declared as she shoved Anastasia out of the way, pushed open the Priestess room door and dressed in her own robe.

Both Princesses pulled the hoods down tightly over their faces to conceal their identities.

"Now keep your head down, do not say a word, and follow me. I don't trust you to not give us away," Alecia growled in disapproval as Anastasia nodded her head profusely.

# Princess Annalyse

It had been several weeks since Princess Annalyse Brandistone, had been crowned Heir and future Queen of Alearia. The people of Alearia were conflicted in their feelings regarding the young Princess's appointment of the prestigious title. In just one short year, tradition dictated that Princess Annalyse would ascend the throne as Queen of Alearia, at the young age of seventeen.

The people questioned how a Quillencian-raised healer could be deemed fit enough to rule the Kingdom in such a short period of time. The current King and Queen of Alearia had done their best to assuage the people's fears. Annalyse was present, front and center at all royal events, and taught the ways of ruling a Kingdom firsthand.

The overnight transformation of Annie's life had been both overwhelming and exhilarating. Princess Annalyse felt fortunate and blessed to be crowned Heir of the Kingdom of Alearia. Though, she struggled to come to terms with her new life and responsibilities. From apprentice healer to future Queen, would certainly be an overwhelming change for any young woman.

*The present day.*

The first rays of light were barely peaking over the horizon of the snow-capped mountains of Alearia, as Annie awoke to a loud knock on her palace suite door. Princess Annalyse's newly appointed Lady's Maid, Ruth, a middle-aged woman dressed in the customary baby blue dress uniform and white apron, drew back the curtains surrounding Annie's golden four-posted bed. Candles around the room had been lit, allowing soft light to flood the chamber.

Ruth quickly re-stoked the fire in the suite's hearth, whilst Annalyse drowsily sat up in bed. The sleep deprivation was slowly starting to eat away at Annie's normally patient demeanor. Regular late nights in training for her future role as Queen, and early morning preparations each day meant that the young Princess was only able to secure a few hours' sleep a night.

*'I'm not sure how much longer I can go on like this,'* Annie thought dismally to herself. *'It is an honor to be chosen as Alearia's future Queen, however, if each day continues like this, I will burn out before I even assume the throne.'*

"Good morning Princess Annalyse," Lady Ruth greeted the Heir after returning to her bedside. "I will prepare your bathing chamber for you whilst you drink your tonic," Lady Ruth hinted, gesturing towards the small bottle of amber colored liquid she had left on Annalyse's bedside table the night before.

Annie nodded her head reluctantly in agreement as the Lady's Maid made her way into the bathing chamber to prepare her bath.

The tonic, Annie had been told, was designed to enhance her fertility. The Queen Mother, Amealiana had gently warned Annie that shortly after being crowned Heir, it was expected she would marry and soon afterwards produce future potential Heirs to ensure the family bloodline carried on.

The thought of becoming a mother at such a young age horrified Annie, and therefore she had actively been avoiding taking the viscous, nauseating, nightly tonic as prescribed by the castle's Head Healer.

'*When I feel ready, I will bear a child and not a moment before. It's times like these that I wonder if Anastasia should have been crowned Heir. My twin dearly wishes to be a mother and she would have no concerns about marrying a stranger and beginning a family of her own.*

'*Surely the King and Queen will permit me to at least choose my future husband. I will not be shackled to someone all my life if I do not love them,*' Annie thought forlornly.

Annie knew it was only a matter of time before the Queen broached the subject again. With Annie's coronation a mere eleven months away, she was sure that the search for her future husband would inevitably begin sooner rather than later.

Lady Ruth walked gracefully from the bathing chamber, the room now exuding the strong scent of lavender oil, reminding Annie strongly of her dear former mentor. Lady Lilliana, an incredibly gifted healer, had courageously given her own life to bring Annie back from near death.

'*I miss you, Lily. There isn't a day that goes by where I do not wish you were here with me. My only wish is that the Goddess had granted us more time together,'* Annie thought to herself as a tear silently fell down her cheek.

Annie felt the tears rise in her more easily these days. The emotional highs and lows of learning to rule an unfamiliar Kingdom, and the lack of sleep compounded by the grief she endured from the loss of her mentor, left the young Princess in a constant emotional state.

After taking a deep consoling breath, Annie slid herself out of bed and picked up the vial of tonic from the bedside table. Removing the glass stopper from the vial, the scent of lavender was quickly overcome by the strong smell of liquorice root. In one quick swig, Annie drank the oily, unpleasant concoction before discarding the vial and making her way to the clawfoot bathtub.

It was customary for a Lady's Maid to assist with a Princess's every need. However, Annie still enjoyed her own independence and solitude, so she gently shut the bathing chamber door behind her and locked it securely. Annie liked Lady Ruth — she just didn't agree with a Lady's Maid being forced upon her just because she was crowned Heir and it was suddenly considered improper for her not to have one.

Annie released a sigh of relief at once again being alone, and without hesitation, threw off her night clothes and enjoyed the blissfully hot lavender-scented bath.

Without warning, the door to the bathing chamber started to groan as an unknown identity began hacking at the wooden door. Splintered wood fell to the ground on the inside of the chamber as the intruder made quick work of destroying the door's lock and surrounding wood, prying open the door.

Annalyse released a horrified scream as she jumped out of the bath, wrapping her night gown around herself, water pooling on the floor around her.

The intruder, dressed in black training leathers and a cape, stalked menacingly through the doorway carrying a hatchet. No doubt a cache of other weapons hidden beneath his cloak. Bloody boot prints followed the stranger along the polished wooden floor, as he slowly stalked towards Annie.

Beyond the doorway, Annie caught a glimpse of her Lady's Maid sprawled out on the floor in her bedroom, blood pooling around her from what appeared to be a stab wound to her abdomen. All life and color had drained from her face.

Annie stood shivering in shock in the corner of the bathing chamber as the assailant approached her. Before Annie could react, the intruder slammed the blunt end of the hatchet into the side of her head and she crumpled to the ground.

## Agnes

Agnes paced impatiently around the confined sitting room of a farmer's cottage on the outskirts of the Alearian city proper.

*'Curse this decrepit hole of a place. I am sick to death of living in filth whilst my family live in their luxurious castle. I caught a lucky break when my naive sisters came to my rescue. Of course, I had no intention of walking to my death. I would have found a way out of the dungeon myself. Gullible Anastasia and Alecia just made my job of escaping easier.*

*'I can be merciful… When I exact my revenge upon my ungrateful, backstabbing family, I may spare them both my wrath… As for that condescending long lost sister of mine, she will pay the highest. That piece*

of Quillencian trash stole my crown, my title, and my life. If I can't be Queen, then neither can she.

I'm not a mind conqueror or fire-wielder anymore, but I don't need a gifting to destroy their lives. I am a weapon both physically and mentally.

'Once Annie is delivered to me, I will make her pay for ruining my life. My family don't stand a chance against me. I will eliminate them all, starting with their precious Annie.

'I will take over the Kingdom and rule as is my Goddess deigned destiny.'

## 3

# *Princess Anastasia*

In the early hours of the morning, Princess Anastasia casually strolled down the empty castle corridors towards her twin's bedroom. Every morning since the Crowning Ceremony, Anastasia had made a habit of escorting her sister down to family breakfast in a show of support for her younger sister's new position. Anastasia knew the adjustment to her new title as Heir was hard for Annie. Anastasia was therefore determined to support her in any way she could.

Anastasia felt light as a feather, as time revealed that no one suspected her or Alecia of releasing Agnes from the dungeon. As far as Anastasia knew, no one had seen or heard of her eldest sibling since her escape, though the city guards were actively on the hunt for her.

For the first time in a long time, Anastasia felt as though a weight had been lifted from her shoulders. She no longer felt under pressure to compete for the crown, and had escaped conviction for the crime of freeing her sister.

Rounding the final corner of the royal family's private wing, dressed in her favorite lavender day dress, Anastasia approached the door to Annalyse's suite. She knocked gently on the carved oak door, awaiting her invitation to enter.

Before the Crowning Ceremony had taken place, Annie had refused to have a Lady's Maid and had always answered the door herself, which Anastasia had found both amusing and refreshing. Since Lady Ruth had been appointed to serve Annie, Anastasia felt less welcome when knocking on her twin's door. If she was quite honest, Lady Ruth intimidated her, though Annie reassured her sister that the Lady's Maid had a sweet disposition hidden beneath her Matron-like demeanor.

Anastasia, however, was less than convinced. She had a strong inkling that the Lady's Maid intimidated most people with her direct, no-nonsense, authoritative manner. After waiting an unusually long time for the Lady's Maid to answer the door, Anastasia gave up on protocol and opened the door herself to her sibling's suite.

Upon entering the royal suite, Anastasia felt her intuition kick into action as she noted the eerie silence of the usually bustling suite at this time of the morning. Anastasia, a well-trained warrior and fire wielder, became acutely aware of her surroundings and shrunk to the shadows of the room. She noted the broken furniture and tousled bed linen on the floor of the usually pristine suite.

"Holy Goddess!" Anastasia swore under her breath, fully absorbing the picture in front of her and laying eyes upon the Lady's Maid sprawled across the floor in front of the bathing chamber.

Abandoning all precaution, Anastasia ran to Lady Ruth's aid, searching for any signs of life, but sadly found none. The Matron had lost too much blood and her skin felt ice cold; her eyes staring vacantly into the distance.

The Princess gently closed Lady Ruth's eyes before adrenaline kicked in and she sounded the castle alarm by ringing the emergency bell in the room, alerting the palace guards of danger. Running into the bathing chamber, she continued searching for Annie and noticed the bloody boot prints all over the floor, and what appeared to be a blood splatter trailing down the far wall. With no sign of Annie's body, Anastasia assumed she had been abducted.

The fire-wielding Princess took a moment to examine the situation, searching for clues as to where the intruder may have taken her twin. Anastasia prayed that wherever she was, Annie was still alive.

*'Best case scenario, Annie has been taken hostage, and the King and Queen of Alearia will pay a handsome ransom for the safe return of their Heir. Worst case scenario, something more sinister is afoot… Where could they have taken her? How did they escape without raising an alarm?'*

Walking out of the bathing chamber, Anastasia noticed blood spots along the floor and followed them like a trail of breadcrumbs. The path led towards the hidden passageway behind her mother's portrait.

Anastasia flung open the concealed door and began to sprint down the passageway, lighting a flame from her hand to guide her way. Reaching the bottom of the stone stairs, Anastasia followed the corridor which she knew led to an emergency underground evacuation passageway.

Rounding a corner ahead of her, Anastasia caught a glimpse of the intruder carrying the motionless Heir over their shoulder. Anastasia threw a wall of fire across the ceiling, hoping to stun the intruder into dropping her sister, but onwards he continued to flee.

In hot pursuit, Anastasia unsheathed the dagger she kept strapped beneath her dress before throwing the weapon towards her prey, aiming it towards his thigh but missing by a hair's breadth. The assailant stopped in his tracks, threw Annie to the ground, raised the hatchet he had been holding in his other hand and hurtled it towards Anastasia. The warrior Princess quickly deflected the weapon with a fling of her fire, but when he flung a dagger towards her immediately afterwards, it found its mark in her right shoulder. Anastasia bellowed a sharp, painful scream.

An unfamiliar feeling stirred in her soul, and she released a wave of radiating fire straight into her attacker. The assailant counteracted her fire wall with a shield of water, turning Anastasia's fire to mist. The urge to protect and save her sister built up inside her chest, and Anastasia lunged towards the intruder, ignoring the pain in her shoulder. But instead of striking him with her hands, great big claws wrapped around his neck.

The intruder was forced to the ground, the weight of Anastasia's beast-like form pinning him firmly in place, blood pouring from his pierced carotid artery, all color and life drained from his body.

Anastasia caught a glimpse of herself in the reflection of a puddle; a giant mountain cat with her same blue eyes stared straight back at her. Anastasia froze in shock by the sight of her transformation and failed to hear the approaching guard until it was too late. Struck from behind, a sword ploughed through her chest and the world faded into oblivion. In her final moments, all Anastasia could think of was her twin lying lifelessly, just out of arms reach.

# Princess Annalyse

Annie awoke in the castle infirmary, her head pounding. She felt like her body had been hit by a herd of wild animals. Annie slowly opened her bleary eyes; the light from the bedside candles enraging her migraine. Resting her head on the bed beside Annie, Queen Amealiana awoke from a fitful sleep.

"You're awake!" Amealiana gasped, pain written across her face, her eyes red and puffy from endless tears. "Oh, my poor precious child, I was afraid I would lose you both."

Confusion clouded Annie's head as she looked around in bewilderment, unable to absorb the words her mother had just spoken. Pulling herself slowly into a sitting position, a wave of nausea overcame her, and she instantly regretted her decision. It was then that she first saw her.

Her precious twin lay lifeless on a bed beside her, a bouquet of roses placed upon her chest. Annie leapt from her bed, and ignoring the pain from her head injury, she hurtled herself on unsteady legs towards her twin. A heartbroken rasp escaped her as Annie crawled into bed beside her beloved sister, tears silently pouring down her face.

"Don't leave me Tash, we only just found each other. I can't go on without you. You need to come back to me," Annie begged her twin.

Her heart and soul's energy drained away into her twin like the radiating light of a candle flooding the darkness. She felt the bond between her and her loved one regenerating slowly, and that was when she realized what she had done. Trying to picture her spirit radiating towards her twin once more, and focusing on the bond between them, Annie projected her healing thoughts upon her twin and felt her own body's lifeforce depleting in the process.

"Stop!" Queen Amealiana screamed, realizing what was occurring. "Stop, Annie! This could kill you as well! You cannot save her Annie, the risk is too great," Amealiana begged her whilst attempting to wrench her away from her dead twin.

But the Heir held on firm, and shot out her mind conqueror powers towards Anastasia, as well as her newly awakened healing powers passed on from her former mentor. Annie reignited every brain cell in her twin's frail mind; her healing powers replenishing her twin's blood supply and stitching up the gaping wound in Anastasia's back. With a roar of pain, Annie gave all she could to help save her sibling before falling unconscious beside her, drained of all energy, her arm still draped across her sister's body. Annie appeared as though she had aged by at least a decade.

Magic always has a price.

# Queen Amealiana

Queen Amealiana held her precious daughters, shielding them from the world. Offering the one thing that no one else could — the love of a mother, as her beloved twins lay heartbreakingly lifeless beneath her.

"Help! We need a healer! Save my daughters, please!" Queen Amealiana begged to the healers now rushing into the royal infirmary suite to offer their assistance.

The royal infirmary's Head Healer, accompanied by one of her apprentice healers, gently pried Queen Amealiana away from her daughters before quickly lifting Annie and placing her gently back on her own hospital bed.

The Head Healer quickly assessed the Heir. Satisfied that Annie was still alive and merely in a deep restorative sleep, the healer turned to look back at Anastasia across the room. She was astounded to see signs of life in the formerly pronounced dead Princess.

The irregular, slow, shallow rise and fall of Anastasia's chest and slight color that had returned to her cheeks, had the healer running back to the fire-wielder's side. She placed her hands firmly over the young Princess's heart and pumped healing energy into her body, electrifying her heart back into a regular, steady rhythm. The healing apprentice, mirroring the senior healer's actions, held the young Princess's hand and shared the load of the healing with her mentor, sending her gifting's energy into the fragile young woman.

The infirmary was comfortably warm thanks to the blazing fire in the suite's hearth, however, the Queen's heart felt frozen, suspended in time as she anxiously waited to find out if one or both of her blessed children would survive the ordeal. Margarette, the Queen's Lady's Maid, assisted the Queen into a chair between her two daughters' beds and took her position beside her, holding the Queen's hand gently in support.

Princess Anastasia's wooden bed groaned as the Head Healer and apprentice leaned more of their weight on the bed, struggling to maintain the intensity of their healing magic blazing into the fire-wielder.

Princess Alecia burst into the room and rushed to Anastasia's side, taking her free hand in her own and demanding to know what happened. Terror filled her eyes as she beheld the lifesaving measures the two healers were taking to save her beloved sister.

The bond that Alecia and Anastasia shared was like no-other. Bonded at a young age through their fire-wielding training, the girls had depended on each other all their life. In the last year their family had seen more heartbreak than most would experience in a lifetime. Alecia uncharacteristically began begging the Goddess to save her precious sister. Shocked and bewildered by all that was taking place, she clung to the hope that her precious fire-wielding sister would survive.

"We have done all we can," the Head Healer regretfully revealed as she collapsed after some time, bone-weary, into a chair beside the Queen.

Heaving deep breaths, she let her eyes rest for a moment, attempting to recover from the energy she had just exhausted while completing Annie's healing work. The healer apprentice quietly excused herself, and on swaying feet, stumbled out of the room in search of a place to rest.

The room felt as though everyone was waiting with bated breath. Queen Amealiana, holding vigil by her daughters' sides, petitioned the Goddess in prayer, her voice cracking with each heartfelt word.

"Blessed Goddess bring my daughters back to me," she prayed. "Save Anastasia and revive my precious Annie. I could not live without either of them in my lives. My heart cannot take any more loss. Holy Goddess, please, save my daughters. I already feared that I had lost Anastasia once today, do not let Annie and the healers' sacrifices go in vain. If it means that they will live, take me instead".

Tears poured from the Queen's eyes. Holding tightly to her twin daughters' hands, she continued to pray with all her heart.

"If a soul must be taken into the After World as payment for their lives, allow me to pay the debt," Amealiana begged. "They have so much to live for, their lives have just begun. Please Goddess, I beg you, with all my shattered heart and soul, heal my daughters."

# Princess Annalyse

The air felt thick and muggy, which was unusual for a cold winter's night. The hearth was burning, the candles were lit, and the two wooden beds in the infirmary had been pushed together to allow the twins to heal side by side.

Annie slowly opened her eyes, allowing her vision to adjust to the low lighting. Turning her head to the side, she felt Anastasia's warm hand in her own and released a sigh of relief. Her chest ached from the deep exhalation.

*'Apparently healing others is detrimental to your own health,'* Annie joked internally, softly smiling.

"Hey big sister," Annie yawned at her twin. "How are you?"

"Grateful to see you awake," Anastasia sighed. "What in the Goddess happened? I was halfway to the After World when I felt you tugging on my soul. How did you save my life?" Anastasia asked in awe of her sister.

Annie looked deep into her twin's eyes, warmth and relief filling her heart.

"I'm not really sure... My mind and heart wanted nothing more than to save you. I couldn't be separated from you so soon, not after we have only just been reunited. I have a feeling that when Lily saved my life, her last spark of healing gifting was passed on to me and that's how I could save you. I doubt I could heal anyone like that ever again. I can't feel that spark inside me anymore," Annie sighed. "But that doesn't matter. What matters is that you are alive, and we are together again. Promise me you will never scare me like that again. I remember during a moment of semi-consciousness that you came to my rescue. Anastasia, you transformed into the most beautiful, strong mountain cat I have ever seen. How in the Goddess's name did you do that?!"

"I don't know," Anastasia replied honestly, and a look of bewilderment crossed her face.

"I wanted to save you," Anastasia explained. "The water mage who kidnapped you rendered my fire-wielding powers useless. I tried to stab him with the dagger I always keep on me, but I missed. Then my natural instincts just took over. I lunged for him and suddenly my hands were replaced by paws and claws. I wasn't going to let another sibling be taken from me. I have lost too many people I love already. I wasn't going to lose you too. I love you Annie. You are the other half of my soul. You are my twin. I have lost you once, I can't lose you again," Anastasia spoke from her heart.

A gentle knock at the door, followed by a healer entering the room, drew the two sisters from their reunion.

"Pardon my interruption Princesses" the young healer spoke whilst gently falling into a curtsy. "The King and Queen are here to see you."

"Thank you, miss, please show them in," Anastasia gently replied.

"As you wish, my Princess," the healer replied with a respectful nod, opening the door for the Alearian rulers to enter.

"Presenting their Royal Majesties, Queen Amealiana and King Titian," the healer formerly introduced.

"Thank you, Emily, but enough with the formalities. My girls, how are you?" The King asked, masking his concern with his usual stoic tone.

"I am as well as can be expected, thank you Father," Anastasia replied, pulling herself up with a wince.

"What happened my darlings?" The Queen asked with great concern, rushing over to give both of her twin daughters a warm embrace.

"Hello Mother and Father, it is so good to see you," Annie croaked, pulling herself up alongside her sister, leaning against the headboard for additional support.

"I think Anastasia can tell you more than I can. I practically slept through the whole drama," Annie attempted to joke.

"I would hardly call your near-death experience and Anastasia's actual death a '*little bit of drama*'," King Titian chided the Heir, completely unamused. "An intruder broke into our castle and tried to abduct you. Now is not the time to make jokes." The King roared.

Annie released a sigh. "But we didn't die. We are both alive and safe and that is all that matters," Annie groaned exasperatedly.

The Queen rose from her position on the bed next to her daughters to comfort her husband by his side.

"I think what our Heir is trying to say is, now is not the time for questioning. Let's allow the Princesses time to rest and we can talk about this in the morning," Amealiana tried to reason.

"Very well," the King relented, "but don't think for one second I am letting this go. Guards will be posted inside this room all night and wherever you go to afterwards, until I can figure out who was behind this dreadful attack. Mark my words, if I find any link between the attack and Agnes, I will hunt her down myself. I will personally kill her where she stands for the pain she continues to inflict upon our family!"

The Queen gave her husband a gentle hug before taking his hand and guiding him over to his daughters' bedside so that he could embrace them. The gesture seemed out of place; the male Royal was not known for displaying his affection, though he swallowed his pride and gently hugged each of his daughters briefly. A gesture which touched the young ladies' hearts.

The King slowly exhaled a breath and bid his daughters goodnight before whispering into Anastasia's ear: "I am so proud of you my daughter. I am so proud to not only call you my fire-wielding daughter but also my shape-shifting prodigy. You are a true gift from the Goddess for our people."

Anastasia offered a small smile in thanks, no doubt feeling at a loss for words, taken aback by the rare praise she had received.

"Goodnight my darling daughters," Queen Amealiana farewelled her children, pressing a kiss to each of their cheeks before leading her husband arm-in-arm out of the room to allow the Princesses the rest they needed.

*'Praise the Goddess that we are both alive,'* Annie thought to herself as she gently lay back down, Anastasia following her lead, before taking hold of each other's hands and falling into a blissful deep sleep.

*6*

*Agnes*

Just past the edge of the city proper, in a small farmer's cottage, Agnes paced in frustration. The stone, two-bedroom cottage usually housed a family of three. The family's main form of income came from hunting; selling the pelts and meat off at market. This was supplemented with the meagre healer's wage that the commoner's wife, Antoinette, earned as a castle healer.

Antoinette sat upright in a sturdy wooden dining chair, her hands bound tightly behind her back, dried tears tracked down her face. Her right eye shone with a fresh mottled bruise from Agnes's most recent assault. Her hair hung unkempt and her uniform was filthy and bloodstained from spending hours tending to Princess Anastasia's wounds before she was deemed beyond saving. Her care had been taken over by the Head Healer and new apprentice.

The couple's ten-year-old son usually attended school during the day whilst his mother worked in the castle, but was presently locked in the single bedroom as Agnes's hostage.

"Your beloved husband has disappointed me Antoinette," Agnes drawled. "One small task I set him, and he could not even achieve that. Such poetic injustice that he was murdered by the Princess you tried so desperately to save. All the while, you were completely unaware that it was your dear beloved husband who was behind the attack."

Agnes crouched to menacingly whisper in the healer's ear. Antoinette flinched at her closeness.

"How does it feel to know that he was so brutally murdered, several floors beneath you in the castle, whilst you attended to your daily healer duties completely unaware?" Agnes taunted rhetorically.

"The whole city is on high alert," Agnes continued, straightening once more to her full over-bearing height, "trying to find answers regarding your husband's traitorous ways. You can thank the Goddess that his identity remains unknown or else your time would have run out too. The problem I have now… Is that with more guards on duty, it makes it even more difficult for me to move around the city undetected. Since your husband has failed me, that only leaves you to carry out my plans. That is, if you want your precious child to live."

Antoinette's eyes flared at the threat. Agnes pulled up a chair in front of the healer so she could stare at her directly in the eyes.

"But I will be merciful," Agnes scoffed. "If you deliver me the Heir of Alearia alive, I will leave you in peace. You will be free to live out your mundane life caring for your son. Though no doubt you will have to relocate to some remote community after your husband's identity is discovered. Of course, without the money brought in from your husband, and working as a healer for a few silver coins a month, I fear you will soon run out of money to feed your precious little son, so your future must seem quite bleak… Any future is better than no future at all though, isn't that right Antoinette?" Agnes smirked, ripping the gag from the middle-aged woman's mouth.

"Please!" The woman pleaded, her voice horse, "let my son go! He has done nothing to harm you. He is just an innocent boy. I will send him away to live with my family, please, just let him go, and I will do anything you want!"

"Now why would I do that," Agnes drawled, "when I can already make you do whatever I want whilst your son remains here? There is no guarantee that once your son is out of the picture, you won't go and do something stupid like reveal my identity to the guards or take your own life… No, I don't think I will be releasing your son. Not until you have carried out my demands."

"Please!" The woman continued to beg, "please release him! He is all that I have left in this world! Without my husband's income we will surely perish. There are hardly any food stores left. If I don't get to the market soon with the little money we have left, we will all starve. Please, he is only a little boy, he has his whole life ahead of him, just let him go!" Antoinette pleaded in between heaving sobs.

"I see you are not yet desperate enough to follow through on my demands if you are so focused on your son, so I shall make a deal with you. If you do not meet my demands by sunset tomorrow night, I will kill your son in front of you. I will make him suffer and then I will make you suffer for failing me. Don't think for one minute about calling out for help. The moment a single palace or city guard arrives at your quaint little home, I will set your home on fire with your child tied up in it. So… I will tell you one last time Antoinette, for my patience is running thin. Bring me the Heir of Alearia, or you and your son will die," Agnes demanded menacingly, her eyes staring straight into the healer's soul.

The healer was now trembling, her body quaking from fear.

"As you wish," the farmer's widow reluctantly agreed.

Agnes released a wicked cackle, severing the binds that held the widow captive and slicing the woman's delicate healer's hands in the process with her dagger. The widow released a small whimper of pain before attempting to compose herself. Steel filled her eyes as her protective motherly instincts took over.

"If you dare harm my precious Arthur, whilst I carry out your dirty work, I will find a way to end you. Goddess damn you!" The healer spat at the former Princess's feet before sprinting from the cabin, heading straight for the city proper.

Agnes smiled to herself with intense satisfaction as she crossed the room and unlocked the boy's bedroom door, which opened with a loud creak.

"Arthur, you may come out now," Agnes cooed at the entrance to the now unlocked bedroom door. "Mother has just gone to the market to gather some food and then we shall have a feast. There is nothing to fear, you are safe here with me," Agnes said gently, incongruent with the nasty smirk she had painted across her face.

The boy lay huddled in a foetal position in the far corner, underneath his single wooden bed frame from where he had heard all that had transpired. Trembling in terror, his eyes squeezed shut, hyperventilating, he fully realised the danger he and his mother were in.

His father was dead, and no-one was coming to save him.

7

## Princess Annalyse

The castle was on edge after the recent attempted abduction. Princess Annalyse, however, was still expected to perform all her duties as Heir; one of the unfortunate realities of being a royal. After two short recovery days, Annie was thrust back into her duties, feeling bone-weary. Her head felt permanently clouded from sleep deprivation, but what uneased Annie the most was that she hardly recognized herself in the mirror.

The healing the Heir had performed upon her twin had aged her appearance significantly, and she had transformed from a sixteen-year-old girl into the body of a woman in her late twenties. Her figure had filled out, and small wrinkles around her eyes had appeared. Everything about her reflection seemed unfamiliar. It would be an adjustment she would have to grow accustomed to. Magic always has a price; her grandfather King Julian had once told her. Evidently, losing years off her own life in exchange for Anastasia's regained life was the cost she would have to pay, but it was a sacrifice she would gladly make again without a second thought.

Unfortunately, the effects of her premature aging left questions regarding her fertility, and therefore her dosage of her daily fertility tonic had been doubled. The pressure to find a husband and produce an Heir was now more pressing than ever.

In the tallest tower of the Alearian castle, Annie stood beside her mother, the crisp mountain breeze ruffling their hair. Soft snowflakes drifted around them. The centuries-old castle was a mix of sandstone and traditional bricks, giving the castle a slight luminescence as the sunlight reflected off the surrounding snow and pale sandstone, outer turret towers.

The Alearian Kingdom was a mountainous rugged land, not for the fainthearted. Nestled upon a mountaintop, the Alearian castle stood proudly, and further down the mountain was the city proper. Scattered among the oaks of old, the city's estates and cottages were situated; sprinkled with white delicate snow.

Annie looked out towards the horizon to watch the sunrise with her mother, dreading the conversation she undoubtedly felt was coming.

"Mother, I do not feel like myself. The person I see in the mirror looks somewhat like me, and sounds like me, but she doesn't feel like me. I do not regret what I have done… But I am afraid. If I cannot feel comfortable in my own skin, how can I feel comfortable with anyone else?" Annie dared voice.

"My dear Princess," Queen Amealiana began, "you are the Heir of our mighty Kingdom. You are strong and you are wise. What you see on the outside does not reflect any of your internal qualities. You are a beautiful young woman. Some of your years may have been taken away from you, but that only saddens me because they are years we will never get back together, and I have already missed so much of your life. Saving Anastasia's life came at great sacrifice and I am eternally in your debt for bringing my beautiful daughter back to me. To see you, Anastasia, and Alecia, alive and well, brings me such joy as a mother. I only wish that I could ensure your safety. To strengthen your position in our Kingdom, you need to ascend the throne. To protect your legacy, you must find a suitable husband to crown King and begin your own journey of starting a family," Amealiana warned.

"Not only does producing an Heir protect our family's legacy," Amealiana continued, "but it also avoids uncertainty for the Kingdom's future. The people need to know that if something were to happen tragically to yourself or your future husband, that someone else will be there to rule Alearia. Above all else though, being a mother is the most rewarding role you will ever fulfil. If I had to choose between motherhood and being Queen, I would always put my children first. I love you all dearly with all my heart. Now, come. It is time we head down to family breakfast. We can talk more over delicious pastries and fruit platters. Sweets always make difficult discussions easier to stomach," Amealiana promised.

"Come on Annie! This will be fun! Think of matchmaking like choosing a meal from a menu that you get to enjoy for the rest of your life!" Anastasia cheekily exclaimed to her sister over family breakfast.

"A man I am expected to live the rest of my life with, no pressure," Annie replied. "And what if I don't like the noble or Prince, or whoever they are? What if they don't like me? What if they hate the smell of my breath in the morning? What if he hates the way I have aged so quickly? There is so much pressure placed on one decision. I always imagined I would marry for love, not out of duty. I grew up in a small town among young men who used to tease me. I don't have any male friends. How am I meant to know how to act around potential suitors?" Annie asked, exasperated.

"Annalyse Brandistone," King Titian fumed. "You are the Heir to our Kingdom, and you will perform your Goddess deigned duty. Marriage in royalty is not about love. It is about alliance, protection, security, and maintaining a strong bloodline," King Titian insisted firmly over his cup of tea.

"My dear Annie, have another pastry," Queen Amealiana offered attempting to smooth over the conversation with the lure of sweet treats. "The King and I only want was is best for you and for Alearia, and that is why we need to start addressing this issue. I am sure your sisters can offer you some advice on courting. The suitors will begin to arrive soon, and it is up to you to decide who becomes our future King. Whoever you choose as your husband is up to you, but the Kingdom will be watching. You have made steady progress in your leadership training, but a large proportion of our Kingdom's people are still unsure about a Quillencian raised healer becoming our next future Queen. It is up to you to prove them wrong," Amealiana insisted.

"Very well, Your Majesties," Annie conceded reluctantly, pausing to indeed take another bite of a raspberry tartlet. "I will meet these suitors. But the idea of marrying a stranger is abominable to me. I will not marry someone I cannot see a future with."

"Oh, give me a break," Princess Alecia drawled from across the table, quiche in hand. "You had the crown handed to you on a silver platter, and you want to throw all of that away because you don't want to marry someone unless it is for love? For Goddess's sake Annalyse, you are rubbing this opportunity in our faces. It is time that you put aside your idealistic small-town values, and start thinking more about what it means to be a ruler. Our people need a strong ruler, not one ruled by their feelings," Alecia stated matter-of-factly.

"I understand that, sister," Annie sighed through gritted teeth. "But I will not change who I am and what I stand for to appease the people. I will gladly give all I have to serve Alearia. I think I have already proven my loyalty time and time again as I heal each of Agnes's mind conqueror victims. I am left exhausted by the end of each day, from doing so. I don't have time for myself, let alone time to court potential suitors. Frankly Alecia, I thought we had moved past this sibling jealousy after I appointed you the next leader of the Alearian Legion Army," Annie said frustratedly.

Alecia slammed her glass of juice down on the table in front of her, the contents spilling over the sides.

"For Goddess's sake Annalyse, did you really think you could buy my loyalty with a title?" Alecia stood from her chair and bellowed, "I am not some cheap trophy. I have thanked you time and time again for returning my gifting to me, but at the end of the day if you refuse to satisfy your role as Queen, then I will gladly take your place. Our people need a strong leader they can rely upon."

"Right, ladies," the King interjected, attempting to restore peace. "Before we start any matchmaking, I need Annalyse and Anastasia to report to the infirmary for a health review with the healers. I want to make sure that you are both as fit and healthy as possible. We must all be at our best in this coming year before Annalyse ascends the throne. After their health review, we will meet in the war council chamber to review our plan to re-capture Agnes. I am sure that she is behind the recent attack and whilst she is still at large in the community, no one is safe," the King declared. "Alecia, as our future Army General, I need you to be front and center, leading this meeting. I want your opinion on all tactical matters from this point onwards."

"Very well Your Majesty," Alecia proudly agreed. "At least someone takes my experience seriously," she mumbled under her breath.

"Your Majesty," Anastasia requested, "would it be possible to schedule some training time with you? I am aware that you are extremely busy, but I would like to train with you in my new shape-shifter gifting if you approve?"

"My daughter, nothing would make me prouder," the King responded, sitting up with renewed vigour. "I am sure we can make the time. It is important that you learn to harness your new gifting. As a matter of fact, given your newfound gifting, I think it is time that we start looking into finding you a suitable husband as well. Your blood is worth bottling, my Princess!" The King exclaimed.

"Pardon me, Your Majesty," Anastasia objected, "but I wish to train my new gifting, that is all! I am sixteen years old. I am not the Heir of Alearia, and I am not ready to be married yet. Please my King, do not send me away just yet, I have only just got to know my twin. I couldn't tolerate being sent away to live the rest of my life with a stranger in another country. I want to live here and train with you," Anastasia pleaded frantically.

"As far as I can tell," the King roared, rising from his seat and slamming his fists on the table, "none of you are mature enough for the responsibilities bestowed upon you. You are not children any longer. The Crowning Ceremony is over. You must all step up and take your royal duties seriously. I am still the King, and I will not tolerate disobedience. If I hear one more ungrateful word or disagreement, I will marry you all off, send you all away and pass on my crown to someone who will put the needs of our people above their own. You are all excused!" The King roared.

Antoinette

The castle grounds were bustling; full of groundsmen tending to the gardens and shovelling the paths clear of snow. The stablemen were out exercising the horses in the surrounding forest.

After running through the city proper and up the mountain towards the main castle gates, Antoinette was exhausted and bedraggled. Heaving deep breaths, she was drenched in sweat beneath her thick white healer's uniform despite the cold winter temperature.

"Help me!" Antoinette panted, banging on the wooden gates of the castle's surrounding wall. "I need to speak with the Head Healer."

A young guard dressed in the House of Brandistone royal colors of red and gold, a solid iron breastplate worn over the top of his guard's uniform, peered through the peephole in the gate.

"The castle is in lockdown. Only essential staff are permitted entrance into the grounds," the guard firmly declared.

"Please Sir, my name is Antoinette. I am one of the castle healers," she replied flashing him her identification paperwork that was thankfully still in her top pocket. "I am rostered on duty today, but I was mugged and assaulted on my way here, so I am terribly late. I need to speak with the Head Healer urgently, or I will surely be punished. Please, I have a clean uniform in the infirmary healer's office to change into, please let me in," Antoinette begged.

"Very well... But clean yourself up as soon as you are inside. After you have finished your shift, I will need to take a statement from you, so your attacker can be identified and held accountable for their actions," the guard instructed her as he began to unlock the multiple complex gate locks. Finally, he pulled the door inwards for the healer to enter.

"Thank you, Sir. As soon as I have finished my shift, I will return to deliver my statement," Antoinette replied with relief. "Thank you for your help kind Sir. Now, I must be going, please excuse me."

Antoinette released a sigh of relief as she began the trek up the main road leading towards the castle building. The healer's head throbbed from dehydration, her body sore and weary.

*'Goddess, guide me, show me what I must do. Help me save my son, Arthur. Please forgive me for my sins. If today is the last day of my life, please welcome me into the After World with loving arms and protect my son until we meet again.'*

Antoinette continued to follow the cobblestone path around the side of the castle, slipping occasionally in the sludgy wet snow, her feet numb from the cold. Many of the groundsmen stopped to stare at her bedraggled appearance. Antoinette glared at them in response.

*'How dare they judge me. The Goddess knows what I have been through. If only the world knew too and instead of judging me, they would rush to offer me their assistance.*

*'I am the Goddess's vessel for healing, but to keep my son alive, I will do anything. He is my world. Without him in it, I would have no reason to exist. As soon as I have done what needs to be done, I will pack our things and we will flee Alearia. Together, Arthur and I will travel abroad and start a new life.'*

The healer clung to the small sliver of hope that she would be reunited again with her son. Approaching the staff service entrance, Antoinette removed a bronze key from her side pocket, thankful that the key had not fallen out during her torture at the hands of Agnes.

Gently turning the key in the lock, she pushed the door open and held her breath; anxiety and panic stirring in her chest. Antoinette made her way through the main service corridor. Keeping her head down to avoid making eye contact with anyone else, the healer took the first right turn and followed the next corridor all the way to the end.

Antoinette crept through the back entrance to the infirmary office, locating the spare uniform wardrobe and quickly changing her clothes in the designated healers' bathing chamber, her bones and muscles aching with every movement. The healer quickly disposed of her dirty uniform in the laundry basket, and went over to the supplies closet where she knew the enchanted ointments were kept.

Antoinette knew it was a waste of resources to use the enchanted ointments for personal gain, but as she was unable to heal herself, she had no choice. If she entered the infirmary with her black eye, she would only raise suspicion, so she quickly snatched the cream she needed and rubbed it vigorously around the affected area on her face. The bruising and swelling disappeared in a matter of moments. After taking a comb from the store cupboard, she brushed out her matted hair before tying it up in a bun and securely pinned a clean starched healer's bonnet in place.

Taking a deep breath to calm herself, Antoinette peered into one of the bathing chambers mirrors. Staring back at her was a new woman. It was as though the past few days had been erased from her body entirely, thanks to the healing ointment. Antoinette still appeared weary but for all intents and purposes, she looked like a woman who was frazzled from being late for her shift, rather than someone on a devious mission for Alearia's most wanted fugitive.

The Head Healer walked into the room and stopped abruptly, taking in the sight of her missing healer.

"Antoinette! What a relief it is to see you. We missed you yesterday. Where have you been? If you were sick you should have sent word of your intended absence. I was dreadfully worried about you after you attended to Princess Anastasia's care, to no avail. I was worried you were blaming yourself for the young Princesses death, but I have some terrific news!" The Head Healer cried.

Antoinette turned to the healer matriarch, a surprised look upon her face.

"I apologize for my absence, Head Healer. Please, what is your news?"

"Princess Anastasia and Princess Annalyse are both alive, praise the Goddess!" The Head Healer exclaimed. "It is a long story, but Princess Annalyse saved her twin. It is a Goddess given miracle. I have never in all my years seen anything like it. Both Princesses are just about to come in for their health reviews. Would you like to assist me? Perhaps it would help to bring you some closure, to see the Princesses alive and well," she suggested.

Conflicting feelings rushed through Antoinette's heart, but she attempted to hide her inner turmoil and painted a fake smile across her face. She felt like a lion being handed her prey, as her conscience fought a battle between what was right and wrong.

"Praise the Goddess. I would be honored to assist you," Antoinette replied, her mission to save her son's life, winning over her internal debate.

"Thank you for the opportunity Matron. You are right, I have been blaming myself for Princess Anastasia's passing. I should have sent word of my absence. Praise the Goddess that she is alive," Antoinette responded.

"Very well, come with me," the Head Healer offered.

Antoinette followed the Matron from the healers' bathing chamber into the main infirmary and through the last doors into the royal infirmary suite. Awaiting inside the doors to the suite were two palace guards.

"Excuse me gentlemen, but the Princesses will need their privacy for their assessments. I am afraid I will have to ask you to wait outside," Antoinette stated authoritatively.

"I apologize healer," the senior guard responded, "but we are under strict orders not to let the Princesses out of our sight. It is protocol while the castle is in lockdown. I am sure you understand."

"Very well," Antoinette replied, "but please turn around so that the royals may at least have the illusion of privacy," Antoinette granted.

The Matron chuckled at her response.

*'How on earth am I possibly going to carry out Agnes's plan with two guards supervising my every move?'*

Antoinette took a deep breath before walking into the royal infirmary suite. Princesses Anastasia and Annalyse were waiting in chairs beside the two infirmary beds.

"Your Majesties," Antoinette and the Matron said together whilst curtseying before the royals.

"Arise," Princess Annalyse responded, taking the lead.

Anastasia nodded her head in acknowledgement of the two healers.

"We were advised to attend for a health review today," Princess Annalyse explained, "but I assure you, we are both well. There is no need to waste your time on us, when I am sure there are people who need your care far more than we do."

"With all due respect Your Highness, we are here to serve you," the Matron responded. "You are both just as important as all of our other patients. Please allow us to quickly examine you and you may be on your way," the Matron politely requested.

"Very well Matron, thank you for your assistance," Princess Annalyse politely replied.

"Thank you, Your Majesty," the Matron began. "If it would be permissible, I would like to assess you whilst Antoinette, our senior healer, examines Princess Anastasia. You see, Antoinette was the first on the scene to attend to both of your injuries as she was on duty at the time. Unfortunately, until now she thought that Princess Anastasia had sadly passed away and was relieved to find out that was not the case."

"Thank you so much for trying to save my life Antoinette, that means the world to me," Anastasia responded sincerely. "I cannot explain how miraculous it is that I came to live again, other than I felt my sister tugging on my soul, and I knew my time in this Kingdom was not over. For helping to heal my sister, Princess Annalyse, I am eternally in your debt, for if she were not healed, I certainly wouldn't be here today. Thank you, from the bottom of my heart," Princess Anastasia spoke earnestly.

"Agreed. Thank you, Antoinette, for all you tried to do for my sister and for helping to heal me too," Annie responded. "You are a true hero. In fact, all the healers that bestowed their healing gift upon us are heroes to me. I was unable to complete my sister's healing and if it were not for you, I am told Matron, then my sister might not be with us today. Thank you both for the roles you played," Princess Annalyse thanked the healers.

"You are very welcome Your Highness, you honor us with your praise," the Matron responded with a warm smile. "Princess Annalyse, if you would kindly please follow me, I will examine you in one of our other private infirmary rooms," the Matron requested.

Annalyse nodded her head in acknowledgement and began to follow the Matron. Antoinette hesitated for a moment, fear creeping once more to the forefront of her mind.

*'Holy Goddess, how am I possibly going to carry on with my mission for Agnes now…'*

"Forgive me Matron," Antoinette hesitantly interrupted the Head Healer as she was exiting the room. Under hushed tones she whispered shakily, "Matron, I know this is unorthodox, but do you mind if I assess the future Queen instead? I feel uneasy caring for Princess Anastasia after losing her so recently. I would feel much more reassured if you examined her yourself."

"Sister Antoinette, you need to tackle your fear head on," the Head Healer said firmly. "If you do not care for Princess Anastasia today, that fear will continue to fester inside of you. If you are not able to carry out your duties, I am afraid you will be reassigned to another healer's post," the Matron firmly cautioned the senior healer.

Antoinette reluctantly nodded in understanding before mumbling her apologies and returning to Princess Anastasia's bedside.

*'What am I to do now? I must save my son, but I have lost my only opportunity to see to the Heir on her own. Perhaps Agnes would accept Princess Anastasia instead? Surely one Princess is just as valuable as the other…'*

With the Princess's permission, the healer began her ministrations.

# Princess Anastasia

The infirmary room felt sterile; the usual bedspreads had all been discarded and replaced with plain white linen. Anastasia noted the blood-stained wooden bed frame and the varnish that had started to rub away, presumably from the intensive cleaning process following the twins' previous admission.

Princess Anastasia hated the infirmary. She hated the feeling of constantly being examined. As a Princess, she was used to having a level of authority. As a patient she felt as if all power was stripped from her, and a sense of vulnerability plagued her.

In the past year, Anastasia had spent more time in the royal infirmary suite than most. Between her reoccurring anxiety attacks, visiting her sisters during their admissions, and then most recently returning from the dead in this very room, likely on this very bed, being in the infirmary made the hairs crawl on Anastasia's arm.

*'I need to get out of here. This room holds far too many ghosts from my past. I have only just begun to feel comfortable in my own skin. I cannot afford to regress again. A short assessment, that is all that needs to be done and I can get out of here. I can do this, I just need to breathe,'* Anastasia attempted to reassure herself, but her intuition told her that something was not right.

Anastasia couldn't explain why this feeling of dread plagued her, and therefore put it down to general anxiety from being back in the infirmary.

"Healer Antoinette, I would like to thank you again for your previous care of my sister and me. However, I feel fine today. There is no need to concern yourself with assessing me. I will be on my way now," Anastasia stated, abruptly standing up from the bed and beginning to leave the room.

"Just a moment Your Highness," Antoinette interrupted the young royal. "You seem tense. May I make you a cup of tea to help calm your nerves? The Matron would be upset with me if I let you leave without assessment. It is no trouble at all, I assure you," Antoinette reassured her.

"Very well," Princess Anastasia reluctantly agreed. "Please bring me some tea and then we may begin."

"Certainly, Your Highness," Antoinette responded, curtseying and leaving the room in the direction of the healers' office.

*'Goddess, bless me, relieve this anxiety, help me to move on from my experiences and not associate this room with such dread and disdain. I know everyone believes I have overcome my struggles with anxiety and a lot of the time I have. I felt such relief when I wasn't crowned Heir. I expected to feel dissatisfied, but I couldn't be happier for Annie. She will do wondrous*

*things for Alearia, she just needs me to teach her our Alearian ways and customs and she will fit in perfectly.*

*'Today's anxiety is a completely rational response after everything that I have been through. I am still me. I can feel however I need to feel, to process through these emotions in whatever way works best for me. Healing has no time limit. Please Goddess, just help me through today.'*

While Anastasia waited patiently for her tea, she practiced her deep breathing relaxation techniques with closed eyes. She tried to distract herself by making a list of suitable potential suitors for her twin, sadly the list was not very long.

"Thank you for your patience, Princess," Antoinette stated, drawing the Princess from her thoughts as she walked purposefully back into the room, carrying a silver tray with a small tea service. The healer gently placed the tray on the bedside table before pouring the royal a cup of soothing tea. Anastasia eagerly sipped it, feeling her nerves float away on a cloud of fog.

"Antoinette, can you please assess me as quickly as possible? I am feeling a little lightheaded. I suspect it is just anxiety. I hate being in here, but I would like to go and lie down if that is ok?" Anastasia asked, suddenly slurring her words.

*'Whatever was in that tea is a lot stronger than I am used to,'* Anastasia thought drowsily to herself with a slight tinge of concern. However, the soothing properties of the tea quickly eased her worries.

"In fact, I might just lie down for a moment, if you don't mind…" Anastasia slurred as she crumpled onto her bed, falling into a deep sleep.

# Antoinette

A mixture of guilt and hope fought a battle in Antoinette's mind. The sedative had acted far more quickly than the healer had anticipated, but she had brewed the tonic much stronger than usual to bide her some more time.

"Guard," Antoinette called out calmly.

The guard posted beside the door came quickly over to the Princess's bedside. "Is everything alright Healer?" The guard asked uncertainly as he beheld the unconscious Princess lying in front of him.

"Everything is fine," Antoinette warmly reassured the guard. "The Princess was feeling anxious, so I gave her a sedative to help calm her and she is now in a restorative sleep. Can you please carry the Princess to her room? She needs a long rest and she will be much more comfortable in her own bed. I will monitor her while she sleeps," the healer directed the guard.

"Very well Healer…" the guard replied sceptically, "but once she is safely in her bed, I will remain outside her bedroom suite at all times. My number one priority is the Princess's safety and she is at her most vulnerable whilst asleep," the guard firmly concluded.

"Of course, Sir! The health, wellbeing and safety of the Princess comes first. That is why I will remain by her side."

"Very well," the guard responded, leaning over and gently scooping the sleeping Princess into his arms and carrying her gallantly to her suite.

'Goddess forgive me for what I must do.'

# 10

# Princess Annalyse

Annalyse's examination had been conducted quickly. The young Heir had made a remarkable recovery since her recent incident. The Matron confirmed to Annie that she had in fact aged approximately 10-15 years through saving her twin's life. A sacrifice she would willingly make again.

For her twin, there is nothing she wouldn't do. Having family had brought a new depth of fulfillment to her life. Having been raised as an orphan, Annalyse counted every new day with her family as a blessing.

After the examination was complete, Annie walked back into the main royal infirmary room to re-join her twin, only to find the room empty.

*'Anastasia must have completed her assessment earlier than anticipated. How strange that she did not wait for me... Though she probably didn't*

*want to be in here one moment longer than absolutely necessary.'* Annie sighed and reluctantly made her way up to the war council room.

The war council chamber was a secluded room, hidden down a secret passageway leading from the throne room. It was the beating heart of the castle, and maps of the Alearian Kingdom and surrounding Kingdoms were hung around the brick walls. Alearia had been at peace for many years now, but since Annalyse had been crowned Heir, uncertainty was plaguing the Kingdom, and with uncertainty often comes unrest.

King Titian, as always, sat at the head of the war room table on his throne. Queen Amealiana sat calmly to his left and Annalyse assumed her newly appointed place to his right.

The room was typically cold as there was no hearth, however, King Titian suspended multiple small flames around the room, blissfully warming the chamber to a cosy temperature. Unfortunately, on days when the conversation became more heated, his flames would often reflect his mood and flare up in response. Once, the General lost his eyebrows when he questioned the King's decision on a matter of security protocol... An accident of course, but the King had only recently resumed suspending his flames around the room during meetings.

"Thank you for meeting today everyone," the King said.

Annie looked around the room. All the usual members of the council were present except for Anastasia, though Annalyse suspected that she had likely gone to rest after her examination. Annie knew the infirmary made her twin anxious, and cursed herself for not going to check on her sister before attending the meeting.

"As you all know, there was a recent attack on the castle," the King recalled. "We highly suspect the traitor, Agnes, was behind it. I have guards combing through the city proper, searching door by door for any information on her possible whereabouts. Unfortunately, as we were unable to question the intruder prior to his justified death, we cannot yet confirm a link to Agnes. We are still unable to identify the man. However, the guards are also showing a sketch of the intruder as they door-knock, in the hopes that we can glean more information from the public," the King continued. "Alecia, as future General of the Alearian Legion, how do you propose we speed up the process of finding the traitor, and what new security measures do you propose we put in place to ensure everyone's safety?"

"My King," Princess Alecia began, "I have begun planning the new training schedule for the Kingdom's people with Your Majesty's permission. The Alearian people will be offered up to two training sessions per week in their gifting. The schedule will be posted on the city notice boards, and citizens may attend as they are able. Sessions will begin at the end of Spring."

"More training translates to stronger giftings and better defense of our Kingdom," Alecia reiterated. "For those particularly gifted in defensive and offensive magic, they will be offered the opportunity to join the Alearian Legion. However, many citizens with elemental giftings, such as water mages and fire-wielders, are already valued members of the community contributing to crop growth, fire management and emergency services, and they will need to remain in those valued roles."

The King nodded his head approvingly, gesturing for Alecia to continue.

"Those not blessed with offensive or defensive magic, such as the sage gifted, healers, and non-magically gifted community," Alecia continued, "will be offered combat training instead, so that they too will be able to defend themselves. Thankfully, as mind-conqueror giftings are no longer a threat to the people now that Agnes's mind conqueror gifting has been eliminated — thanks to the brave Quillencian King's sacrifice — we do not need to train the people to defend themselves against mind attacks," Alecia spoke confidently.

"As you all are no doubt aware," Alecia continued, "based on recent reports that have come in from our under-cover palace guards, discord is stirring among the Goddess's temples around the Kingdom. It seems that the High Priestess, despite her supportive front at the Crowning Ceremony, has been whispering treasonous gossip in her subjects' ears. The church does not seem convinced that Annalyse's appointment was the will of the Goddess, and its acolytes are trying to garner public support to their side. It is in my opinion that we will need to monitor the temples more closely. I feel that it is in the Kingdom's best interest that we squash this problem before it becomes a real issue. Therefore," Alecia declared, turning to face the entrance sentries, "guards, can you please show our guest in?"

Confusion filled the King and Queen's faces, which they attempted to mask with little success as High Priestess Elizabeth was escorted into the room and directed into the remaining spare chair around the table beside Princess Annalyse.

Annie shifted uncomfortably in her place at the turn of events. She had never been fond of the High Priestess or her uncanny ability to stir trouble during the Crowning Ceremony rituals. The personal attacks she had launched upon each of the Princesses during their final ritual revealed the Priestess's true nature, and the young Heir did not trust her in the slightest.

"Your Majesties," High Priestess Elizabeth said, dropping into a shallow curtsy before taking her seat. "What a pleasure it is to have received your invitation to the war council meeting. There are many issues I would like to raise, and I am grateful to be given this opportunity."

The King and Queen of Alearia briefly made knowing eye contact with each other before masking their faces and posture into the picture of authority.

"Greetings, High Priestess," King Titian stoically replied.

"Welcome High Priestess Elizabeth, what a pleasure it is to have you with us today," Queen Amealiana attempted to welcome her subject more sincerely.

"Thank you for accepting my invitation, High Priestess," Princess Alecia interjected, standing from her seat and taking the lead in the conversation.

Alecia directed her attention towards the religious matriarch, who was now seated across from her. Inhaling deeply and drawing herself to her full height, head held high, the future Alearian Legion leader began.

"Prior to your arrival, High Priestess," Alecia recapped for her, "I was detailing to the council my plans to introduce gifting training for our people, with the additional option to undertake combat training for those with non-defensive type giftings, and for the non-gifted. This new program will teach the people how to defend themselves, which is a valuable skill for anyone to possess," Princess Alecia summarized.

"Quite right Princess Alecia. This is especially vital as it has become clear that our leaders may not be as capable of protecting our people as they once were," High Priestess Elizabeth spoke boldly.

The King stood from his chair and slammed his fists on the table before reigning in his temper.

Through clenched teeth, he seethed, "are you accusing your rulers of failing to protect their people? Because surely a member of the church would not question her Goddess appointed rulers?"

The High Priestess mocked shock, raising her hand to her chest, "I would never question *you*, Your Majesty. I am merely communicating the concerns of your people. Given the recent '*Magical Disease*' caused by a former royal, and then the war council's failure to capture the escapee, the people are beginning to question their rulers' abilities to keep them safe. Particularly the future Queen, given her lack of *experience* in the area."

Queen Amealiana laid a gentle hand upon her King's arm in reassurance, before standing beside him as a sign of unity.

"Our people," Queen Amealiana strongly and sincerely voiced, "are as always, our number one priority. We have guards searching every inch of this city for Agnes, and sooner or later we will find her, and she will be held accountable for her actions. As for the risk to safety that she poses to the Kingdom, without her powers we will not see a repeat of the *magical disease*, you can be assured."

"With all due respect Your Majesties, surely the recent attempted abduction of our *potential* future Queen demonstrates ongoing safety concerns," the High Priestess alleged. "Perhaps it was Agnes, or perhaps it is the people's way of showing their disapproval of the recently appointed Heir... Either way, the people need a leader who can protect them. If Princess Annalyse cannot even protect herself from an intruder, what hope does she have of protecting Alearia?"

"There is nothing *potential* about Annalyse's future ascension to the throne," the King declared. "She will be crowned our next Queen and you, High Priestess, will fall in line and support her, or I will have no choice but to charge you with treason. As for her inability to protect herself, Princess Annalyse has been progressing well in her combat training as well as her mind-conqueror training. The trespasser caught our Heir off guard and rendered her unconscious before she was able to defend herself. Princess Anastasia was able to save her life and Annie in turn saved Anastasia's," the King concluded proudly.

The High Priestess smiled sweetly in response as she continued to spit her poisonous accusations. "How fortunate we are that Princess Anastasia, even with her *challenges,* was able to rescue her twin."

Princess Alecia and the King glared at the High Priestess's sly criticism.

"Even more fortunate," Elizabeth continued, "is the newly awakened second gifting of Princess Anastasia. Perhaps her newfound confidence and newly awakened gifting suggests that the Goddess may not agree with the newly appointed Heir?"

"So, this is the rubbish you have been spreading among my people?" the King stated. "You openly admit that you do not agree with Princess Annalyse being crowned Heir!"

"I have said no such thing, Your Highness," the High Priestess meekly replied, a small smirk across her face. "I am merely pointing out that the evidence suggests the Goddess may disagree with the Princess's appointment. As High Priestess, I would not be performing my duty if I did not raise these concerns on the Goddess's behalf."

*'Goddess above, this is the last thing we need right now. I am finding it hard enough to learn my duties as future Queen. How am I meant to win over the temple as well… Think Annie… What can I do to help ensure the High Priestess's support? Ah ha!'* Annie snapped her fingers in delight.

Annie straightened in her chair and turned to face the scheming woman sitting beside her.

"High Priestess, thank you for raising your concerns," Annie responded. "My greatest desire is to serve the Goddess and our people. You are wise in all matters. I have learned much from our current rulers, the King and Queen of Alearia, in terms of what is involved in the day to day running of our Kingdom. In order to better understand my peoples' needs and the views of our sacred Goddess, I wish to work with you over the coming months, in regular weekly meetings, so I may receive feedback from yourself and the temple. At such meetings, we may discuss the best interests of our people and work towards strengthening the relationship between the royal family and the temple. How would you feel about this working partnership High Priestess Elizabeth?" The Alearian Heir confidently proposed.

The High Priestess's smirk grew wider, triumph burning in her stark green eyes.

"Very well, *Princess*," the High Priestess replied coyly, "we shall trial this new partnership, as you call it, and see where it leads."

"Then it is settled," Princess Alecia voiced. "Thank you for your attendance today, High Priestess, we look forward to working more closely with you in the future," she said, abruptly dismissing Elizabeth from the meeting.

"As you wish. Thank you for your time Your Majesties," the High Priestess replied before escorting herself from the War Chamber; a palace guard following closely behind to escort the matriarch from the castle.

"For Goddess's sake!" The King roared once the door was shut securely after the High Priestess's exit. "I cannot stand that woman. She seeks to undermine our family at every turn. Only the Goddess knows what her true intentions are behind spreading such treasonous slander."

"Agreed, my King," Princess Alecia voiced. "You cannot trust her Annalyse. Who knows what schemes she is concocting? Let us hope that we find Agnes soon so we will at least have one less threat to worry about."

Annalyse nodded her head in agreement.

"Now that the meeting is over, I will take your warning under advisement. For now, I think a training session is in order, don't you Alecia?" Annalyse winked at her sister. "I'm sure we could all use a workout after this meeting. I will attend Anastasia's rooms and see if she would like to join us."

"Very well," the King agreed. "Enjoy your training session. Alecia, as soon as you hear any news regarding Agnes, I want to know straight away."

"Certainly, King Titian," the future general replied.

Agnes

Sunset was approaching with no sign of Antoinette or her prize. Agnes sat by the hearth, glass of wine in hand. Antoinette's ten-year-old son, Arthur, was sitting in the opposite chair trying to make himself appear as small as possible as he trembled in fear.

The room felt toasty and warm, thanks to the roaring hearth, which was quite a feat considering the limited remaining firewood in the cottage. Agnes knew that the wood stocks were likely meant to have seen the family out until the end of winter, but she did not care. By the end of today, the family would either be on the run, or dead. Neither option required firewood stores, so she frivolously threw another log on the roaring fire.

'I shall miss my time in this quaint little cottage, teasing and torturing these miserable peasants. But after tonight I will be a mind conqueror once more, and I will overthrow my pitiful excuse of a family and claim my rightful place as Queen. Assuming the damned healer does not fail me… Though what better motivation than to have her son held hostage. Arthur, no doubt the light of this woman's world. Without him, she would have no reason to live, so for her sake, I hope that motivates her to move quickly as I am growing impatient of these babysitting duties.

'The boy needs to go. I can smell the urine soiling his pants from over here. What a poor excuse for a young man, shaking like a leaf and saturating himself from fright like an infant. When I was his age, I was already taking up combat training. This boy needs to grow up fast, or he will not survive the coming years ahead. That is, if he lives out the night,' Agnes wickedly thought to herself, whilst indulgently taking another sip of her wine.

'At least the wine stores have not yet run out…'

"Please Miss," Arthur squeaked. "Can I have something to eat or drink? I haven't eaten more than a small bowl of broth in days, and my stomach aches."

Agnes lifted her eyes from her glass of wine to slowly assess her prey. Like an Alearian mountain cat sizing up its next meal.

"So, you do speak," Agnes drawled. "Certainly, I am nothing but merciful. You can eat anything you can find… though the last time I checked the shelves were bare. There is a dead rat in one of the cupboards, perhaps that would sate your appetite," Agnes mischievously taunted the boy. "Your mother will be home soon with some food and if she is not, let us just say, that you won't have to worry about ever feeling hungry again…" She cackled, a wicked grin painted across her face, her teeth gleaming.

The boy's pupils dilated as he fully comprehended the danger that he was in. What he had felt prior was fear. Agnes could tell now, that for likely the first time in his life he realised what it meant to feel terror.

The moon shone overhead, and the town's emergency bells had been chiming loudly throughout the evening. A good omen, Agnes thought to herself. A strong easterly wind was blustering throughout the alps. Snow fell heavily, the combination making visibility in the dead of night near impossible, even with a torch or exceedingly good navigational skills.

Given the current weather conditions, Agnes allowed the healer a little longer before deciding what to do with the boy. Arthur had passed out from fatigue or lack of sustenance a few hours earlier, which made his presence more bearable now that he was unconscious.

*'The only good child is a sleeping child. Honestly, who would want to be a mother...'*

The creaking of the front steps drew Agnes from her thoughts as a moment of anticipation filled her soul. With a loud thump and kick flinging open the front door, in walked the healer carrying what appeared to be a person wrapped in a bundle of linen. Antoinette collapsed to her knees from exhaustion, an unconscious woman falling in a heap on the floor, the linen pulling away from her face to reveal Princess Anastasia.

The loud thud roused Arthur from his deep sleep. Through his bleary eyes, from his position on one of the single sitting room chairs, Arthur beheld his mother. The sight instantly jolted Arthur into alertness as he stumbled quickly over to his mother and collapsed on her lap, throwing his arms around her, heaving tears. Antoinette remained slumped on the floor, her healer's uniform stained in dirt and blood, but Agnes did not care.

"That is not Annalyse!" Agnes shrieked.

# Antoinette

Antoinette threw herself over her son's body protectively. She had no strength left after carrying the sleeping Princess for miles from the castle down to her home. Her journey began down a staff secret passage, carrying the lifeless Princess wrapped in a bundle of linen. Sneaking her out of the castle grounds to make her way back home, the healer dodged guard patrols and avoided the main areas of town to avoid raising more suspicion. She was mentally and physically exhausted, but she vowed to herself that with the last of her strength she would not go down without a fight. She would try to protect her son until her very last breath.

Antoinette shielded her son in her arms from Agnes as much as she could, and from her position still slumped on the ground, the healer raised her head and with her last ounce of bravery declared, "take it or leave it. I have done all I can. Now release me and my son and I swear on the Goddess herself that I will not breathe another word of this. I will take my son and we will leave Alearia and never return."

Agnes tilted her head to the left, then to the right, analyzing the healer. Her mind surely rolling over ways to punish Antoinette for her insolence.

"What happened?" Agnes finally asked with a deathly calm demeanor, and so Antoinette told her story.

# Queen Amealiana

In her palace suite, the Queen sat in stunned silence as Annie revealed that her twin was missing. An alert had soon after sounded around the city, and all available non-essential guards were ordered out on patrols to search the castle and city proper for any sign of the missing Princess. Alecia herself took charge and led one of the city's search parties, desperate to find her closely bonded sister.

The Queen sprang into action, sprinting to her daughter's room, followed by Lady Margarette, in search of a beloved item of the Princess that she could use to help trigger a vision of the Princess's whereabouts. Skimming through the Princess's wardrobe and snatching one of Anastasia's preferred lavender day dresses, the Queen held it up to her face and inhaled the blessed lingering scent of her darling daughter.

"Goddess I beseech thee. Please holy one, reveal to me the whereabouts of my beloved Anastasia. I have lost her once this week, I will not lose her again," Queen Amealiana vowed.

Clutching the soft material of the dress, the Queen focused her concentration on the item and the scent of her daughter that flowed from the garment. Her vision clouded over as her Goddess given prophetic gifting began to reveal a vision to her.

*Anastasia was tied to a double wooden bed with thick chains stretching both her arms and legs taught. The room was dark; a single candle shining on the bedside table. The wind howled against the small glass window frame.*

*Agnes stood over her captive sister and dumped bucket after bucket of mushy snow over the barely conscious, moaning Princess… Presumedly to hinder her fire-wielding gifting. Superficial wounds could be seen along the Princess's mostly bare legs and arms. Her soaked dress clung to her body, making the Princess appear even more frail and thin than usual.*

Anastasia was a warrior in her own right, though many people often forgot that, but the vision Queen Amealiana saw was of a woman who had little left to give — of a young woman who, despite all odds, and all that she had previously survived, was now struggling to hold on.

Anastasia appeared as though she could take no more. As though she had finally been defeated. The Queen's heart broke at the image of her suffering beloved daughter. Queen Amealiana focused on the vision once more despite the pain it caused her to look for any identifying factors that may help to locate her daughter.

*In the vision, Agnes turned to face the Queen as though she expected her to be present as she declared: "If you want to see your precious Anastasia alive again, absolve me of all my crimes and bring me Annalyse. I will not kill either of your precious twins if you do as I say. We have unfinished business, Annalyse and I,"* Agnes cackled. *"Bring her to the graveyard tomorrow at sunrise. Only you and your pathetic Heir may come. If I see any signs of palace guards or any of the other family, you will never see your precious Anastasia again."* The vision faded before Amealiana's eyes.

"Holy Goddess! That clever little witch is using my visions to communicate. Is there no limit to her cruelty? Margarette, summon Annalyse and Alecia to my chambers immediately, and tell no one else. We have plans to make," Queen Amealiana shuddered.

# *Princess Anastasia*

Anastasia lay helplessly on the bed. Whatever tonic the healer had given her, had neutralized her giftings in addition to rendering her unconscious. Anastasia struggled to recall how she had come to be in this room. Neither did she know how she had acquired the wounds to her limbs that stung when kissed by the snow that Agnes ritualistically threw over her, to ensure that her powers remained nullified.

The sheets felt ice cold from the frequent drenching. An unfamiliar sensation for the fire-wielding Princess. During an earlier moment of consciousness, Anastasia recalled seeing the healer cower in the corner of the bedroom, huddled over who she presumed was her son.

The next time she roused to consciousness the woman and her child were gone, a trail of blood left in their wake. Anastasia had no idea where they had gone, or if they were still alive, but she would think more about that another time. Now was the time to draw upon her training, to reach deep within and draw out any ounce of courage and strength she possessed. Now was the time to be brave, to survive.

*'If I had access to my powers, I would dry myself and this frigid bed and transform into a creature that could break free of these damned chains. I set Agnes free and this is how she repays me for my mercy. What a fool I was to have thought that my kindness could change her, bring her back to the light, grant her a clean slate.*

*'She is deranged beyond reason. Grandfather was right, the Agnes I knew is gone forever and there is no way for her to come back. Her sanity was exchanged for her frivolous expenditure of her gifting for selfish vengeful purposes. She doesn't deserve the second chance I gave her. This woman, this shell of a human, is not my sister. She is a mad woman, destroyed by her own envy and need for revenge…*

*'I am a warrior; I do not need to rely on my powers to survive. For now, I just need to breathe, resist my building anxiety and look for an opportunity to escape.*

*'I am strong, I am brave. On my darkest days, I will look to the light. Even if today seems hopeless, I know deep down in my fractured soul, that someday soon I will find myself again. I will feel joy again. I will cling to that sliver of hope that each new day brings. I am strong. I will get through this. This is not the end. I will escape.'*

*Agnes*

The snowstorm had died down, and several feet of fresh snow lay in its wake. The moon was high in the still overcast night sky. Agnes dressed in the peasants' hunting clothing and a pair of Antoinette's fur-lined rabbit skin boots to help keep out the chill. To avoid identification on her travels, Agnes had smudged soot across her face to help disguise her features. She also tied a thick scarf around the lower half of her face and tugged her hair beneath the hood of the hunter's warm winter coat.

In the wooden cart lay a gagged Princess Anastasia, her hands and feet bound together with metal chains. No matter how much Anastasia tried to scream, only a muffled sound could be heard. Agnes piled several layers of animal furs over the Princess, hiding her from peeping eyes. Agnes hoped the guise of heading off to the morning markets would avoid any suspicion as to why she was out so early in the morning. The first rays of daylight were no-where in sight.

Agnes brought the peasant family's lone horse around from the small side stable. She attached the horse to the cart before assuming her position upon the wooden bench seat. With a whip of the reigns, the horse lurched into a canter, pulling the open top, wooden cart from the farmer's cottage, through the forest and down the snow covered, dirt road around the outskirts of the city proper.

The mountainous Kingdom, coupled with the deep fresh snow, made the trek slow and slippery, the cart threatening to topple if the horse went too fast. Multiple times the cart got caught in the snow and the wheels needed to be dug out, much to Agnes's utter frustration.

Deciding that the cover story was more effort than it was worth, Agnes unhitched the wagon from the horse, heaved Anastasia out of the cart and threw her over the back of the horse, piling the furs over her body, hiding her once more from curious eyes.

Jumping into position on the horse behind Anastasia, Agnes urged the horse into a gallop to make up time, the first light of dawn starting to peak over the horizon.

# Queen Amealiana

The crisp morning air normally awakened the Queen and invigorated her with a sense of renewed energy. Today the cold air soaked through to Amealiana's bones as she was filled with anxiety and apprehension about the coming meeting with her eldest daughter, turned traitor to the crown.

The Queen and Annie slunk in the shadows of one of the old oak trees surrounding the perimeter of the cemetery. Gravestones as old as the first settlement of Alearia, almost 450 years ago, could be found scattered amongst the graveyard.

Nearby, the Queen could see a particularly old and neglected gravestone, weathered away by time and the intense climatic conditions of the rugged mountainous Kingdom. The descendants of the deceased long since passed, with no one left alive who would remember them or come to pray for their souls. The idea of a graveyard was still quite strange to the Queen, even after living in the Kingdom of Alearia for most of her life.

Having been raised in Quillencia, her home country's tradition dictated that all deceased be honored through the fire burning ceremony. The tradition allowed the deceased's final sins to be cleansed away, and their remaining soul allowed to freely pass with the Goddess from this world into the next.

The Queen often wondered how the Goddess collected souls from the people of Alearia, if they had not had a chance to be cleansed in the Holy Goddess's flame. However, she kept her musings to herself as Alearia was her home and their traditions were now her own, no matter how puzzling they may seem to her.

The graveyard was on the outskirts of the city proper, downhill from the city's water supply to ensure the water was not contaminated by the remnants of the fallen. The cemetery itself was originally quite small, but as the population had swelled thanks to the healers' giftings, people were living longer and procreating more often, praise the Goddess, and thus the graveyard had grown along with the population.

What was once a small cleared area, was now the size of a small acreage. The resting place of the deceased was surrounded by the old oak trees that guarded the city and castle from invaders, making the terrain more difficult to traverse, and concealing most of the city from prying eyes.

The Queen's horse Ebony, sniffed around the tree, looking for any sustenance to feed upon while it patiently waited for its master to attend to her business. The Queen wore a long black cloak, the hood pulled low over her face, concealing her identity from prying eyes. Not that anyone was around this early in the morning, but the Queen remained cautious and vigilant all the same.

Annalyse wore a similar cloak as advised by her mother. Both women — scarcely trained in combat or defense — were wary that they were likely walking into a trap, but it was a chance that the Queen had to take to bring her beloved Anastasia home. The Queen was no fool though, her sage wisdom had guided her to make a backup plan for their protection.

Hidden on the opposite side of the cemetery, upon a tall tree's snow-covered branch, crouched Princess Alecia, dressed in white to camouflage herself amongst the snow. Her weapons remained concealed under her clothing, her fire-wielding gifting simmering beneath her skin, at the ready for any sign of betrayal from Agnes should she attempt to harm any of her family.

It was unclear to Amealiana why her eldest daughter had kidnapped poor Anastasia in the first place, but she highly suspected she knew what Agnes would want from Annie in exchange for her sister's safe return. The thought made her anxiety peak. Giving Agnes any more power would be disastrous. A risk they were not willing to take. Therefore, it was crucial that the Queen find another way to retrieve her daughter without giving into the traitor's demands.

A crunch in the snow was the first sign of Agnes's arrival. Approaching from behind them in the forest, a horse stalked towards the awaiting royals. Agnes sat straight-backed upon the horse, a large mass slumped across the saddle in front of her, presumably Anastasia. The Queen's heart rate quickened as she began to fear the worst for her daughter.

*'Holy Goddess, please let my Anastasia be alright. Help us to all escape my evil daughter's intentions. Help her to see the error of her ways, and if there is any way to heal her, then please do it,'* Queen Amealiana silently beseeched the Goddess.

The Queen pushed Annie behind her protectively, leaving herself exposed to the approaching traitor. A concealed blade hidden in her boot was her only form of immediate defense against any potential attacks. Amealiana felt her youngest daughter trembling behind her. Though, she knew that Annie was doing her best to put on a brave, confident front.

*'If only Annie wasn't so scared of using her mind conqueror abilities, she could eliminate the threat that is Agnes once and for all. But I understand it completely. Annie's gifting has a cost and to use her mind conqueror gifting for anything other than healing would go against every moral code she possesses.*

*'How could I ever judge her for her decency and morals? She is the future hope of our Kingdom and I will protect Annie at all costs. Agnes will not have her,'* Queen Amealiana promised herself.

Agnes elegantly jumped down from her horse, dressed in common peasant wear, holding the reigns of her horse in one hand and unsheathing a dagger from her hip with the other. A smirk crept across her face, her eyes menacing. The empathetic Princess her mother had once known had been replaced by this shadow of a person driven by revenge.

"Stop where you are!" Queen Amealiana ordered as Agnes approached, with a fierceness that none of her daughters had ever seen. "We have come as you requested. Now hand over my daughter," the Queen spoke fearlessly. Her need to protect her children her sole driving force.

Agnes ignored her mother and continued to slowly creep towards the Alearian royals, until she was a mere ten feet away from them.

"I believe I am in the position of power here *mother,*" Agnes spat, the title tasting like dirt upon her tongue. "Hand over the Heir and I will give you back your other precious twin."

"Never!" The Queen declared, "you may have whatever you want, but I am not here to trade one daughter for another. Return Anastasia to me and we will allow you to leave peacefully. It will be as though we never saw you. I do not want to see you dead my daughter, but you are forcing our hand with your ceaseless cruelty. You are beautifully cruel my child, not a good trait for anyone to possess, and I am deeply sorry that I have failed in my duty as your mother to raise you into a strong selfless woman."

Agnes barked a sinister, mocking laugh. "Ha! Your words are worthless to me! You dare criticize my choices, my morals, when it is you who has clearly chosen your other Goddess blessed children over me. You haven't changed. You still think yourself almighty and honorable. You do not deserve to be Queen and she," Agnes spat, directing her attention to Annie, shivering behind her mother, "does not deserve to be the Queen! I should be Queen! I am the only one who has what it takes to rule a Kingdom, to make the tough decisions. In time you will see how wrong you all were in appointing her as your Heir. I am merely here to speed up the process.

Hand over Annalyse, or I will slit Anastasia's neck right here, right now and there is nothing you can do to save her."

"That is not going to happen. This is your last warning Agnes. Hand over Anastasia now, or face the consequences," Queen Amealiana confidently declared, taking a brave step forward towards Agnes, though internally she could feel herself falling apart, feeling trapped in a situation she did not know how to navigate.

Agnes's smirk grew wider as she dropped the reins of her horse and closed the gap between herself and the Queen.

Before Her Majesty had the time to react, she pulled the Queen into a headlock, stabbing the unsheathed dagger brutally into the Queen's side, just narrowly missing her heart.

Amealiana attempted to scream in pain, but all sound was suffocated as Agnes put more pressure on the Queen's neck, holding her more tightly. The Queen's vision blurred, and her light faded away.

Amealiana dropped to the ground, blood seeping from her stab wound onto the freshly fallen snow.

## Agnes

Annalyse screamed in shock, diving towards her mother to try and catch her before she hit the ground but failing to do so. Throwing herself across the Queen's body she began heaving sobs, seemingly oblivious to what was going on around her, consumed in her new grief.

The snow soaked into her clothes, leaving her wet and freezing, not that the young Heir noticed. Blood seeped endlessly from the Queen's wound; her pulse weak, breathing shallow.

Annalyse ripped a section of her cape off and attempted to staunch the bleeding from her mother's wound, but the damage was too great. The Queen's eyes glazed over as the Goddess's spirit took Her Majesty by the hand as she passed from this world to the next.

Agnes paused for a moment, a glimmer of remorse flashing briefly across her face as she beheld her mother lying lifelessly before her. Another life lost at her hands in rage.

Quickly turning her attention to the task at hand, Agnes grabbed the Heir's blond hair, dragging Annie towards her horse. Annie uselessly attempted to gain traction in the snow, clawing at Agnes's hands to try and free herself.

A wall of fire suddenly erupted in between Agnes and her horse and turning furiously in a fit of rage, she noticed for the first time, her sister Alecia's presence. Alecia was sprinting towards her, sword in one hand, the other directed towards Agnes, controlling the fire wall she had just created.

Alecia was fire incarnate. The Kingdom's future General a living weapon, rage and purpose devouring her senses. Agnes made a sharp turn, running horizontally along the fire wall, pulling her sister along helplessly behind her.

"You will pay for this Agnes!" Alecia screamed, hurling her sword with all her might towards her eldest sister, aiming for her heart but falling short by several feet as she misjudged the distance between herself and her target.

Using her remaining free hand, Alecia sent a volley of fireballs towards her traitorous sister, all missing their mark. Agnes ploughed through the snow purposefully, even with the added weight of hauling Annie behind her by the hair.

Alecia quickly closed the distance between her and her sisters. Finally, Alecia landed a fireball against Agnes's side, narrowly missing Annie in the process.

Agnes bellowed out a scream of pain, releasing her grip on Annalyse's hair in the process. Annalyse instinctively rolled away from Agnes, but then rolled up a snowball and threw it at her sister's back to help douse the fire that was spreading over Agnes's cloak.

Agnes threw off her cloak and before Alecia had the chance to catch her, she threw herself through the wall of fire. Shielding her face with her arms, she rolled on the snow on the other side of the firewall, extinguishing the flames that clung to her clothes and cooling her various burns.

With a last burst of energy Agnes dashed towards her horse, heaving herself up behind Anastasia once more in the saddle and coaxing her horse into a gallop. Away from the fire, away from her sisters, away from her mother's body, and off into the safety of the dense ancient oak forest she rode in search of a new place to hide and plan her next move.

# Princess Alecia

After Agnes's miraculous escape, Alecia was enraged. Anger and adrenaline were her driving force. Alecia would not allow herself to be consumed by grief — she would save those feelings for later after she had captured the traitor and made her pay for kidnapping her sister and ending her mother's life.

The soon-to-be General escorted Annie and the Queen's body safely back to the castle and then spent the remainder of the day relentlessly searching for signs of Agnes and Anastasia. Much to Alecia's hindrance, snow had fallen softly during her search, concealing any tracks she may have been able to follow to locate the traitor and her captured sister.

Upon returning to the castle at dusk, Alecia ordered the Queen's personal guard to search the forest high and low for signs of them. She brutally instructed the guard not to return to the palace unless they had discovered the traitor's whereabouts and returned Princess Anastasia safely back to the castle.

Powered with anger and remorse for failing to protect their Queen, the former Queen's guard searched the Alearia city proper and surrounding areas endlessly, seeking out revenge on Agnes. Amealiana's guards mourned the loss of their Queen, especially head guard Tomlin, who had always been closely bonded to the Queen since his initial appointment to the position ten years prior.

Sir Tomlin blamed himself for the Queen venturing unescorted into the forest with her two daughters, and Alecia blamed him too.

*'It wasn't fair to place so much responsibility on my shoulders. Tomlin should have been there to protect her too. If he had paid closer attention to the Queen's whereabouts, Mother might still be alive, and Agnes's body might have been lying cold in the castle instead.'*

As soon as Agnes was brought to justice, Tomlin informed Alecia that he intended to take full responsibility for the Queen's passing and would honorably accept any punishment the King deemed fit. Alecia and Tomlin both knew that his life would likely be forfeit.

*'A life for a life.'*

The Kingdom of Alearia felt as though it had stopped, its people collectively mourning the loss of their beloved Queen Amealiana. Candles were lit in each of the residence's front windowsills, in honor and remembrance of their former Goddess blessed ruler.

Black mourning banners once again hung around the castle grounds and along the halls. The King had locked himself away in his suite, furious over Alecia and Annie's deceit in accompanying their Queen Mother to attempt to negotiate with Agnes. And all for nothing. The Queen had ascended to the After World, and precious Princess Anastasia was still held captive by their evil sister. The King was in mourning, entrenched deeply in the anger stage of the grieving process.

Alecia paced around the Queen's room as Annie lay curled in a foetal position on the Queen Mother's bed.

*'How can Annie just lie there as though she has nothing left to give? I will save my tears, those unnecessary emotions, for after I have exacted my revenge.*

*'I understand that life has been especially cruel to Annie. Seemingly taking away everyone she has ever loved. But now is not the time for crawling into a miserable pit of grief.*

*'Giving in to my emotions will help no one, least of all Anastasia. She needs me to stay strong, she needs me to find her. I will not bury my mother and sister in the same week.'*

Margarette, Queen Amealiana's former Lady's Maid, attempted to comfort Annie through her loss, but so entrenched in her own grief, she had little emotional energy left to offer the young Heir. Margarette had served her Queen faithfully throughout the years and had loved her like her own family. Her life was devoted to serving Her Majesty. Margarette had witnessed the Queen grow into a strong, empathetic, leader and her love for the Queen, just like the Kingdom's, had only grown stronger as the years went on.

Uncertainty now plagued Alearia, Alecia had heard whispers of it in the streets as she searched for Agnes. Their people felt as if their rock, their solid foundation, had been taken from them. With the King's noticeable absence since the Queen's tragic passing, the Kingdom was starting to fall into disarray. The war council and senior Legion members were trying their best to uphold the peace and to keep the Kingdom running, but without their King taking control or Annie as the Alearian Heir reassuring their people, murmurs and unrest had starting to spread.

Horrible treasonous gossip had spread about the Queen's premature demise, rumours Alecia feared were likely fuelled by the High Priestess Elizabeth. Whispers were beginning to spread far and wide, that the royal family were no longer be capable of protecting the Alearian people. They themselves were incapable of protecting their own Queen, who was beloved by all. The first signs of a coup were bubbling under the surface and Alecia was busy strategizing how to proceed in managing the situation before it became too out of control.

*'Of course, if my bloody father and sister would do their job, the people would have no reason to question our royal family's ability to rule. One silly reassuring speech to the people, a public acknowledgement of the Queen's passing, anything, would help smooth over this whole situation. What a fool they were to appoint an empathetic healer to the position of Heir when she clearly is out of her depth, falling into a mess over the loss of our mother. Selfish, that is what she is!*

*'Doesn't she realise that I am grieving too, that I miss our mother. But I must focus. I do not have the luxury of giving in to my grief. For now, I need to concentrate on getting Anastasia back, and then I will destroy Agnes!*

*'How stupid I was for assisting Anastasia to free her in the first place! If we hadn't released Agnes, our mother would still be alive, and Anastasia would be safely here with us. My poor grandmother, Queen Annalyse, first she lost her husband and now she must grieve the loss of her only daughter.'*

# *Princess Annalyse*

It was late evening the day after the Queen's passing, and Annie remained curled up in the Queen's bed, her suite connected to the King's chambers. Alecia had left the room hours ago, frustrated with Annie's lack of action.

*"Don't you realize that I am grieving too,"* Alecia had fumed at Annie before she stormed out of the room. *"The whole Kingdom is grieving! I have known our mother my whole life and yet you who have known her for five minutes, just lie there helplessly like you have given up. Stop feeling sorry for yourself and get up! We need to find Anastasia; we need to plan our mother's funeral, and you need to step up and help me deal with the civil disturbance that is brewing, or your reign will be over before it has even begun. Is that what you want? Stop being a coward! You have your people to think about. As Heir, you no longer have the luxury of self-pity."*

*"Besides, if it wasn't for you, our mother might still be alive,"* Alecia yelled.

Those words had hit Annie the hardest, like stabbing a dagger straight through her heart.

*"You have the greatest power in the entire realm, and yet you refuse to learn to use it for defense. You could have saved our mother if you had just learned to use your damn mind conquering abilities under pressure! Why didn't you just render her unconscious like you did in the interrogation*

room? Were you overconfident that the Queen could handle the situation with no support? Or were you just too stupid to act?" Alecia had roared at Annie, tears welling in her own eyes — a rare moment for Alecia —before she had stormed out of the room. Her patience with Annie had come to an end.

'A coward, that is exactly what I am. She's right… Mother would still be alive if it weren't for me. Why didn't I save her? Why couldn't I save myself? Once again, I needed someone to come and rescue me… Once again, a loved one has died to save me.

'I am a curse to anyone who gets too close. What sort of a ruler will I ever be if I can't even protect myself?

'Enough, Alecia is right! I need to stop feeling sorry for myself, pick myself up and get on with it! I once proclaimed I would be the mind conquering healer our people need, now I must become the Queen that they deserve,' Annie declared to herself, pulling herself up from her mother's bed, slowly rising and placing the Queen's crown that lay on her bedside table, upon her own head.

"I will make you proud mother, I swear it." Annie declared, looking straight into the Queen's ornate hanging mirror. "Be at peace, reunited with your son, father and my dear Lilianna."

# Queen Annalyse of

# Quillencia

The first light was beginning to peak over the horizon on the second day following Queen Amealiana's departure from the realm. Queen Annalyse, accompanied by her son Prince Joshua, stood at the foot of the funeral pyre.

The Quillencian Heir and Queen Matriarch had arrived only a few hours earlier, after traveling day and night on horseback to attend Queen Amealiana's funeral ceremony in Alearia. The alpine conditions of Alearia prolonging the final part of their journey and leaving their traveling party feeling bone weary.

As Agnes's decision to murder her mother in cold blood was spontaneous, neither Queen Amealiana herself or her mother Queen Annalyse, had foreseen her tragic demise and were helpless to prevent it. After Agnes had made the decision to end her mother's life, Queen Annalyse felt the final piece of her soul shatter as she was shown a brutal vision of her daughter's passing.

Only a few moments later, carried by the wind, the Queen felt her daughter's spirit whisper the words; "I love you," as her soul was carried to the After World with the Goddess.

Queen Annalyse wasn't sure her heart could bear any more loss, but for her family, and to farewell her only beloved daughter, she had made the long journey to Alearia with a heavy heart, barely having a moment to herself to process this loss.

Queen Annalyse was a strong woman, whose sage wisdom and prophetic gifting had guided her vigilantly throughout her life. Years of endless visions, of which she could often not prevent, had left a heavy burden on the elderly Queen's shoulders, and she knew in her heart that her reign would also soon come to an end.

*'A mother should never have to bury a child, a loss my daughter knew all too well, that I must now learn to endure.'*

Standing in the Alearian royal family's private rose garden by the fountain, Queen Annalyse stood regally beside her son. For the benefit of the Alearian people, a public ceremony would be held later that day at which the family would be expected to wear the traditional black gown and veils. However, this morning's fire burning service was for family only. A private service commenced at sunrise on the second day following the Queen's passing, as per her home Kingdom of Quillencia's tradition.

Regrettably, the Queen's personal guard who had searched incessantly without rest, had been unable to locate the Alearian Queen's murderer or the kidnapped Princess Anastasia. The Quillencian Queen had offered for her own personal guards to join the search for the lost Princess following the burning ceremony.

Queen Amealiana's personal guards, including her head guard Sir Tomlin, were granted special permission to pause their search to attend this morning's ceremony. All however, had politely declined the offer, intent to not rest until their lost Princess Anastasia was returned. This would be their final act of service in honor of their beloved fallen Queen. Tomlin had spoken briefly with the Quillencian Queen upon her arrival to Alearia to offer his sincerest condolences for her loss, and to offer his apologies for failing to protect her daughter Queen Amealiana.

"My daughter was very fond of you all, especially you Sir Tomlin," Queen Annalyse responded thoughtfully, "and if she wanted to go off and save her daughter without your protection, then she must have had a very good reason. I doubt anyone could have stopped her. Do not blame yourself for something that you cannot change. My daughter Amealiana is at peace now with her father and son, and we must all take comfort in that. You served my daughter honorably and I am grateful for your years of loyal service. Now go in peace Sir Tomlin, do not burden yourself with guilt. Go forth and bring my granddaughter back to us," the Quillencian Queen wisely spoke, her sage wisdom a guiding light in her time of need.

Tomlin thanked Queen Annalyse sincerely in turn for her forgiveness and kind words. His shoulders relaxed as though a weight had been lifted from him, as he bowed deeply in respect to the Queen, before setting off back into the forest on horseback to continue his search for the missing Princess.

As the sun rose over the horizon, near the woodland border of the castle grounds, High Priestess Elizabeth stepped forward to stand beside the pyre on which Queen Amealiana was laid to rest. The fallen Queen wore an emerald green gown, that used to remind her fondly of her home Kingdom of Quillencia; her necklace and crown adorned with jewels that reflected the early morning rays of light, as though the Goddess continued to shine though her ever resting body. A bouquet of lilies and roses rested over her now still chest and her long blond tresses hung gracefully down the sides of the silk pillow on which her head was gently laid. Only the soft whinnies of the stable horses in the distance and the morning song of the birds filled the air.

*'How Ebony will miss her master's morning rides with her. Ebony was Amealiana's confidant, her faithful companion, she was more than just a horse to my daughter. They were soul bonded. I wonder if the whinnies she makes are her own mourning song, for the friend she too has lost…'*

Princess Alecia and King Titian of Alearia stood either side of the pyre, heads bowed respectfully. Princess Annie chose to stand beside her grandmother, a few feet away from the base of the pyre. The Quillencian Queen held Annie's hand in her own, occasionally squeezing it gently to remind Annie that she was not alone.

"Good Morning your Majesties, King Titian, Queen Annalyse, Princesses Alecia and Annalyse, and Prince Joshua. Thank you for allowing me the honor of presiding over this remembrance service of our beloved Queen," the High Priestess spoke respectfully. "Queen Amealiana was cherished by all. Her life was lived with integrity, kindness and compassion. Her Goddess blessed sage wisdom and prophetic giftings guided her loyally throughout her life. May Queen Amealiana's values and wisdom live on through her descendants forevermore."

The High Priestess paused for a moment to allow those in attendance to reflect on the impact the Queen had upon their own lives before continuing.

"Our lives were all the richer for having had the privilege of knowing her. Though your hearts feel heavy, be reassured that our dear Queen is now at peace in the endless tranquillity of the After World with her loved ones who have passed before her. I would now like to invite Queen Annalyse to speak on behalf of the family here today," High Priestess Elizabeth concluded.

*'Goddess grant me the wisdom to graciously speak words that bring honor to you and my daughter,'* Queen Annalyse prayed silently as she stepped forward, leading Annie along by the hand, to walk up the steps of the pyre and stand beside her fallen daughter.

The Quillencia Queen reached out to take Amealiana's hand in her own, releasing Annie's as she did so. Annie walked around to the other side of her mother and took her mother's other hand in her own.

Princess Alecia and King Titian left their places standing at the base of the pyre to climb the stairs to the Alearian Queen's resting place. King Titian chose to stand beside the Quillencian matriarch and Alecia took her place by her mother's resting head. Alecia began to softly stroke her hand through Amealiana's long silky tresses, cherishing her final moments with her dearly loved mother.

Prince Joshua, the Queen's only sibling, remained hesitantly at the base of the pyre, trembling slightly whilst attempting to remain composed. As the Quillencian Queen began to speak, Prince Joshua took a deep breath and slowly climbed the stairs to stand beside his mother, his eyes glazing over as he attempted to hold back his tears. Leaving only the High Priestess standing at the base of the pyre and the Quillencian guards standing discretely in the shadows.

"Holy Goddess," Queen Annalyse of Quillencia spoke with age old wisdom and grace. "We thank you for your blessed presence here today. Thank you for welcoming my daughter into your loving embrace and guiding her to the endless bliss of the After World, where she is free to spend eternity in the loving arms of her father King Julian, and her dear son

Prince Alexander. All of whom were tragically taken from us before their time."

"Queen Amealiana Caston Brandistone, was a venerable woman who dedicated her life to serving her Kingdom and her family," Queen Annalyse spoke fondly. "Amealiana was a gifted sage and prophetic, who worked hard to hone her giftings to bring the Holy Goddess glory. Amealiana lived a hard life, sacrificing her time with her beloved daughter Annie, to ensure her safety and laying to rest her only son and father, which all left irreparable stains on her heart. My daughter was loved by all who knew her. The Kingdoms of Quillencia and Alearia were stronger for her presence and her leadership. I am a worthier woman for having been Goddess chosen to be her mother. My grandchildren are stronger, wiser, more compassionate and open-minded, for having been raised by such a loving, generous, kind mother."

"Amealiana, I am proud to call you my daughter. You will never be forgotten. We will cherish our memories of you. For family and Kingdom, you dedicated your life, and now we dedicate ours to continuing your legacy. I love you my daughter, and I always will," Queen Annalyse solemnly spoke, her strength beginning to fail her as she felt the weight of her grief come crashing down upon her.

Knees threatening to give way beneath her, Queen Annalyse grasped the Alearian King's hand for support whilst she leaned over her daughter's body, placing a gentle kiss upon her forehead, tears ran down her cheeks. Not a dry eye could be seen amongst the family.

"I love you mother, and I am grateful for the precious time we had together," Annie spoke barely louder than a whisper, as she leaned over to embrace her mother, kissing Amealiana's cheek one final time.

After sadly releasing her mother's hand, she slowly made her way back down the pyre steps, escorting Queen Annalyse on her way, offering her arm for support. Prince Joshua chose to follow them, no doubt keeping his farewells private, trusting that his sister already knew his heart's wishes.

Princess Alecia and King Titian now stood alone beside their beloved Amealiana. Alecia whispering her final goodbyes to her mother before turning towards the pyre stairs. However, King Titian quickly grasped the back of Alecia's shoulder, preventing her from leaving, taking her by surprise as she turned around to see her father.

It was only then that Queen Annalyse noticed for the first time, the dark circles below his eyes from lack of rest, hidden behind red tear-streaked eyes, a look of utter despair on his face. The rare vulnerability he never allowed the world to see beneath his usually overconfident mask.

"Remember father, that mother has not truly left us. She remains with us in spirit and in our hearts," Alecia spoke softly but with conviction as though she would accept nothing else.

"I can't carry on like this any longer. My heart cannot bear anymore loss," the King revealed broken-heartedly. "I need you to promise that you will find Anastasia, that you will bring her back, and then you will stop Agnes. Teach Annie to be the Queen the people need. Protect our Kingdom as our General Alecia, this responsibility I could only entrust to you. Can you do all of this my child?" King Titian implored Alecia with a level of sincerity and desperation that his family had never seen before.

Alecia swore upon the Goddess that she would do as the King had asked of her and always strive to serve her Kingdom above all else.

"Thank you, Alecia, I love you," King Titian whispered whole-heartedly.

"I love you too father," Alecia responded, embracing her father and ever so slowly walking down the pyre steps and back towards the castle, not stopping to look back.

Queen Annalyse looked on as the broken-hearted King lay protectively across his beloved wife's body, no longer feigning any false displays of strength when he had none left to give.

Titian whispered his love and devotion to his wife. A rare moment of vulnerability shared with the world, and he vowed to be reunited with her again soon in the After World.

A wall of flames spontaneously ignited around the entire pyre, cocooning the Alearian King and Queen inside before an almighty burst of flame overcame the entire structure, burning brightly and as high as the castle turrets from the King's Goddess given flame.

Hours later, when the flames slowly began to dissipate, the only sign of the King and Queen remaining were their wedding rings that had been forged in dragon fire and passed down from generation to generation.

# Princess Anastasia

In a long abandoned Legion watchtower atop Mount Lizabeth, situated in the mountain range surrounding the Alearian City proper, Anastasia lay on a threadbare rug, locked in a tiny storage room, her limbs bound in chains. Anastasia could feel flickers of her fire wielding power pulsing faintly beneath her skin; the only thing preventing her from succumbing to hypothermia. However, due to her recent malnourishment, and the potion Antoinette had slipped Anastasia days earlier, her body was severely depleted of the strength and ability required to wield her giftings.

Anastasia knew she would only have one chance to make an escape and so she kept resting, kept conserving her energy, allowing her giftings to ever so slowly return to her as the potion slowly but steadily wore off. Anastasia was filled with rage. The time for self-pity had passed. It was unlikely rescuers would find her in this isolated location, so Anastasia was determined to find a way to save herself.

Agnes had gloated to Anastasia upon their arrival to the watchtower, of how she had murdered their own mother in cold blood. Agnes likely believed the impact of her mother's death would destroy any remaining sanity Anastasia was holding on to but instead it had restored fire to her heart and powered the hatred she now felt towards her eldest sister.

It would have been easy for Anastasia to fall into a depressed state and succumb to the grief threatening to consume her. But Anastasia vowed to the Goddess that she would avenge her mother's death, and she could not do that from inside a storage room. So, for now she focused on her plan, conserving her energy.

Anastasia would not allow herself the luxury of giving in to her feelings. She would strategize as the warrior she had always trained to be, in honor of her mother.

# Princess Alecia

Pacing around the war council chamber in her Legion leathers and fur lined boots, Alecia stopped every so often to re-assess maps of the Kingdom. The General personified, was focussed on forming a list of the unsearched locations her lost sister could be held captive. Every day that Anastasia was held captive by her eldest sister was utterly deplorable. Alecia was a born leader. Her ability to remain clear-headed in times of adversity was one of her greatest strengths.

Alecia pushed aside her thoughts regarding her father's passing. She knew King Titian better than most. They were kindred spirits in terms of their headstrong, stubborn, aggressive personalities. Alecia knew that once he had decided upon something, nothing she could have said would have changed his mind. So, even though she felt her father had let her down, and his decision to take his own life made her blood boil, blaming him or feeling sorry for herself would not change the outcome. Alecia had therefore decided the only thing left to do was to find her sister.

*"If you want something done right, you have to do it yourself,"* King Titian had installed in Alecia from a young age.

*'Now is the time to act,'* Alecia vowed to the Goddess, *'I will find my sister Anastasia and bring her back. I will carry out the King's final wishes, and I will get this Kingdom and family back on track before there is nothing left worth saving.*

*'Father was right about one thing. I am a woman of action, a general by nature and birth right. I will destroy Agnes for all she has done. Setting Agnes free, indulging Anastasia in her wishes to forgive and forget, was a mistake I cannot take back, but I can try to rectify it by making sure that no one else dies at her hands ever again.*

*'Now, where have the guards already looked and where would I go if I were trying to hide?'* Alecia thought to herself, staring at the largest map pinned to the council room wall.

A knock on the door drew Alecia from her thoughts. As she turned around to see who was there, the door pushed open and in walked Annie, dressed in her training clothes, a heavy pack in one hand and a black winter cloak hanging from her shoulders.

"You were right," Annie declared in a strong, firm voice that left no room for misinterpretation. "We need to take down Agnes and bring our sister back. The only way I can be of any help is if I push aside my high and mighty morals and fight as a mind conqueror. So, what's the plan General?" Annie asked in a cocky tone, a fake smirk painted across her face, her strong determined gaze staring Alecia straight in the eyes.

"Well, well, look who has finally decided to step up. Shut the door and sit down! We have a rescue to plan and revenge to enact. This time, Agnes does not make it out alive," Alecia declared devilishly.

# Princess Anastasia

Furious, Anastasia lay on the stone floor in a dried pool of her own excrement. Her clothes were filthy from lying on the floor for days, with minimal food and water provided. The sustenance she was given, she had no choice but to eat like an animal from a bowl whilst her hands remained bound. Anastasia had no idea of the time of day or how much time had passed as she lay in a vault-like windowless storeroom within the mountain. Her hands remained chained behind her back; her feet also chained tightly together.

Anastasia could feel her fire-wielding gifting humming strongly once more beneath her skin, a blessed sense of relief and security returning to her. Without her fire-wielder gifting, Anastasia had no doubt she would have already succumbed to hypothermia. She mused that Agnes was likely counting on that as well to keep her alive. A dead hostage was as good as no hostage at all. Such a risk to allow Anastasia's powers to return but likely a risk Agnes felt she had to take to lure her true prize, Annie.

*'I will not be a helpless Princess stuck in a tower waiting to be rescued. I will escape from this wretched room and rain hell upon Agnes for treating me this way. Agnes is no kin of mine. Grandfather was right, there is no coming back from what she has become. I will escape from this hell hole and make Agnes pay for what she has done to me, and for taking the life of our mother.*

*'I will not be a meek and mild bystander any longer. I am a trained warrior, just as strong as Alecia. I will get out of here the first chance I get. But I will not give myself away. Agnes must not know to what extent my powers have returned or she will leave me here to rot in this iron cage of a room and never open the door again.*

*'After I am reunited with my father, Alecia and Annie, we will mourn the loss of our Queen Mother together. Curse Agnes for denying me the right to attend my own mother's burning ceremony.*

*'Goddess, I pray that my mother has found peace in the After World with Alexander, Grandfather and Lilianna. I also pray that when the time comes, you give me the strength to do what needs to be done.*

*'Now is not the time for compassion or self-doubt. Now is the time to fight for my survival, to overcome my struggles and embody the Goddess's warrior spirit.'*

# Agnes

Sleet fell over Mount Lizabeth, and the surrounding mountain ranges. Agnes lay atop the watchtower roof, Alearian mountain cat furs protecting her from the elements.

Ever since Agnes had been a young girl, hiding had always been her biggest asset. She had mastered the art of melting into the shadows, often listening in to council meetings through vents of the castle's secret passageways.

Atop the watchtower roof, Agnes spent most of her time gazing out over the surrounding countryside, on the lookout for the palace guards that were sure to be hunting her down. If Agnes was completely honest with herself, she was quite surprised it had taken her prey so long to find her. But she resolved that the more time her pursuers spent out in the elements hunting for her and their stolen Princess, the more drained of energy and reserves they would be.

Agnes had pilfered preserved food stores from each of the nearby watchtowers over the past several days. The supplies were enough to keep her and her captive well-nourished for an extended period, not that she had any intention of waiting in isolation much longer.

*'If the search party doesn't come to me then I will go to them and take what is rightfully mine. Of course, if Antoinette had managed to abduct the right sister in the first place, I wouldn't be in this situation. But I can't change the past. I can only focus on the present. I will get my revenge and powers back one way or another.'*

Several hours later, Agnes saw the first light of a torch flickering off in the distance beneath the forest trees. She knew a search party must finally be approaching. So, Agnes watched and waited, silent and stealthy beneath the night sky as she eagerly waited for her plan to play out.

The biggest risk to her now was a wind whisperer discovering her location, so Agnes made sure to breathe into her coat that was pulled up over her mouth and nose, so the noise of her breathing could not be carried upon the wind. She remained deadly still, comforted by the weight of two daggers concealed at her hips.

*'I am a weapon, deadly and efficient. Pity the fool who thinks they can defeat me in battle. I am death itself, ready to wage war.'*

# Princess Anastasia

"Princess Anastasia, is that you? Please, you must wake up!"

The Princess awoke, startled from a fitful sleep as her shoulder was shaken by a stranger in the darkness, the husky male voice whispered with urgency. "Who are you? Stay back," Anastasia voiced, anxiously trying to squirm away from the intruder, her chains hindering her movement.

"Shh... We must be quiet, Princess. I am Sir Lawrence, here to rescue you. I was searching the fort for you when I heard you breathing beneath the gap between the lead door and the floor. If it were not for my gifting, I never would had thought to search a storage closest for you. Thank the Goddess you are alive!" Sir Lawrence spoke in hushed tones.

"Is there anyone else with you? Where is Alecia?" Anastasia enquired urgently, a glimmer of hope filling her chest.

Sir Lawrence helped Anastasia to a sitting position on the floor and attempted to break her chains, but without a key or anything stronger than a blade, his efforts were futile. The knight's voice was shaky as he repeatedly tried and failed to break her chains.

"Princess Alecia is here, she led the search party for you, and Princess Annalyse as well," Sir Lawrence tried to reassure her. "They are searching the other floors for you. We have seen no sign of Agnes. She may be out scavenging for supplies under the cover of night, but we cannot be certain so we must be cautious. We suspected we would find you here after we saw fresh bloodstains at the entrance to the watchtower. We have been searching the mountain watchtowers for the past couple of days desperately trying to find you," Sir Lawrence replied urgently.

Alarm crossed Anastasia's face as she took in the guard's story.

"You mean to tell me you brought Annie here, straight into Agnes's trap? What were you thinking?! Annie is in great danger," Anastasia exclaimed.

"We must find her now before Agnes does! Do you think Agnes would really be stupid enough to leave me unguarded? You have all walked straight into her trap. None of us are getting out of here alive if Agnes has her way," Anastasia alarmingly but furiously declared.

Desperate to find her twin, the fire-wielder focused all her gifting on her chains, heating them to boiling point, burning her hands and those of Sir Lawrence's in the process, forgetting to warn him to move away.

The knight groaned in immense pain from the sudden second-degree burns. Noticing the bowl of water in the corner of the room on the floor, he hurried over to immerse his hands and alleviate some of the pain.

"My chains!" Anastasia barked through gritted teeth, her hands still burning, "smash the chains!"

Sir Lawrence painfully grabbed his dagger with one burnt hand, and with the blunt end, smashed it into the glowing hot chains wrapped around her wrists and ankles. The chains crumbled into tiny pieces, finally releasing the Princess from her bonds.

Straining to hold back the tears of pain, Anastasia too dowsed her burning hands and feet in the bucket of water, taking the edge off the pain. Both the guard and Princess were thankful for the cool air now flooding the room through the open door.

The knight removed his cloak and methodically tore six strips of cloth from the bottom hem. He then soaked the make-shift bandages in the remaining bloody water, binding each strip securely around each of their burnt hands as well as Anastasia's ankles. The wet dressings felt like a soothing balm to their damaged bodies.

Distracted with tending to their wounds, neither the wind whisperer nor warrior Princess noticed the slowly dissipating breeze coming through the open storage door until it was too late.

Before either Knight or Princess had time to react, the door slammed shut behind them, locking them inside.

# Princess Annalyse

Due to the unvarying watchtower layouts, Annie felt comfortable navigating the levels of this latest tower on her own. After searching a few of the lower levels with no luck, Annie had made her way down to the dungeon to continue her search. Annie's intuition and sage gifting told her they were getting closer to finding her sister. Annie could feel the bond between her and her twin growing stronger with every passing minute.

The air was stale in the watchtower's dungeon. Two rows of cells were buried deep into the heart of the mountain. Annie imagined that they would have been used during times of war to house and interrogate prisoners of invading armies.

It seemed as good a place as any to search for her missing twin, however, the eerie darkness and silence of the dungeon caused Annie to regret her decision to split away from the group.

"*We can cover more ground if we split up,*" Alecia had reassured her despite Sir Tomlin's warning that they were safer as a united group.

Annie hadn't seen or heard from the others since.

She continued her search, whispering repeatedly; "Tash, are you here?"

Walking further into the depths of the dungeon, only a small candle to light her way, Annie's sage gifting warned her that something was not right.

"*Run! Get out of here! It's a trap!*" A message carried upon the air warned.

"Sir Lawrence?" Annie whispered into the darkness. "Is that you?"

But there was no response.

A moment later, Annie heard light footsteps descending the stone steps towards the dungeon. Thinking quickly, Annie blew out her candle and hid in one of the cells amongst a haystack previously used as a prisoner's bed.

With the room now in complete darkness, Annie reached out her mind conqueror gifting to attempt to identify her pursuer but was met instead with an impenetrable, adamant black wall.

Fear began to fester in Annie's heart, as she realised how helpless she was without the ability to use her gifting as a defensive weapon.

Taking a deep, slow, silent breath Annie decided in that moment that she would not allow fear to win and in the darkness, she listened and waited as the footsteps approached.

# Agnes

*'I can sense her, like a missing piece of a puzzle, her gifting calls to my soul. Years of training have honed my senses to seek out my prey. Even without my mind conqueror gifting I can feel her aura. In a matter of moments, Annie will be mine and I will become a mind conqueror once more.'*

Fingers scraping against the rock wall of the passageway, Agnes navigated her way down the forty stone steps she knew would take her to the dungeon floor. There was nothing standing between her and her prey now that her protectors had been dealt with.

The lingering smell of excrement soaked into the ground from previously held captives, filled Agnes's nostrils as she reached the dungeon. The smell was surprisingly strong, despite the watchtower being abandoned since the last attempted invasion during Agnes's early childhood.

Agnes remembered those days well, despite her young age at the time. She recalled watching the knights prepare for battle in the training yards before being dispatched to their designated posts. Another failed invasion attempt by another insignificant, power hungry Kingdom. Countless lives were pointlessly lost on both sides. To take on the Kingdom of Alearia was suicide. No matter how many dents they made in the King's army, the Alearian forces always triumphed from sheer numbers. Alearia was a powerful, mighty Kingdom, and it did not yield.

It was watching those valiant knights prepare for battle that inspired Agnes to become a warrior. Even without a Goddess given gifting, Agnes was determined to never be weak. She trained and honed herself into a weapon hidden beneath the guise of a meek and mild, gift-less Princess. The Alearian people considered her a pitiful potential Heir, seeing only what she allowed them to see. All the while, she watched and waited for her moment to shed her disguise and claim the title and power she deserved.

"Come out, come out, wherever you are little sister," Agnes taunted in the darkness. "I only want what is rightfully mine. Give me your gifting, and I will show you mercy. I will let you all go free. You can take Anastasia with you and return to the privileged lifestyle you have so quickly grown accustomed to. No one is coming to save you Annalyse. The others are... *indisposed...* shall we say. But before you get any clever ideas about attacking me with your gifting, know that while I am conscious your efforts are pointless. I have trained my mental defenses, and you will not break past them again. You have lost the element of surprise."

Stalking through the darkness, Agnes could sense she was drawing closer to her target. The hum of power radiating from Annie's mind sent thrills down Agnes's spine in anticipation.

Daggers now poised in each hand, the former Princess stalked deeper into the dungeon corridor, allowing her daggers to scrape against each of the iron doors she passed to incite fear in her target.

Stopping short in front of the fifth cell door to the left, Agnes felt her head beginning to throb as a mental attack was launched upon her in another failed attempt to breach her mind's defenses.

"Nice try little sister, but you will have to do better than that!" She taunted, throwing her right-handed dagger directly towards the haystack where she sensed Annie was hiding.

A piercing scream filled the dungeon as the dagger found its mark.

# *Princess Annalyse*

The pain of the weapon penetrating Annie's left leg was like nothing she had ever experienced. The darkness concealed the degree of damage caused by the blade, but that didn't stop the burning sensation thrumming up her thigh. Annie could feel the wound seeping blood through her pants and into the hay. The dagger, thankfully, must have missed an artery or else she would likely be close to death.

The apprentice healer turned Heir, wrenched out the protruding dagger from her thigh and attempted to slow the bleeding by applying direct pressure to the wound with both hands. Annie's screams were soon replaced by muffled moans and grunts as she attempted to deny Agnes the satisfaction of her reaction.

*'Goddess, if it is your will that I join my family in the After World today, please take me quickly. Agnes will never claim my gifting for her own. I will never give it to her. At least I can pass on from this life knowing that she will never be able to ruin anyone else's life as a mind conqueror. The last of our bloodline's gifting will fade away into the eternal light. Perhaps that is as it should be.'*

Agnes laughed sadistically in triumph as she stalked across the cell, fumbled around in the haystack and pulled her youngest sibling by her blond tresses out on to the cold stone floor. With her right hand she held Annie's head back and positioned her remaining dagger to Annie's throat with her left.

"Give me your gifting or you will never see the light of day again."

*'Goddess have mercy on my soul.'*

# High Priestess Elizabeth

By fire-wielder light, twenty senior Priestesses gathered in the Alearian city temple. Ravens had been sent across the Kingdom two days earlier to each of the five different Alearian temple sites, summoning the senior Priestesses from each sisterhood to represent their cohort at the meeting. Wind whisperers laid a cloak of air over the colosseum-like place of worship, preventing curious ears from eavesdropping.

"Senior sisters of the Goddess, and temple leaders," High Priestess Elizabeth proclaimed from the alter towards the holy women filling the first two rows of the vast sandstone temple. "Thank you for gathering here tonight. It is after much prayer and consideration, that I have summoned you all here. As you have all overheard, Queen Amealiana has transcended from this world into the next at the hands of her own daughter. Shortly afterwards, King Titian also entered the After World. The Alearian Heir is no-where to be found. Our Monarchy has abandoned us, leaving a foreign ruler to take over. The Brandistone Heir promised us more input into our Kingdom and has instead left us to the wolves. Queen Annalyse of Quillencia has no place leading our Kingdom, and if our Heir will not assume her place as Queen, then we need an Alearian who will."

Whispers around the room began; a mixture of agreement and apprehension surrounding their leader's declaration.

"I know what you are all thinking sisters," Elizabeth placated them. "The Crowning Ceremony exists because it is the Goddess's will. However, our future Queen has neglected to take her Goddess given responsibilities seriously. I do not believe that the Goddess would approve of her chosen Heir abandoning her own people in their time of need."

More whispers rose amongst the sisters, the High Priestess's claims gaining more sway with her subordinate's.

"The Goddess has called for us to be more than spiritual counsellors to the throne," High Priestess Elizabeth declared. "If Princess Annalyse was as devoted to our Kingdom as I am, she would not have run away. Sadly, she has proven what I predicted all along. Princess Annalyse is not fit to be our Queen. Neither of the remaining Brandistone royals are either. The signs have been written in the wind for a time. First, our treasured Prince was murdered at a public event, then our eldest potential Heir inflicted torment and pain upon our people with her magical gifting. Alecia proved her unpredictable nature when she had that poor servant girl frozen and Anastasia, though sweet, suffers from mental illness. The time has come my sisters, for us to rise and take control of Alearia. We must return our Kingdom to its former glory," High Priestess Elizabeth concluded.

The Priestesses rose as one from the pews, applauding their religious leader. The High Priestess stood tall and proud from the alter, absorbing their praise, allowing the anticipation in the room to build.

"Sisters. Beloved representatives of our Goddess. I cannot act alone; I need your help," Elizabeth announced. "I call upon each of you to act in the best interests of your Kingdom. Follow your Goddess given duty. Spread the word amongst your temple sisters and worshippers. Rally the people, and we will take control of our Kingdom. In two days, we will meet at the castle gates to protest. We will demand to be heard and we will rally the people. If our peaceful attempts at a resolution do not wield results, we will have no choice but to take further action. We are the voices of our people and we will be heard. In the Goddess's name, for family and Kingdom, go forth and carry out your Goddess's work."

"For family and Kingdom," the room roared in unison as one voice for one people.

"I will see you in two days at sunrise at the castle gates. Go in peace and serve our Goddess well."

# Princess Anastasia

Bounding down multiple stone steps at a time, the fierce Alearian mountain cat leapt, tracking the scent of her twin. Her powerful body jumped effortlessly down staircase after staircase, floor by floor, the others left trailing behind, restricted by their human body's limitations.

The mountain cat's eyesight allowed her to navigate through the darkness with ease. Approaching the dungeon, her twin's scent mixed with the tang of blood, grew stronger. Anastasia brushed that thought aside, letting her animal instincts take over.

Reaching the dungeon on silent feet, the mountain cat paused to listen, allowing her enhanced hearing to guide her next move. The tang of blood mixed with urine overwhelmed the giant cat's senses as she began stalking silently through the dungeon corridor, following her sister's scent.

The mountain cat entered the already open fifth dungeon cell. Kneeling on the floor in a pool of her own blood, held up by her hair in the traitor's hand, was Annie. A knife held threatening to her throat. Annie appeared weak, barely conscious as she hazily begged her captor to spare her life. Furious with the scene before her, Anastasia released a mighty warning growl which echoed off the dungeon cell walls.

Agnes turned on the spot, pulling Annie along with her, "what in the realm?!" Agnes exclaimed, eyes wide, turning the dagger she previously had pointed at Annie, towards the giant cat.

Without hesitation, Agnes hurtled the dagger through the air towards the fierce beast. The giant cat dodged the dagger and then leapt towards the traitor, pinning her to the ground under her immense weight. Without a second thought, she ripped out Agnes's throat with her mighty jaws, blood dripping from her maw. Revenge was finally hers.

Annie hit the stone floor with a thud, moaning in agony. The blood flowed more freely now that she had momentarily released pressure from the stab site. Despite her dire condition, the sight of Anastasia in mountain cat form, seemed to bring her twin a sense of relief.

With a flash of light, the giant mountain cat perched upon her victim's body transformed back into her bare human form. Anastasia pulled the clothes off the traitor's dead body and threw them on, wiping most of the blood from her mouth onto her sleeve.

"Hello Annie," Anastasia grinned at her twin before helping her up into a sitting position against the cell wall, Annie trying to suppress a moan in the process. "I thought you were meant to be saving me?" Anastasia attempted a joke whilst applying pressure to Annie's wound with her own hands.

"I missed you too," Annie softly spoke in reply.

"Never mind," Anastasia chuckled before solemnly declaring, "it's my turn to heal you this time. Take a deep breath. I'm sorry but this will not be pleasant."

Annie did as she was told, and Anastasia allowed her fire-wielding gifting to surge though her palms.

The Heir screamed as her twin soldered the wound to stop the bleeding. After several minutes, the wound closed over, and Annie released a thankful sigh now that the excruciating pain had finally come to an end. With a moan of exhaustion, Anastasia slumped against the wall next to her twin. The two girls rested their heads against each other, taking a moment to recover.

"Annie, I need to tell you something," Anastasia spoke hesitantly after a few extended moments of silence.

Annie squeezed her sister's hand reassuringly, encouraging her to continue.

"It was Alecia and I that broke Agnes out of the dungeon," Anastasia confessed, unable to make eye contact with her twin, fearing her reaction. "I'm sorry I trusted her..." Anastasia continued. "This is all my fault. At the time, I couldn't bare for her to be sentenced to death, but I was wrong. If I didn't break her out, you wouldn't have needed to rescue me and mother would still be alive," Anastasia spoke softly.

She could feel the cold tears slide down her cheeks and her shoulders sagged as a weight she hadn't known she had carried was lifted from her through her confession.

Annie opened her eyes and turned her head to face her sister sitting beside her. "I knew it was you."

Anastasia sat stunned.

"You care so deeply for everyone that I knew it had to be you," Annie continued. "It was the right thing to do. Mother would have wanted for her to have another chance to redeem herself, but sadly Agnes fooled us all. Her heart was beyond healing, her soul shrivelled. It is not your fault Anastasia. None of it is. We can't change the past, so do not burden yourself with regret, because it will only eat away at your soul. Misplaced guilt is a waste of time. It is a trick of our mind that anxiety installs. It is not the truth. Take comfort in knowing that finally Agnes got what she deserves. Thanks to you, we are all free of her. I just pray that the Goddess takes pity on her soul because an eternity in limbo is a fate I wouldn't wish upon even her."

Anastasia embraced her twin for what felt like the first time in a long time. "Thank you for forgiving me Annie. Thank you."

"There is nothing to forgive Tash. Thank you for once again saving my life."

Alecia burst into the cell, flame in hand, ready for any threat, followed by Sir Tomlin with a noticeable limp, arm wrapped around Sir Lawrence for support.

Alecia took in the scene before her; Agnes splayed dead across the floor, Annie and Anastasia embracing, slumped against the wall.

With a wicked grin Alecia apologized, "sorry we missed all the fun."

Anastasia just rolled her eyes at her older sister and replied, "took you long enough... Now get over here and give me a hug."

# Queen Annalyse of

# Quillencia

"Your Highness, the crowds are growing more boisterous by the front gates. High Priestess Elizabeth is preaching traitorous gossip to our people. How do you wish for the Alearian Legion to proceed?" Lord Ashcott, General of the Alearian Legion asked.

Lord Ashcott had served his country proudly during many attempted invasions as the Alearian Army Legion General, and prior to that, as a leader in the Alearian Legion's command. Over the last two decades, in times of peace, Lord Ashcott had assumed an advisory role, due to his mature age.

Following Princess Annalyse's ascension of the throne as Queen of Alearia, Lord Ashcott would formerly hand over the Legion's reign to Princess Alecia, who would officially be declared the Kingdom's first female General of the Alearian Legion. She had been working side-by-side with Lord Ashcott recently, learning from him, preparing to take on her future as Alearian Legion General.

Queen Annalyse of Quillencia, stood lost in thought by the window of the throne room, staring off towards the horizon. Towards her home.

"Do nothing," the Queen responded after some time. If the General was surprised by her response, he did not let it show. Ever the professional.

"As long as the protests remain relatively peaceful," Queen Annalyse continued, "we can do nothing to interfere. If we act too brashly the people will only revolt further and the foothold of influence the High Priestess possesses will grow stronger, which is exactly what she wants. We must beat her at her own game. Rather than punish the people and the Priestesses for their protests, I want you to arrange for water and food to be taken down for the people. With full stomachs perhaps the crowd will become more reasonable. We need to soothe the peoples' anger long enough for Princess Annalyse to return from her journey. Once Alecia and Annalyse have returned, united, they will resolve this issue."

"As you wish, Your Majesty," Lord Ashcott responded, bowing low.

"Two more things, Lord Ashcott," Queen Annalyse specified, turning away from the window to stare into his eyes. The Lord stood upright, attention wholly on the Queen.

"Ensure that the remaining castle Priestesses are rewarded handsomely for their loyalty," the Queen said. "We will need to call upon their services for the Heir's formal coronation when she returns. Send ravens out to all the potential suitors that were due to arrive over the coming months and schedule their arrival to be brought forward immediately. Our future Queen will need a King by her side," Queen Annalyse stated, a glimmer of cunning in her eyes.

"Have the Alearian ambassador send out invitations to the rulers of Alearia's allied Kingdoms, to the nobility, Lords and Ladies, and to the senior priestesses of Alearia," The Quillencian Matriarch added. "There will be a wedding following the next new moon. Alearia will soon be celebrating the reign of their new Queen and King."

*'Let us hope and pray that Alearia's Goddess appointed Heir can restore balance as prophesized. A new reign to reunite a dark and twisted Kingdom. I pray it will be just as my daughter foresaw at Annie's birth. Amealiana, guide your daughters safely home, so together they may restore peace and harmony to your Kingdom.'*

# *High Priestess Elizabeth*

High Priestess Elizabeth stood proudly upon a temporarily erected stage beside the castle gates at the end of her first day of protesting.

"People of Alearia, the Goddess gives you thanks for your support of her Holy mission. It is our role as servants of the mighty Goddess, to speak up, to demand justice, and make the wishes of the people known. Alearia needs a mighty leader. If Princess Annalyse cared for her people and valued her Goddess appointed responsibilities, then she would be here with us, hearing our concerns and requests," The High Priestess declared.

The crowd hung on her every word, cheering in support.

"The Goddess demands absolute service from her leaders," she continued, "and our Heir is not meeting those demands. Our Goddess has shown me visions of a new Alearia, one where the Goddess and her people once again live in peace and harmony. The Goddess cannot do her work through our leaders if they do not make themselves available to serve her. Earlier, the palace sent us gifts of food and water to reward us for speaking freely and making our concerns known. They recognise that their reign is nearly over, and new leadership is required for our Kingdom to once more thrive and flourish."

Cheers ascended from the crowd, fuelling the flames of distrust in their Monarchy.

"The time has come," the High Priestess continued, "to choose where your loyalty lies. You must decide if you choose to stand by a Monarchy that has fallen apart — a new member of the royal family dead every other week. Or, you can wholly put your faith and trust in the Goddess and by extension your High Priestess and fellow sisters. Trust us to always put your needs first. Under the Goddess's guidance, we can restore peace and unity to our Kingdom. The time has come for new leadership! The time has come for change!" Elizabeth declared, wind whisperers carrying her message across the city proper so that every noble, every peasant, could hear her call to rally the people.

'*The crowds grow by the thousands as my message is relayed. My influence spreads far and wide amongst the people. We will stand strong as a united people against a Monarchy that has failed to provide stability, failed to protect their people. Any attempt the castle makes to win back their people's allegiance, I will twist to suit my means.*'

"All hail the Goddess! A new Alearia!" The people chanted, adopting the battle cry begun by the Priestesses.

The sun set and the bonfire flames grew. The people set in for a long night of protesting. The cold air of night fuelled their tempers as the crowd grew rowdier and the protests continued.

"All hail the Goddess! A new Alearia!"

*'Our people will be heard, and I will be crowned ruler of all Alearia. I will be High Priestess and Queen, and a new reign will begin.'*

# Princess Anastasia

After the conflict in the watchtower, the three Princesses and two knights tended to their wounds as best they could thanks to Annie's apothecary skills and Anastasia's diathermy fire power. During a confrontation with Agnes, Sir Tomlin had acquired a broken ankle. His injury was sure to make the journey home slower and more gruelling.

After Annie had finished making a brace for Sir Tomlin's left foot, Alecia took Anastasia for a short walk amongst the trees surrounding the watchtower. Anastasia could tell there was something weighing on Alecia's mind and so she had not questioned her sister when she suggested they go for a stroll, even though all she wanted to do was rest.

"I have missed you, Tash. Not a moment that went by, that I wasn't thinking of you," Alecia whispered sadly.

Anastasia stopped walking, grabbed her sister's hand and pulled her into a warm embrace.

"I missed you too, sis. I knew you would come for me. Nothing gets between you and what you want," Anastasia attempted to joke, whilst trying to hold back the tears she felt welling in her eyes

Alecia pulled away from her sister's embrace and held both of her younger sister's hands. The first light of morning was just hedging over the horizon. They had been awake all night and exhaustion had set in.

"Anastasia," Alecia began hesitantly, "there is something else I need to tell you."

Alecia took a deep slow breath; her bottom lip began to tremble uncharacteristically. Taking a seat on a nearby boulder under the cover of a tree, she beckoned her sister to join her.

"What is it Alecia? You can tell me anything. I can handle it," Anastasia promised, though as the words escaped her lips, she wasn't sure she could.

"At our Queen Mother's burning ceremony, father ordered me to find you and bring you home. He told me to take care of our Kingdom. As hard as our father found it to express his feelings, we always knew how deeply he loved our mother," Alecia spoke sorrowfully.

She paused to take a deep slow breath, trying to regain her composure.

"I don't think he could bear to be parted from her," Alicia sadly continued, "and so, as our mother's spirit was carried from this world into the next through the cleansing pyre flames, our father joined her... Only their wedding rings remained after the fire had burnt out. Mother and father are forevermore reunited in endless peace with Alexander and the Goddess now," Alecia reflected, releasing the first tears Anastasia could recall seeing her sister shed since Alexander's passing.

Anastasia embraced her sister once more. At a loss for words, she finally allowed herself to shed the tears she had been holding back so bravely.

*'How could our father die from his own flames? He was fire incarnate. I didn't think it was even possible… And why would he leave us?*

*'Surely his children were just as important to him as his wife, though father changed after Alexander's passing. He was a shadow of the ruler he had once been. Perhaps we weren't enough for him anymore.*

*'Perhaps I wasn't enough for him anymore.'*

An hour later, as the sun fully rose over the Alearian Alps, Anastasia and Alecia sent billowing flames over their eldest sister's body as it lay to rest atop an animal fur they had found inside the tower.

"Goddess forgive our sister of her sins and grant her an eternity of endless peace in the After World," Annie whispered in prayer to the sky.

Alecia had protested Agnes's right to have a burning ceremony initially, but there was no room for argument once Annie pointed out that their mother would be horrified if her living children denied her eldest the chance to pass on to the After World.

Even Anastasia had to agree that an eternity in limbo was a fate she would wish upon no-one, not even the traitor who had used her as bate to lure her twin sister into a trap.

A day of rest followed by three gruelling days of travel through the Alearian alps on their way home, had taken its toll on the weary travellers. Approaching the crest of a mountain bordering the Alearian city proper,

Anastasia couldn't be more relieved to see her home atop the adjacent mountain peak in the distance.

'*Home... What an odd notion when almost everyone I care for has departed from this world into the next. What is home without our King and Queen to lead us...*'

"You are not alone," the voice of her departed mother echoed upon the whispered wind. "Follow Annie and she will lead you home. She is the Queen that will restore balance to our Kingdom."

Anastasia looked around to see if anyone else had heard the message from the fallen Queen. After it became clear that the message was meant solely for her ears only, as the group continued looking towards the city proper, Anastasia turned slowly towards Annie and dropped to her knee. The knights followed her lead in respect.

"My Queen," Anastasia declared, startling her twin with the use of the formal title. "Your Kingdom needs you. We need you. Help us restore peace and stability to our home. For family and Kingdom, take us home."

"For family and Kingdom," the knights and Alecia echoed.

Annie took a deep breath and turned back to face the city proper.

"I cannot do this alone," Annie spoke honestly. "I will need you, Alecia, to be my Legion General and protect our people from harm. And Anastasia, I need you to be the gentle voice of reason, who speaks for those who cannot speak for themselves. You will be the voice of our people. For family and Kingdom. Let's go home," Annie proclaimed.

# 24

## *Princess Annalyse*

"I was naive to believe I was in any way capable of leading a Kingdom," Annie claimed, exasperated. "We have been *home* for only a few days and already I feel more like a caged animal than a Queen preparing for her coronation. The idea of choosing a King in the next two weeks is unthinkable. I am not ready for this Queen Annalyse. Why did you insist upon making these decisions without me?" Annie complained like a child to her grandmother.

The Queen of Quillencia straightened in the wing back chair she was seated upon in the young Heir's private suite, flattening out an invisible wrinkle in her forest green gown.

"Young lady," the Queen spoke calmly but authoritatively, raising her eyes to look directly at her granddaughter. "Sit down and stop pacing around like a child."

At the Queen's remark, Annie halted her steps and turned to stare dumbfounded at the Queen before meekly moving to sit opposite her grandmother.

"I apologize, Grandmother. I spoke out of turn," Annie replied like a scorned child.

"Yes, you did, but you are also entitled to. Tomorrow you will be crowned Queen of Alearia, and as Queen your voice matters," Queen Annalyse reminded the Heir. "Yes, your formal public coronation and wedding will not take place for another two weeks but to protect the Kingdom you must be crowned earlier to secure your reign," the Queen responded now in a tone more like a grandmother scolding her grandchild.

"To earn the people's trust back you must marry," Queen Annalyse reminded her granddaughter, "and an alliance with another Kingdom through marriage will help to strengthen your claim to the throne."

Annie inhaled and exhaled deeply and straightened her back.

"You are right Queen Annalyse, every fibre of my sage gifting tells me so, but I am not even seventeen years of age. I am far too young to marry, rule a Kingdom, and..." Annie almost choked on the words she had not yet allowed herself to voice, "conceive a child."

The Queen of Quillencia relaxed her posture and called for the Lady's Maid to bring more chamomile tea. When the room was empty of all but the two royals, the elderly Matriarch leaned forward and took her granddaughter by the hand, gently caressing her cheek with the other.

"You are stronger than you think, Annie. Your Grandfather gave his life for this Kingdom because he knew that you were the future hope of your people. Your mother, Amealiana, believed in you from the day you were born and right until her last breath, she devoted her life to serving you, your family and Alearia. Your father left this world for the next because he knew that you and your sisters could lead the Kingdom," Queen Annalyse reassured her. "You are a mind conqueror and sage gifted. Regardless of your age, you must not underestimate yourself."

"You have overcome many obstacles in your life Annie. Those experiences have forged you into a wise leader," Queen Annalyse continued. "You are the Queen the people need, Annie, and you will prove that to them. You will find a way to stop the riots and calm the civil unrest. You will ascend the throne, and the people will accept you as their new Queen after you have earned their loyalty. Alearia will be a peaceful Kingdom once more. You will make a just and fair ruler Annie. You just need to have faith in yourself," Queen Annalyse concluded.

Annie squeezed her grandmother's hand gently, "thank you, Queen Annalyse. Your support means more than you could ever know."

As the women sat in silent contemplation, Annie's temporary Lady's Maid, Lady Margarette, formerly her late mother's Lady's Maid, re-entered the room. She carefully placed a fresh pot of tea beside the royals, their teacups still by their sides where they had left them.

The Heir of Alearia turned towards her Lady's Maid, "thank you Margarette for all of your help, I realise you are still grieving my mother's loss as we all are."

The Lady's Maid offered a small smile and nod of her head in thanks. "Thank you, Your Majesty. It is an honor to serve you."

"Lady Margarette, could you please deliver a message to Princess Alecia?" Annie continued. "Please request that she schedule a meeting in the war room in an hour. Then please invite all the potential suitors to the family dining room for dinner this evening with the royal family. I wish to welcome our guests formerly to Castle Brandistone."

⁓⁓⊰❈⊱⁓⁓

# 25

## Princess Alecia

In the centuries-old, beating heart of the castle, the Alearian war council members gathered. Once the room was full of mature delegates of the Alearian Legion, led by the mighty King Titian and supported by Queen Annalyse. In its place, now only Lord Ashcott, Sir Tomlin, Princesses Alecia, Anastasia, and Annie, remained. Queen Annalyse of Quillencia had also been invited to attend to offer her insight.

Much to the war council's dismay, many of the senior Legion officers had abdicated their titles in the Legion following the King's death. The news had spread that Alecia would be appointed the next General and many of the Legion's warriors, behind closed doors, questioned her entitlement to the position. The gossip amongst the lower ranking Legion members was that her nobility was the only reason for her appointment to the position.

Whilst Alecia conceded there was some truth to the rumours, she was indeed a fierce warrior in her own right, with an immense fire-wielding gifting. She had trained in tactics, combat, diplomacy and weaponry skills her whole life, and had honed her own body into a physical weapon. Alecia felt she was unquestionably the perfect person to take over the role following Lord Ashcott's retirement.

*'If only the Legionnaires could see my worth too. See that I am a weapon in my own right. Being female and of royal blood does not negate my level of training or my tactical decision making. I have been trained by the best to become the best. I will prove the gossip hungry, sexist pricks wrong.'*

The soon-to-be General sat to the left of Annie's side, who now occupied the King's former place at the head of the table. To sit to the left of the Crown was a great honor, but the sense of privilege was lost on Alecia, who still couldn't help the feelings of jealousy she held towards the Alearian Heir, though she masked her feelings well.

Opposite Alecia sat Lord Ashcott and beside him sat Sir Tomlin. To the left of Alecia sat Queen Annalyse of Quillencia followed by Princess Anastasia.

"Thank you for gathering so promptly," Princess Annalyse began. "As you are all aware, whilst I was away, a decision was made for the betterment of our people that I shall marry and appoint a King upon the next full moon. I stand by the decision that was made on my behalf, which is one of the reasons I have called this meeting today."

"Additional security measures," Princess Annalyse continued, "will need to be put in place for the event. To earn the peoples' trust, I have elected to hold the formal ceremony in the main city temple. It is a risk, I know, to hold the ceremony in such a public venue given the current civil unrest, but to be a Queen of the people means I must be amongst my people. How can the people grow to trust me if I do not put my trust in them? Furthermore, I would like to travel on horse, with escorts of course, in a procession to the ceremony from the castle, so that the people may feel included in the celebrations," Annie concluded.

*'A completely arrogant and misguided decision. She makes these proclamations without putting any thought into the logistics of such an event.'*

"I appreciate the sentiment Your Majesty," Lord Ashcott interjected before Alecia had the chance. "It is a noble gesture to go through with this elaborate event, however, your safety is paramount. I cannot guarantee that there will be enough time before the event to arrange such an elaborate safety plan given the current, *leadership* issues we are experiencing within the Legion. I have tried my best to stamp out any dissent amongst the Legion. However, forgive me for saying this, but just as you wish to earn the trust of the people, so does Alecia need to do the same amongst the Legion, or there will be limited senior commanders left to lead the Legion's squads."

The Alearian Heir sat upright in the throne; her brow furrowed. Sir Tomlin pretended to rub an invisible mark from the table to avoid participating in the suddenly awkward conversation.

*'Typical... blaming the current lack of unity amongst the Legion on myself even though I have yet to even take up the post. It is such a male dominated Legion, that our commanders don't know how to trust a woman in charge. But I will show them I am no ordinary Princess.'*

Annie schooled her features into a picture of calm.

"Forgive me Lord Ashcott," Princess Annalyse began, "but for many decades you have served this Kingdom, through attempted invasions, civil unrest, and attempted assassinations. I would have thought a man of your extended experience would find maintaining security for a wedding and coronation child's play."

Alecia bit her lower lip to hold back the laugh that was threatening to escape.

*'Annie may be reckless and arrogant for wanting to carry through with such a risky public event, but you have to hand it to her, she can be a clever, manipulative snow fox. A Queen needs backbone, perhaps we are seeing the first sign of hers.'*

"Very well, Your Highness," Lord Ashcott regretfully accepted defeat to save face.

"Thank you, Lord Ashcott," Princess Annalyse responded serenely. "Princess Anastasia?"

"Yes, Your Majesty?" Anastasia responded.

"This Queen needs a King. I need you to remain by my side as my adviser and discrete security guard over the coming week whilst I choose a King from the prospective suitors. Do you feel you are up to the task?"

"It would be my honor, Your Majesty," Anastasia blushed as she responded.

*'I somehow doubt Tash will mind in the slightest, being surrounded by eligible suitors all day long,'* Alecia thought mischievously.

Alecia turned to Annie, "and what task do you have in mind for me, *Your Highness?*" Alecia drawled over the formal title.

"Alecia, when you are not working alongside Lord Ashcott, leading the Legion and planning the ceremony security, I would like you to investigate the backgrounds on each of our potential suitors. Find out what their motives are for wanting to be King, and who is the most trustworthy," Annie directed.

"As you wish, Your Majesty," Alecia responded.

"Very good," Annie stated. "The next topic on the agenda is city security. What are the latest updates on the civil unrest and riots brewing in the city, Alecia?"

Alecia felt herself squirming a little in her seat at that question. She had always desired for this level of responsibility but now that she was accountable for ensuring the peoples safety, she found delivering unfortunate news quite difficult.

All eyes around the table were expectantly focused on her, awaiting her response with bated breath. All except for Lord Ashcott, who stared knowingly at his hands crossed in front of him upon the table.

Alecia took a deep breath and maintained her composure.

"Overnight, two palace guards attained serious injuries while attempting to maintain security on palace grounds," Alecia explained. "At the time, a group of approximately ten rioters were attempting to break into the castle grounds through the back-service entrance gates. The attempted intruders were apprehended before they could harm anyone else and are all currently being held in our quickly overcrowding dungeon cells."

"I see…" Annie trailed off, maintaining a cool mask of composure, "and what is the latest news on the city's movements?"

Alecia felt her palms grow sweaty as she avoided direct eye contact with her sisters.

"As well as the attempted breach of the castle grounds last night, another group of rioters launched a handful of attacks on a noble's manor in the city proper," Alecia revealed. "Our city guards called for reinforcements, but unfortunately they took some time to arrive on the scene. In the meantime, one rogue peasant managed to break through the guards' lines and assassinated the son of a noble."

Annie was quiet for a moment, pausing in thought.

"Who was the poor gentleman that passed away?" Annie asked.

"His name was Sir Riley Thornley, Your Majesty," Alecia informed her. "Agnes and Sir Riley had a romantic history of sorts, though she was promised at the time to another noble. We believe that Sir Riley was murdered for his past connections with the traitor. Sir Riley had proved he was ignorant of Agnes's crimes and severed ties with her as soon as her crimes became known, but some townsfolk still held a personal vendetta against him. It is a tragic loss for the house of Thornley. He was the Lord and Lady's only living Heir," Alecia concluded.

"The Thornley's," Lord Ashcott continued, "have been loyal to the Brandistone family for many a generation. It is due to their strong connection to the royal family and past connection to Agnes, that we feel Sir Riley was assassinated. The protesters and rioters are gaining more of a foothold in the city and their actions are becoming more violent and unpredictable," Lord Ashcott warned the future Queen.

"To murder a noble due to their connection to our family," Alecia carried on, "suggests that dissent amongst the people is rooted far deeper than we had believed. Sir Riley's death brings the current death toll from the recent unrest to twenty. Most of these deaths have been attributed to injuries obtained during protests or untreated illness. However, three of the deaths can be attributed to physical injuries obtained during altercations with city guards trying to restore law and order. Sir Riley's death is the first known assassination."

Alecia noticed the way Anastasia, who was previously excited by her set task, now sat pale and slumped in her chair.

*We grew up alongside Sir Riley. He was a regular guest at the palace. His passing has surely shocked Tash, just as it has to me.*

"Thank you Alecia and Lord Ashcott for that report," Princess Annalyse replied softly, drawing Alecia from her thoughts.

Queen Annalyse of Quillencia rose from her seat to address the group. "Your Majesty, in times of civil unrest death is sadly inevitable. We have been fortunate in Quillencia to have maintained peace for many generations. If it would please you, I would like to make a couple of suggestions?" Queen Annalyse requested towards the Alearian Heir.

Annie nodded in affirmation of her request.

"To earn the peoples' trust," Queen Annalyse stated, "a ruler cannot show favouritism amongst her people. As it seems nobles with connections to the crown may be targeted, additional security will need to be implemented. To evacuate the nobles from their homes would be a sign of mistrust towards the general population, so I advise against it. Might I suggest instead stationing a small number of the Alearian Legion within the grounds of each of the key nobles' estates who have connections to your family, as well as increasing the Alearian Legion presence around the city proper. The Legion can work alongside the city guards to help maintain order. By increasing guards in all areas of the city you will not be showing favouritism, but you will also be able to effectively protect those that are most vulnerable to attack."

Annie nodded her head again, likely internally weighing up the pros and cons of the Quillencian Queen's suggestions with her sage wisdom.

"To help foster trust between the Alearian family and the people once more," Queen Annalyse of Quillencia continued, "might I suggest opening the grand city hall to the public each day to serve fresh water and food to the people. Whilst the people are protesting in the streets, the work balance has been interrupted and valuable jobs such as planting crops and harvesting vegetables have been neglected, and food stores are sure to be running low. By feeding the people, you will show them that you care about their wellbeing."

"Thank you for your sage advice Queen Annalyse," Annie agreed. "Lord Ashcott, please see to it that this community service is arranged. Employ local woman to prepare the food and provide stock from our castle stores. The Alearian Legion can oversee the project to make sure peace is maintained. Can you also please arrange for Alearian Legionnaires to be utilised as suggested by Queen Annalyse?"

"As you wish Your Majesty," Lord Ashcott nodded in respect.

"Thank you. That concludes our meeting. Anastasia and Alecia, would you please accompany me to my suite to prepare for this evening's meal? We have company to entertain," Annie smiled playfully, trying to lighten the mood. Rising from her seat, she signalled that the council was dismissed.

"For family and Kingdom," Annie stated.

"For family and Kingdom," the council echoed.

# 26

## *Princess Annalyse*

*'Lady Margarette has outdone herself,'* Annie thought in awe as she took in the room before her.

Waiting for Annie, in her suite, were a team of three seamstresses and their assistants. In the center of the suite was a table overflowing with various exquisite and expensive dress materials.

Officially standing guard in the room was one of the few female Alearian Legion warriors, Clara. Annie first met the legionnaire in the training arena. When Annie's usual combat trainer was away on official duty for the Legion, Clara would train Annie in his place. Leading up to the Crowning Ceremonies, Annie had only trained with Anastasia, but after her appointment as Heir, a formal combat trainer had been appointed to her services.

The three Princesses examined each of the beautiful fabric rolls laid out across the table. All manner of material from delicate silk to embroidered taffeta, lay spread out before them. Alecia beckoned for the Lady's Maid to serve the wine as they made their choices.

Anastasia picked up a roll of deep red silk, before hastily discarding it back on the table, and quickly gulping down a large mouthful of wine. Annie suspected that after all her twin had been through recently, seeing any shade of red would likely evoke feelings of anxiety for her.

Annie recalled vividly, the blood crusting her twin's body after she had rescued her from Agnes. The horrors her sister must have lived through, Annie was ashamed to admit, that she did not feel ready to know the full extent of. It was not a topic either twin had raised since their return to Castle Brandistone and Annie respected her sister's right to privacy.

*'She will talk to me when she is ready.'*

"Do you remember the last time we were gathered like this?" Anastasia asked. "Times were easier back then. Mother was with us and our only worry was who would be crowned Heir. It seems a lifetime ago now," Anastasia stated, her voice trailing off in thought.

"I miss her too," Annie spoke softly.

Not one to give in to her emotions easily, and eager to restore the relaxed mood to the room, Alecia exclaimed, "I'll have this one if you don't want it Anastasia!" Before snatching up the roll of red silk her sister had just discarded. "Perhaps in a gown made of this, I will find my own doe-eyed husband," Alecia smirked wickedly, handing the roll to one of the assistants and moving to a block to be measured for her dress.

Annie gazed over a range of gorgeous shimmering blue tulles, organza and silk materials. "Anastasia, have a look at these. You would look a vision in a ball gown made of these."

"I do believe I would," Anastasia offered a smile in appreciation. "But perhaps a gown that extravagant would be better suited to your wedding? That's fine though, I already have a gown I can wear tonight," Anastasia commented, picking up the fabrics and handing them to one of the assistants.

"Yes, this will do perfectly for the coronation and wedding. Thank you," Anastasia nodded to the assistant in appreciation.

"Seamstress," Anastasia added, stepping upon a measuring block with false bravado, as one of the seamstresses beside the block dropped into a curtsy. "Design me a gown that makes the gentlemen blush."

With butterflies in her stomach, Princess Annalyse entered the dining room in a stunning silver gown with an empire neckline and a long, draping, shimmering cape trailing behind her. Upon her flowing blond tresses, sat Queen Amealiana's emerald crown. Due to the young Heir's style of gown and aged appearance from healing her sister, anyone who didn't know Annie's history would believe she was a mature young woman in her late twenties.

The room felt much smaller than Annie recalled it being at breakfast that morning. Along the royal family's dining table, members of the royal family and five prospective suitors stood in respect as Annie made her way gracefully across the room to her seat at the head of the table.

After Annie was seated, with the assistance of a servant, her guests all resumed their seats. To avoid giving the impression of favouritism towards her home country of Quillencia, Annie had politely excused Queen Annalyse of Quillencia from the introductory dinner party with her suitors.

"Good evening everyone," Annie began rather awkwardly. "Welcome to Castle Brandistone. I am Princess Annalyse Brandistone, though I am sure you already know that. Oh dear, that was not very Queenly of me, forgive me," Annie blathered, "I do believe my nerves are getting the best of me. I apologize for the unorthodox group meeting. I was hoping to have more time to get to know each of you during separate visits, however, after the Alearian King and Queen's passing into the After World, the coronation and wedding are required to be brought forward."

*'Oh, my goodness, why am I rambling? I don't know how to be a Queen or host a dinner party or court suitors. Nothing says romance like 'I'm a young Queen about to assume a throne that I am not ready for… Or, be my King, I am to wed for pure expediency,'* Annie panicked, kicking her sister Anastasia gently beneath the table, signalling for help.

Anastasia choked on a laugh but quickly composed herself. "I believe what our eloquent future Queen means to say, is thank you, to all of you who travelled far and wide to be here with us. We look forward to getting to know you all over the coming week. I am Princess Anastasia Brandistone, pleased to meet you all. Now, please join us in a feast to celebrate your arrival."

*'Thank the Goddess for Anastasia!'*

"Thank you, Princess Anastasia. I hope you all enjoy your meal," Annie attempted to recover from her previous comments, signalling with a raise of her goblet for everyone to do the same.

"A toast to our guests, may your stay in Alearia be blessed by the Goddess. For family and Kingdom," Annie concluded.

"For family and Kingdom," the room echoed.

*'This is going to be a long meal…'*

# *Princess Anastasia*

After the first course was over in near silence, Anastasia decided it was time to save the dinner party.

"Perhaps, Princess Annalyse," Anastasia spoke softly towards her twin, "now would be a good time for the gentlemen to introduce themselves," Anastasia hinted.

Annie looked like a mouse caught in a trap.

"You can do this Annie, show them some of your country girl charm," Anastasia gently encouraged her sister with a wink.

Annie swallowed a large sip of wine before painting a smile across her face.

*It's times like these that make me remember just how little experience Annie has courting gentleman. It's time to turn on the Brandistone charm.'*

"Gentlemen, forgive me, but I am afraid we have not all been formally introduced," Anastasia spoke to the group. "As I said earlier, my name is Princess Anastasia. I was born and raised in Castle Brandistone. The Goddess has chosen to bestow upon me both fire-wielder and shape-shifter giftings. Princess Alecia, our older sister, is to be our Kingdom's future General and she also possesses an incredible fire-wielding gifting."

"Thank you, Anastasia, you are too kind, but yes... It's all true," Alecia declared, batting her eyelashes towards the eligible bachelor beside her. "But alas, this party isn't all about me. Our future Queen, as I am sure you have all heard, is an incredibly talented mind-conqueror and sage."

Annie blushed awkwardly at the praise she was receiving rather oddly from her older sister. But what Anastasia knew though Annie likely didn't, was that Alecia was a proud woman and would not let her Kingdom's reputation be tainted by a shy Queen. So, Alecia would put aside her differences with her sister for one night and, together the two fire-wielding sisters engaged their guests in conversation, relieving the tension from the room.

"Your Majesty," the dark haired, blue eyed gentleman sitting next to Princess Alecia began to introduce himself. "My name is Lord Andrew Amidon, from the Kingdom of Quillencia. I wish to thank you, Princess Annalyse, for your kind hospitality and for welcoming us to your beautiful Kingdom. I too am sage gifted, descending from the Amidon bloodline. My late Grandfather, Lord Aloicious Amidon, was Queen Annalyse Amidon Caston of Quillencia's brother and your late mother's Uncle."

"Goodness gracious me, Sir Andrew," Annie began, "forgive me but I am completely confused," Annie chuckled.

The table joined her in laughter. "That is completely understandable Your Highness. I find I am often confused myself. In fact, I carry a list with me in my pocket just to keep track of my family tree," Lord Andrew joked, earning a surprised laugh from the Heir herself.

"I must get you to make me a copy of this list of yours Sir Andrew, it may come in handy," Annie joked in return, finally relaxing into the conversation.

As the dinner party continued, each of the remaining four potential suitors, including a fellow noble from Alearia, introduced themselves one after the other. Representatives from each of Alearia's allying Kingdoms, including Stanthorpe, Shadows Peak, Isle of Treseme, and Quillencia, were all in attendance.

Throughout the dinner, Anastasia caught herself accidently flirting with the representative from Shadows Peak, who sat beside her at the dining table. Prince Cimmeris Davis was endearing. His deep brown eyes felt as if they could penetrate her soul, his deep, dark chocolate skin and rich black hair made him appear striking amongst the incredibly pale complexions of the Brandistone sisters.

*'Those eyes... He's a shadow walker and a wind whisperer, who could resist his mysterious nature? What secrets does he keep? Why has he, a potential Heir of his own Kingdom, ventured so far from the safety of the shadows to be here? Perhaps he is not favoured to be crowned Heir of his own Kingdom?*

*'Enough practicalities! Oh, my goodness he would make gorgeous Heirs.'*

Anastasia couldn't help but feel drawn towards the young Prince, though she regularly reminded herself that she was there to find her sister a future King, not find a match for herself. It didn't help that she had caught the suave Prince admiring her gown, or her in her gown more to the point, several times throughout the evening.

*'Who can blame him though, I look sinfully splendid in this gown. I have been waiting for the perfect opportunity to show off this gown. I must admit, it is nice to be feeling more myself again.*

*'This past month has been hard without mother around, but I must learn to stand on my own feet and help Annie as best as I can. I am no help to her if I am a mess myself, so day by day, I will keep pushing through my anxiety.*

*'I will hold my head high and be the strong warrior Princess that the Goddess intended for me to be.'*

"Prince Liquire," Annie spoke, pulling Anastasia from her thoughts. "Could you please tell us a bit about yourself and your beautiful Kingdom? I'm afraid we were practically neighbors for most of my life and yet I know little of the Isle of Treseme."

"It would be my pleasure Princess," Prince Liquire Ocea responded. "The Isle of Treseme, as you say, is remarkably close to Quillencia, just a short boat ride from the Quillencian south east shores. The Isle is a relatively small Kingdom in comparison to the expansive Alearian Kingdom. Most of our people are wind whisperers or water mages. I have been blessed to inherit my mother Queen Amphirite Gallayous Ocea's, Goddess given water mage gifting. Whilst we are a small Kingdom, our Treseme Sea Legion is incomparable to other fleets. We know the water and the wind as well as we know our family. Our people cannot survive without either. We need the water and wind just as we need air to breathe. The ocean surrounding our Kingdom protects us and gives us strength; it is the lifeblood of our ancient people. I am blessed by the Goddess to be a Prince of the Isle of Treseme," Prince Liquire concluded graciously.

"Your Kingdom and people sound beautiful, Prince Liquire, I hope to see your wonderful Kingdom one day soon," Annie responded, catching herself blushing towards the handsome blond and blue-eyed, prince.

"It would be our honor Princess Annalyse," Liquire honestly replied to the Heir.

"Your Grace," Sir Igneous interrupted, his accent as thick as his facial hair — his flaming red hair a reflection of his fiery personality. "I am Sir Igneous Margach of the mighty Kingdom of Stanthorpe. Our people are a proud and passionate people. Our Legionnaires are seasoned warriors. As General of the Stanthorpe Land Legion, I take loyalty and respect very seriously. I'd stake my late wife's life on it that my fire-wielding gift equals the strength of the Brandistone bloodline, had she not passed away from the last plague, Goddess rest her soul," Sir Igneous boasted.

"Ahh… very good," Princess Annie replied awkwardly. "My condolences on your late wife's passing. Thank you for enlightening us Sir Igneous about your Kingdom's Legion. Perhaps another time you could share with us more about your Kingdom itself," Annie requested diplomatically, clearly a little unsure of how to respond to such a *well-seasoned* gentleman as he.

"My pleasure, Your Majesty, I must write myself a note to remember to do that. My memory isn't what is used to be," Igneous grunted, respectfully nodding his head.

"Sir Jack," Anastasia interrupted, attempting to divert the attention away from Sir Igneous and save the conversation. "How is your family coping after the recent loss of your cousin Sir Riley Thornley? We offer our condolences; his passing was a loss felt by all who knew him."

"Thank you, Princess Anastasia," Sir Jack Thornley of Alearia responded. "The House of Thornley has been loyal to the House of Brandistone for many generations, and though our Kingdom is transitioning through difficult times now, we remain strong and loyal to the Crown. My cousin will be missed. Thank you for your condolences, Princess."

Anastasia and Annie nodded graciously.

"Mmm… Thank the Goddess dessert has arrived and chocolate cake — my favourite!" Anastasia exclaimed giddily as the servants served the final course of the night.

"More wine please," Alecia requested of the staff before launching into a conversation with Lord Andrew about the latest trade agreements between their two Kingdoms.

The conversation then progressed to debates across the table regarding favourite training techniques and comparing their various Goddess given giftings. Alecia was a born entertainer and her confidence shined at dinner parties and events such as these.

# 27

## Princess Annalyse

Snuggled up, with blankets in front of the cosy fireplace in Annie's suite, the three royal sisters gossiped merrily about the evening's dinner party. Lady Margarette, surprised the siblings with a platter of sweet treats for supper and pot after pot of herbal tea. A knock sounded at the door, drawing the young ladies from their conversation.

Lady Margarette walked over to the door to welcome their guest.

"Queen Annalyse, welcome," Lady Margarette curtsied for their guest before gesturing for the Matriarch of Quillencia to enter.

The mature Queen had the same eyes as her daughter and the detail always surprised Annie whenever she saw her, making her heart long for her mother once more.

Having the Quillencian Queen stay with them since their mother's passing had been a great comfort for the Alearian Princesses. The support and sage wisdom she offered was invaluable. The three royal Princesses stood from their chairs in front of the hearth and curtsied for the Matriarch.

"Welcome Queen Annalyse, what a lovely surprise," Annie greeted their Grandmother.

"Good evening ladies," Queen Annalyse smiled. "I wanted to see how you were feeling after tonight's dinner party Annie and to see how you are feeling about the ceremony tomorrow morning?" The Quillencian Monarch offered sincerely.

"Thank you, Grandmother. That is very kind of you. I am a little nervous as is to be expected," Annie stated.

The Quillencian Royal sat upon the chaise beside Anastasia, her granddaughter offering her quilted blanket for the elderly women to share.

"It is perfectly normal to be anxious; I assure you my dear. But you will make a remarkable Queen. There is nothing you cannot handle," Queen Annalyse responded warmly before turning her attention to the Lady's Maid. "Lady Margarette, how are you? It has been a long time since we have been able to talk. Thank you for serving my daughter so loyally. Amealiana thought very highly of you. I'm sure my granddaughter also greatly appreciates your support and assistance," Queen Annalyse praised her.

The Lady's Maid curtsied again for the foreign Queen, "you are too kind Queen Annalyse. It was my greatest honor to serve Queen Amealiana. I miss her dearly. Sadly, I am beginning to feel my age and regret that I will need to hand over the honor of serving our Heir to a new Lady's Maid shortly."

"I am very sorry to hear that," Queen Annalyse replied, "but age is a plight that sadly none of us are immune to, myself included. Though, how extremely blessed by the Goddess we are to have lived such long, fortunate lives."

Lady Margarette nodded solemnly in agreement. "May I get you anything, Your Majesty? A glass of wine or a cup of tea perhaps?"

"A glass of wine sounds divine, thank you Margarette."

"My pleasure, Queen Annalyse," Margarette curtsied as she poured the Monarch a glass of red wine; former Queen Amealiana's preferred drop.

The Quillencian Queen offered the Lady's Maid a small sincere smile as she accepted the glass and raised it in a toast.

"To Annie, may the Goddess bless her as tomorrow she is crowned Queen of Alearia. For family and Kingdom," Queen Annalyse toasted.

"For family and Kingdom," the three Princesses toasted in return, raising their cups of tea.

*'Goodness gracious me,'* Annie reflected to herself. *'The Queen of all Alearia... A healer's apprentice turned Queen... Who would have thought it? Please Goddess, help me make my mother and Lily proud."*

"Now..." Queen Annalyse continued, drawing Annie from her thoughts, "tell me all the gossip about these suitors, and leave out no details. This old lady needs to live vicariously through you all," Queen Annalyse joked, resulting in laughter all round.

# 28

# Princess Annalyse

The young Heir tossed and turned in her four-poster bed. Eventually abandoning the idea of sleep all together, Annie dragged herself out of bed conveniently forgetting to call for Lady Margarette to assist her with her morning routine. After keeping her Lady's Maid up late while she gossiped until the early hours of the morning with her grandmother and sisters, Annie wanted to give Lady Margarette a well-deserved rest.

Besides, Annie enjoyed her solitude and sometimes it was nice just to pretend for a few short moments, that she was just an ordinary country girl getting herself ready for the day.

'Though I doubt any normal country girl could fathom the idea of grooming herself to be crowned Queen. A bath and tea, is exactly what I need to calm my nerves.'

Annie prepared herself some chamomile and lavender tea with the teapot she kept hidden near the hearth. Then she ran herself a nice hot bath, pouring various natural oils into the water; the blissful floral scents filling the entire bathing chamber. The hot water helped to ease the tension in her body, the tea helping to calm her nerves.

After the water turned cold and her fingers were shrivelled, Annie reluctantly pulled herself out of the bath and wrapped herself in a silk night coat. Catching a glimpse of herself in the bathing chamber mirror, Annie was once more surprised by her reflection. A young woman now looked back at her, rather than the country girl Annie still felt like at heart. It would be a while before Annie felt comfortable once more in her own skin.

'After today there will be no going back. My path will be set in stone, and I will not be able to hide behind my healer's apprentice title any longer. As of today, all decisions, all responsibility, will officially weigh on my shoulders.

'As of today, I will be judged even more critically for every decision and move I make. From today, I will be Queen of Alearia.

'Goddess help me, I don't think I'll ever feel ready for this. How am I to lead my people? How am I to reassure them, to calm the civil unrest? How am I to choose a husband, a King, a father for my children?

'How am I to be a mother, when I am still a child?'

Annie's legs felt unsteady beneath her. She felt herself leaning against the bathing chamber wall, and suddenly feeling overwhelmed, Annie slid down the wall and wrapped her arms around her knees. Crouched on the floor, Annie allowed herself a moment of vulnerability whilst she was alone and allowed the tears of anxiety to pour out of her.

Anastasia knocked on the bathing chamber door, waking Annie from where she had accidently fallen asleep on the floor.

"Come in," Annie yawned, rubbing the sleep from her eyes.

Anastasia entered the chamber, followed by Lady Margarette.

"Annie?" Anastasia spoke softly as she lowered herself down to the floor to sit beside her sister. "Are you ok? Did you spend the night in here?"

Annie yawned into her fist, "excuse me. I was having trouble sleeping so I decided to have some tea and a bath. I must have fallen asleep in here afterwards. I'm fine, no need to worry."

Anastasia crinkled her brow, "very well… If you are sure?"

Anastasia pulled herself up from the floor and both Margarette and Anastasia offered Annie a hand each, lifting her into a standing position.

"Princess Annalyse," Lady Margarette spoke in a gentle tone. "How about a nice cup of tea in front of the fire whilst I style your hair for today's ceremony?"

"That sounds lovely, thank you Margarette. Sorry if I worried you both," Annie responded sincerely.

"There is nothing to apologize for," Anastasia reassured her. "Now sit down, relax, and enjoy your pampering. I have a surprise for you."

Annie sat in one of the chairs by the hearth, tea and a platter of fruit and pastries already laid out for her upon the side table. Margarette began to brush out Annie's hair as Anastasia sat opposite her sister and handed her a small box that she had pulled out of her coat pocket.

"Thank you, Tash," Annie smiled warmly, accepting the gift and opening it gently. "Oh, my goodness Anastasia, they are beautiful! Thank you," Annie exclaimed.

"They were a gift from our mother," Anastasia simply replied. "On our thirteenth birthday, Queen Amealiana gifted me with two pairs of identical sapphire earrings. I always thought it was peculiar that she would give me two pairs of the same earrings. At the time, she told me that they were so gorgeous, she wanted to buy me two pairs in case I ever misplaced a pair. Though truth be told, I never believed her as I would never misplace something so special. I think she secretly hoped that when we were one day reunited, that I would give the second pair to you. Twin earrings for her twin daughters," Anastasia spoke warmly.

Annie lifted her eyes from examining the heart-shaped, sapphire earrings of the deepest blue she had ever seen.

"Thank you, Anastasia, they are the most stunning earrings I have ever seen. They remind me of her blue eyes," she replied warmly.

"You're welcome Annie. I think our mother would have wanted you to wear them today, so you could remember her as you ascend the throne."

Annie pulled away from Margarette's grooming to embrace her sister, "thank you, Anastasia. This means so much to me. I will treasure our mother's gift, always."

"I know you will Annie. Now sit back down and let Margarette work her magic on your frightfully messy head of hair. We have a coronation ceremony to prepare for," Anastasia chuckled.

*29*

*Princess Annalyse*

Floating along the aisle of the castle temple, hundreds of brightly lit candles guided Annie's way towards the throne positioned center stage on the dais. Senior Priestess Lavinia stood proudly beside the throne, dressed in her ceremonial crisp white gown with gold shawl.

To crown a new King or Queen was a great honor for a Priestess. As High Priestess Elizabeth continued to lead the protests against the Monarchy, a replacement Priestess was chosen to conduct the coronation. As Priestess Lavinia, a humble, middle-aged woman, was the most senior Priestess still loyal to the royal family, she was granted the honor.

The crowd of witnesses had been kept to a minimum for security purposes. The guest list was limited to Queen Annalyse of Quillencia, Princesses Anastasia and Alecia, Sir Tomlin, Lord Ashcott, and the five suitors.

Each of the suitors were briefed by Lord Ashcott and Sir Tomlin on the coronation ceremony following the prior evening's dinner party. Each suitor had eagerly accepted their invitation to the private coronation, and offered to attend as official delegates of their respective Kingdoms.

Princess Annalyse, Heir of Alearia, was dressed in her mother's former coronation dress; a cream ball gown with a red and gold sash, the colors of the house of Brandistone. A simple gold circlet sat atop her head, and Queen Amealiana's emerald encrusted crown rested atop a pillow upon the alter behind the throne.

The coronation attendees, led by Princess Anastasia, sung the anthem of Alearia, as Annie gracefully made her way up the aisle, head held high. Reaching the alter, she knelt before the throne upon a silk pillow embroidered with the house crest. Annie bowed her head low in respect for the Goddess; the creator. As the song finished, Princess Anastasia resumed her place beside Alecia and the guests took their seats in the pews.

Senior Priestess Lavinia walked down the two steps to the bottom of the alter stage to stand beside Princess Annalyse. "Thank you, to all who have come today to bear witness to this important moment in our Kingdom's history," Lavinia began in a sing-song rhythm.

"It is my greatest honor to act on behalf of our almighty Goddess to crown Princess Annalyse as Queen of Alearia." Lavinia stood directly in front of the Heir and placed a hand upon each of her shoulders.

"Holy Goddess," the Priestess recited, "we are gathered here to witness our Goddess chosen Heir to be anointed as Queen. We ask for your continual blessing upon her reign, that you will guide her through all her decision making and hold her accountable for her choices. We pray that you fill Her Royal Highness with your wisdom and grace. May she always strive to be a strong, just leader with the courage of a Legion. Let your light shine through her. May the giftings she has been bestowed, continue to be a blessing upon her and her people. May our Queen always demonstrate kindness and compassion. May she always put the people's needs above her own. We pray that she bears children to carry on her legacy. May her reign be long and prosperous. For family and Kingdom, praise be the Goddess," Lavinia declared.

"For family and Kingdom, praise be the Goddess," the room echoed.

"Princess Annalyse," Priestess Lavinia continued, "I now invite you to stand before your Goddess and your people to make your solemn vows."

Annie rose from her position and walked the two steps up to the alter Dais. Standing in front of the throne, Annie turned to face her guests as the Senior Priestess handed her the Goddess's sacred text for her to recite from.

The age-old text was a comforting weight in Annie's hands.

"Holy Goddess, my people, witnesses and honored guests, to you I make these vows," Princess Annalyse began. "I, Princess Annalyse Brandistone of Alearia, vow to always put the Goddess, my family and my Kingdom's needs above all others. I vow to serve my people in accordance with the Goddess's teachings. I vow to lead my people with integrity, to act justly, and to seek the Goddess's counsel. I vow to only use the giftings bestowed upon me by the Goddess, to serve my people. I vow to always put my people's needs first. I vow to produce potential Heirs that will one day participate in the Crowning Ceremonies and thus continue my legacy. I vow to always strive for peace and prosperity. I vow to be the ruler that the people need. I make these formal declarations, as the Goddess is my witness," Princess Annalyse concluded, bowing deeply before her witnesses as a sign of devotion and service to her people.

Priestess Lavinia invited the Heir to sit upon the throne. Taking a small pot full of water from the sacred springs of the Goddess's home temple upon the mountain top, Lavinia dipped her finger into the sacred water and marked the sign of a flame upon Annalyse's forehead, the sign of the Goddess. After setting the pot back upon the alter, Priestess Lavinia then placed the royal ruby encrusted sceptre, into the hands of the Heir.

"This sceptre represents your people," the Priestess declared. "Its heavy weight will act as a constant reminder that the lives of the Alearian people are now in your hands."

"As is the will of the Goddess, I will protect my people," Annie vowed.

Priestess Lavinia then gently placed the former Queen's emerald jewelled crown upon the Heir's head.

"This crown symbolises the weight of the responsibility you now carry," Lavinia advised her. "The Kingdom of Alearia is now entrusted to your care. Praise be the Goddess."

"As it is the Goddess's will, I will always put my Kingdom first," Annie vowed.

Lavinia turned to stand beside Annalyse, so that the witnesses could behold their Goddess chosen Queen.

"By the power vested in me by our almighty Goddess, I declare thee, Annalyse Brandistone, Queen of Alearia. All hail, Queen Annalyse Brandistone of Alearia, for family and Kingdom," Lavinia declared.

The guests and witnesses all dropped to their knees and bowed.

As one they declared, "All hail Queen Annalyse!"

Their declaration then followed by resounding applause, as the witnesses rose to stand and celebrate the crowning of the new Queen.

# Queen Annalyse of Alearia

The private coronation celebrations continued late into the evening. What began as a formal luncheon in the royal family dining room, soon morphed into a garden party in the rose gardens by the fountain. The wine was flowing, and the servants carried around platters of canapés and bite sized desserts.

After a few glasses of wine, Annie felt her confidence build, and even surrounded by the scrutinizing gaze of five suitors, the young Queen felt completely at ease. The sweet aroma of flowers carried upon the gentle breeze reminded Annie fondly of her mother.

"If I could have your attention please, I would like to make a toast," Queen Annalyse of Quillencia began, raising her glass of champagne.

The guests turning their attention to the Quillencian Monarch. "To the new ruler of Alearia, Queen Annalyse Brandistone, may the Goddess guide you, protect you and bless you always. For family and Kingdom, raise your glasses to the Queen of Alearia."

"To Queen Annalyse," the Alearian royals and suitors proclaimed.

Anastasia leant over to whisper into her twin's ear after the group had returned to their own private conversations. The two girls now sat side by side on the fountain ledge, taking in the party around them. "How does it feel, to have all your dreams come true Annie?"

"I didn't even know this was a dream of mine, until recently," Annie sighed blissfully. "But Anastasia, now that I am Queen... What comes next?"

Anastasia looked at twin, a vision of beauty in her pale blue gown and silver tiara, a small smile across her face.

"For now, you take it all in," Anastasia replied softly. "Enjoy this moment. Too often we look to the future and forget to enjoy the present. But if you really want to know what's next... In the coming days we will choose a husband for you. In a week's time, before the whole Kingdom, you will be officially pronounced Queen of Alearia and hopefully marry the man of your dreams. No pressure, sister," Anastasia giggled, lightening the mood, nudging her sister in the side playfully.

"No pressure at all..." Annie drawled, suddenly feeling the need to fidget with her gown to distract herself. "*Queen* of Alearia... *Queen* of Alearia... I don't think I will ever get used to being addressed as such. It makes my heart flutter with anxiety every time I hear it."

"Enough serious talk, the string quartet are now set-up, let's dance!" Anastasia declared as she sprung from the ledge...

But she was quickly pulled back down by Annie. Anastasia turned to her sister, confusion and slight concern flashing across her face.

"What's troubling you Annie?" Anastasia asked softly.

"There has been one thing has been bothering me about today," Annie
dared voice.

Anastasia stood from the ledge once more and leaned forward to whisper
in her sister's ear, "not here. Walk with me, we can talk while we walk."

Annie nodded in understanding, and the two royals began to walk arm-
in arm, seemingly cheerfully around the fountain and off through the garden
hedge maze.

# *Princess Anastasia*

*'I knew something was bothering her. To anyone else Annie would seem
so carefree today, but that is so out of character from the sister that I have
come to know. This was the first private coronation in our Kingdom's
history, it was sure to rattle her a little.'*

"Annie, what's bothering you?" Anastasia asked, pausing along the path
once they had walked far enough away from the party to be out of earshot.

Annie looked up from the ground and broke away from Anastasia's arm,
instead taking her sister's hands in her own and pulling her around the next
hedge maze corner to ensure they were concealed from any prying eyes.

"Do you think I made the right decision in holding the coronation in
secret today?" Annie whispered uncertainly, biting her lip. "What if the
news leaks out of the castle and the people find out I have deceived them?"

Concern shone in Anastasia's eyes.

"The coronation couldn't wait any longer Annie, you know this. A Kingdom without a ruling Monarch is vulnerable. As Heir you did not have the official power to make proclamations for the Kingdom, but as Queen you do," Anastasia responded.

"I understand that," Annie accepted squirming on her feet. "However, if the coronation is not made public knowledge then as far as the people know, I still have no power. Not in the way that counts..." Annie added anxiously.

"Annie, it was our grandmother's advice to have the coronation in secret. She has decades of experience as a Queen," Anastasia reassured her twin. "You can trust her advice. This was the best decision for you and the Kingdom."

"But what if it wasn't what was best for *our* Kingdom?" Annie countered. "What if it sends a message that I have a lack of trust in my people? The people were already revolting against my appointment as Heir."

Anastasia squeezed her twin's hands in reassurance.

"Annie," Anastasia spoke with conviction, "if you genuinely believe that holding the coronation in secret was the wrong idea, then you know what you have to do. You are the Queen of Alearia now and you must do what you feel is right. I will stand by you and support you, no matter what you decide."

Annie squeezed her sister's hands back in thanks, turning to make her way back towards the celebrations, "let's go and get Alecia. Can you please summon Sir Cornell? We have a public announcement to make."

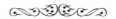

# *Princess Alecia*

'*Despite all of the impulsive, reckless decisions I have ever made, this plan of Annie's takes the cake.*'

Alecia channeled her power, feeling the hum of her fire-wielding gifting singing beneath her skin in preparation, dusk was upon them. After quickly changing into her Alearian Legion ceremonial attire, Alecia was the epitome of a warrior Princess. Her hair still arranged in lose curls from the coronation and her makeup quickly refreshed, Alecia stood tall by Annie's side, gifting at the ready in case of attack.

Sir Cornell had come as soon as he was summoned and stood a little befuddled beside Annie upon the balcony of the watchtower at the front gates of the castle. To onlookers, the former Crowning Ceremony commentator and the Alearian royals appeared to be the picture of composure, as if this impromptu announcement had been planned for days rather than hours. Alecia had made her feelings regarding the announcement perfectly clear, but quickly fell in line remembering that Annie now held power over her as her Queen.

The townspeople and city nobles had quickly gathered at the castle gates after Sir Cornell had sent a message on the wind to every inch of the Alearian city proper, informing the people of the important announcement that was to be made.

Behind Annie, Anastasia stood faithfully in support. The Queen of Quillencia, Senior Priestess Lavinia and five suitors all stood loyally in the wing of the balcony in support of the new Queen.

"Lords and Ladies, people of Alearia," Sir Cornell announced, projecting his voice far and wide with his wind whisperer gifting. "Thank you for gathering here at such short notice for this exciting announcement. I would now like to warmly introduce Her Majesty, Queen Annalyse Brandistone," Sir Cornell announced warmly.

Outcries began spreading around the crowd at the use of the formal title, especially from those who had been protesting Annie's ascension as Heir.

"Thank you, Sir Cornell. Welcome my people," Annie began speaking over the crowds, her voice projected by Sir Cornell, who amplified his gift further to overcome the added noise from the protesters.

*'This will get their attention,'* Alecia wickedly thought as she sent a warning burst of warm air towards the rowdiest of the crowd, their complaints falling silent, and replaced instead by a swathe of accusatory stares.

Annie placed a warning hand gently upon Alecia's arm, sending Alecia sizzling. *'I was only trying to help, ungrateful little sister!'*

"My people," Annie resumed, head held high. The white coronation gown, sash and crown atop Annie's head was not lost on the people. "Thank you for coming here today. I have two exciting announcements to make. Firstly, as of today, our new General of the Alearian Legion is Princess Alecia Brandistone. I wish to thank our former General, Lord Ashcott, for his years of loyal service to the crown. Please make welcome, General Alecia Brandistone, our first female General in Alearian history," Annie announced, though she was met with complaints rising from the crowds, which Annie chose to ignore.

*'The lack of respect regarding Annie's address speaks volumes regarding the people's low opinion of her. Annie has a long way to go to earn the people allegiance.'*

Alecia remained composed, allowing the protests to wash over her like an unwanted breeze, rather than allowing them to affect her.

"Finally, this morning," Annie continued, "in the presence of my beloved family and our guests of honor from our neighboring allied Kingdoms, I was officially crowned Queen of Alearia. The coronation was conducted by Senior Priestess Lavinia, who acted on the Goddess's behalf."

Outcries began once more, some of the protesters throwing food and other objects towards the balcony in protest, claiming her coronation was against the will of the Goddess. A barrier of air was erected by Sir Cornell immediately in front of the balcony, so that all the objects thrown bounced back at the crowd.

Annie continued to stand unruffled and proud, ignoring the interruption as she continued. "I vowed to serve the Alearian Kingdom and its people with honor, integrity and respect. I declare to you all, as the Goddess is my witness, that I will always put family and Kingdom before all else."

The crowd became incensed. The nobles who had attended the announcement in support of the Monarch, noticeably began to flee back to the safety of their homes as the protesters became wilder.

"Enough," a firm, loud voice from the back of the crowd declared.

The protesters parted to make way for the old crone. High Priestess Elizabeth slowly meandered towards the front of the crowd, stopping beneath the balcony where the Queen stood.

"As High Priestess," Elizabeth began, "it is my duty to crown our Kingdom's King or Queen. I therefore rebuke the validity of this coronation. Annalyse is not our Goddess chosen ruler, she is a foreign healer's apprentice who has shown nothing but disrespect for her responsibilities and our traditions ever since being crowned Heir. I rebuke her claim to the crown in the name of our mighty Goddess," Elizabeth declared.

Applause built from many of the protesters in support of the High Priestess's speech.

Annie, rattled by the turn of events, attempted to remain composed. "High Priestess," Annie responded, "thank you for coming here today. Whilst your protest has been noted, our law clearly states that any senior member of the Goddess's sisterhood of Priestesses may perform the coronation ceremony. As Queen of Alearia, I will grant you compassion and leniency as the Goddess would advise me. However, whilst I respect and value your input as a servant of the Goddess, I must also remind you that you are also a servant to the Crown in accordance with the vows you made upon becoming a Priestess," Annie bravely cautioned her.

"I invite my people, including you High Priestess, to meet with me to share your concerns so that we may work together to build a stronger, united Alearia. For family and Kingdom, good evening Alearia," Annie proclaimed, head held high.

"For family and Kingdom," a small percentage of the crowd murmured reluctantly in response. The rest of the crowd once more began voicing their disapproval of Annie's coronation.

Across the crowd, Alecia spotted a flurry of mist and activity brewing in the shadows of the nearest building. The mist quickly spread over the crowd, concealing their actions from the royals on the watchtower balcony. The crowd began to panic as their vision became quickly obstructed.

Alecia grabbed Annie by her arm and yanked her protectively behind her, shielding her body with her own, lighting a flame in each of her hands in warning to anyone who planned to attack.

Alecia started to slowly back away, forcing Annie to retreat with her into the safety of the watchtower; their foreign guests quickly following their lead.

Sir Cornell reinforced his proactive shield of air around the watchtower's balcony, perspiration spotted his brow from exhausting his gifting as the mist crept higher up the castle's barrier walls. Cries of fear continued to rise up amongst the crowd.

"Force the gates open!" Alecia heard one of the rebels declare.

A flash of light temporarily blinded the new General as her sister Anastasia leapt protectively in front of her and the Queen, having transformed into her preferred Alearian mountain cat form.

"Prince Liquire," Alecia called behind her, "can you please do something about this mist?!"

The Prince flashed a grin at her. "It would be my pleasure," he responded proudly, moving to the balcony edge to stand beside the Alearian mountain cat.

Sir Cornell retreated his defensive wall of air a few feet back, giving the water mage Prince room to work with.

Prince Liquire outstretched his hands towards the approaching mist and the balcony shook with the immense strain of his water mage gift building up inside him. With a mighty push of his power, he transformed the mist into a mighty wall of water like a tidal wave out at sea.

With another wave of his arms, he released the full weight and power of the wave upon the outside of the castle gate. Screams were replaced by a thunderclap of water against the iron gate and surrounding stone wall, mercilessly drowning the attempted intruders. The water then dissipated once more into a cloud of mist and floated into the sky as directed by its master from the Isle of Treseme.

With the view of the balcony clear once more, a well-aimed arrow from the remaining upright crowd attempted to strike the Isle of Treseme Prince in retaliation, but was intercepted with a swipe of the Alearian cat's mighty clawed paws. A proud roar followed, echoing across the Alearian city proper. Alecia had never felt prouder of her sister.

Just when Alecia thought the whole saga was finally over, a volley of arrows from the shadows of a nearby building launched towards the balcony. Anastasia and Prince Liquire, who were unprotected by the defensive wall of air, were unable to deflect all the arrows on their own. An iron tipped arrow pummelled into Anastasia's side, and a bellowed roar of pain escaped from the mountain cat as she keeled to the ground. Another arrow pierced the water mage Prince, causing him to bellow in pain.

Alearian Legion guards stormed up the watchtower stairs to assist with the attack, positioning themselves defensively in front of the injured Prince and Princess. They hurled volley after volley of fireballs and water walls without mercy towards the shadows, pounding the attackers with all their might, taking no prisoners. Such was the might and power of the Alearian Legion.

"Prince Cimmeris," Alecia bellowed to the shadow walker Prince behind her, pushing Annie towards him. "Transport the Queen out of here and protect her at all costs!" The General declared.

"With my life," Cimmeris responded. Lifting the startled Alearian Queen into his arms, he transported her through the shadows of the watchtower, and away to safety like a knight in shining armour.

With the Queen out of harm's way, Alecia called for a healer before she launched herself towards the Isle of Treseme Prince and her fallen sister, who lay whimpering in her shapeshifter form, an arrow buried deep in her side.

Alecia and one of the guards quickly lifted the Prince and Princess one at a time into the watchtower building, under the protection of the Alearian Legion on the balcony and Sir Cornell's shield.

Slamming the lead door shut behind them, shame curled in Alecia's gut as she chose her sister over her Kingdom, though she had vowed to protect both.

# 32

# Queen Annalyse of Flearia

The world felt as though it had ceased to exist as Annie stared into the impenetrable darkness. She clung with all her strength to the mysterious Prince's chest, as they shadow walked from the chaotic watchtower into the shadows of a dark room.

After allowing her eyesight a moment to adjust, Annie could make out the outlines of the furniture surrounding her. The sun had now set, and only dim light filtered in through the window.

Annie felt herself being lowered onto a soft bed, the luxurious texture of the linen, a welcome relief against her skin. Annie sat in shock for a moment. The realization hit her that she was sitting in the dark with an acquaintance while her sisters and her grandmother, were out there at the mercy of a crowd rioting against the crown. Her crown.

"You are safe now, Your Majesty," the mysterious Prince reassured her from further away in the shadows, drawing Annie from her thoughts.

A moment later a flame lit in the hearth, casting soft light across the room and revealing the Prince in his impeccable suit, not a hair out of place, his dark brown eyes gazing into her own.

'*Oh, golly gosh, I am in trouble,*' Annie thought to herself.

All feelings of guilt were suddenly pushed aside, as self-consciousness overcame her at the thought of being alone with the foreign Prince, in what appeared to be his personal suite.

'*I must stop staring... But that smile promises trouble in all the right kind of ways... Those eyes have probably gazed over more women in a single summer, than men I have met in my entire life... What am I doing here? I don't know how to court men let alone a Prince like this!*

'*Oh, my goodness, his grin is growing. He can read my mind; he knows I'm checking him out! Goddess save me, I can feel my cheeks heating up... Calm down Annie...*'

"Forgive me," Prince Cimmeris spoke gently but sincerely, "if bringing you here was audacious. I mean you no ill intent. Please allow me to explain. You see, I can only shadow walk to places I have been to in person. This was the safest place I could think of at a moment's notice in your castle, so that is why I brought you here."

"I understand," Annie squeaked awkwardly, suddenly very aware of just how tight she had clung to the shadow walker Prince during their travel. Her cheeks flushed once more. The Prince chuckled in return, a small smirk curving across his face at the young Queen's obvious awkwardness.

"Thank you, Princess Cimmeris, for protecting me," Annie uncomfortably replied before gasping in horror at her mistake in formality.

The Prince burst out laughing, "you and I are going to get along just fine Queen Annalyse. If it is not too presumptuous, may I call you Annie?"

Annie's face blushed bright red in response and the Prince launched into another fit of laughter.

"You will have to work on concealing your feelings more thoroughly my Queen, or you will never beat me at cards," he joked, causing Annie to blush further and release a small laugh herself.

"Thank you for the suggestion *Prince* Cimmeris," Annie replied, feigning interest for a moment in a pulled thread on her dress. "I will remember that if I ever have the unfortunate luck of playing cards with such a mysterious gentleman from Shadows Peak, such as yourself," Annie replied, looking down her nose and raising her left eyebrow, earning herself another laugh from the Prince.

*'Oh, my goodness gracious me, am I actually trying to flirt?! Goddess above I've lost my mind!'*

"I see there is fire after all beneath that dainty exterior," Prince Cimmeris responded with a devious smile. "It is a pleasure to get to know you under more *intimate* circumstances, Queen Annie."

"The pleasure is all mine, Prince Cimmeris, mysterious shadow walker and card playing extraordinaire," Annie teased.

An hour later, after awkwardly exchanging banter whilst Annie tried her best to maintain a cool and calm demeanour, a brisk knock came at the door, followed by Alecia bursting into the room.

"Thank the Goddess, you're alive! I had guards searching the entire palace for you," Alecia exclaimed, staring daggers at Annie. She then turned her attention to the Prince and in a completely different tone that stunned Annie. "Thank you for protecting the Queen, Prince Cimmeris. I am indebted to you for your assistance, but if you could please excuse us, the

Queen needs to come with me urgently," Alecia concluded. Her moment of charm faded away as quickly as she turned it on.

"Excuse us, Cimmeris. Thank you again for helping me," Annie smiled.

"The pleasure was all mine," the Prince charmingly replied, bowing low for the Queen with a small sly wink that only Annie appeared to notice.

"Let's go," Alecia exclaimed, guiding Annie out of the room and promptly heading in the direction of the infirmary.

Annie's heart quickened in her chest as reality hit her and she remembered the severity of the situation she had been whisked away from.

'How self-absorbed could I get?! To allow myself to forget about my poor sister, about the riot, while I was too busy flirting with a foreign Prince. Goddess save my soul because my sage wisdom must be failing me," Annie muttered under her breath.

"The Goddess can worry about saving your soul," Alecia began, "after she saves our sister! I swear Annie, since you came into our lives, nothing but trouble has befallen poor Anastasia and our family."

"Excuse me?!" Annie cried in protest, pausing in the corridor.

"You heard me!" Alecia remarked, a force to be reckoned with, before turning once again on her heel and resuming her journey to the infirmary.

"Goddess grant me patience," Annie muttered under her breath.

"Be careful what you pray for," Alecia advised with a smirk, "before you bring more trials and torment down upon our family. Everyone knows you never prayer for patience unless you have a death wish," Alecia stated matter-of-factly.

"Ha! Very wise advice indeed," Annie chuckled.

"Now hurry up Annie, our sister needs us," Alecia urged impatiently.

# 33

# Queen Annalyse of

# Quillencia

"Get away from me! Stay back!" Anastasia screamed from the corner of the infirmary room, completely bare, clenching a blanket to her chest. A wall of fire erected protectively before her, preventing the healers from coming to her aid.

Blood oozed from the wound in the side of her abdomen where the arrow was still embedded. Anastasia was hunched in pain, that much was clear, but a mixture of fear and rage filled her eyes unlike anything the Quillencian Queen had ever seen in her granddaughter before.

The Head Healer tried and failed to calm the Princess with her reassuring words, but her attempts only aggravated the terrified Princess further.

A water mage had previously attempted to douse the Princess's firewall with water. However, as soon as the Head Healer began to approach the anxious Princess, her gifting reignited the wall, narrowly avoiding incinerating the healer.

The Quillencian Queen had tried to reason with the out-of-control Princess, but nothing could calm the storm that swelled inside of her soul. Mental wounds that had not yet healed had been ripped wide open for the world to see through her re-exposure to the clinical environment.

"Where are the Alearian Queen and General Alecia?" Queen Annalyse of Quillencia roared at the Head Healer.

A rare moment indeed for the foreign Queen to allow her emotions to get the better of her.

"Princess Alecia has gone to find the Queen, Your Majesty," the senior healer responded. "I am sure they will be here as soon as they can. They will be able to calm the Princess; I am sure of it."

"I hope you are right Healer, or else my granddaughter will soon perish from lack of blood," Queen Annalyse said with a mixture of anger and anxiety, whilst she continued to pace around the room.

# General Alecia

The infirmary royal suite door flew open on a roaring hot wind, with Alecia headed in a direct line to Anastasia, the Alearian Queen on her heels.

*'Holy Goddess, what has happened to my sister?'* Alecia thought frantically, taking in the scene before her.

Alecia noticed Annie begin to slow her pace as she carefully approached her twin's wall of fire. Alecia, who was less patient, wrapped a protective layer of her own fire around herself, and walked through the firewall to shake her sister's shoulders.

"Tash calm down! We are here to help you!" Alecia yelled directly at her sister. Anastasia stared vacantly into her older sister's eyes, her firewall flaring up to burn ever more brightly, completely obstructing Annie's view of her sisters.

"They want to hurt me," Anastasia's voice cracked. "They want to take me away again Alecia. Don't let them take me," Anastasia spoke barely louder than a whisper, her voice now hoarse and wavering.

"No one is going to take you anywhere Tash," Alecia replied. "The healers are just trying to help you. That's their job..."

Anastasia's eyes turned from vacant and pleading to furious.

"You don't believe me!" Anastasia screamed disbelievingly. "You are just like them! You want them to take me away again and I won't go! You can't make me! I won't go back to that cell of a storeroom!" Anastasia screamed, hoisting a mighty wall of flame directly into Alecia's chest, sending her soaring back through the firewall and bashing hard into a wall on the opposite side of the infirmary.

# Queen Annalyse of Alearia

The intensity of the flaming wall decreased slightly after Alecia was flung back through it. Annie guessed that her twin's energy levels were beginning to fail, likely related to the blood loss she was experiencing. Annie reached out her mind conqueror gifting towards her twin, closing her eyes to concentrate. Forming a connection with Anastasia's unguarded mind, Annie recognized the disorder of her neuron signals reflecting the anxiety the Princess was experiencing.

"*Tash, it's me. It's Annie,*" she whispered mind-to-mind with her twin.

"*Annie? Annie is that really you? I'm so scared Annie. They want to take me away, don't let them take me away,*" Anastasia begged Annie through their mental connection.

"*I won't let any harm come to you Tash. I promise. I am here to help you.*"

Annie turned to the rest of the room.

"Everyone except Alecia, I need you to leave this room, right now. That is an order," Annie declared.

Following an apprehensive look from the Quillencian Queen and Head Healer, the room emptied, with only Anastasia, Alecia and Annie remaining. Alecia lifted herself from the ground and limped over to stand beside the Queen. Concern for her sister written across her face.

"I am so very sorry for not listening to you before," Alecia spoke softly through the wall of fire. "I just want to help you Tash."

"Everyone has gone Anastasia," Annie gently explained. "It's just you, me and Alecia now. We promise we won't let anything happen to you. We won't let anyone take you away. We swear on the Goddess."

The firewalls intensity decreased slightly further in response.

"Tash," Annie spoke. "Can you please lower the wall so we can help you? You have lost a great deal of blood and we need to help you before it is too late. Please trust us Anastasia. We love you."

"Please Tash, lower the wall and let us help you," Alecia added, a rare plea from the usually stoic, sassy sister.

The wall flickered for a moment, allowing Anastasia a quick glimpse of the infirmary room to ensure her sisters were telling the truth. When Anastasia was satisfied that they were alone, she lowered her firewall and slumped to the ground in exhaustion.

"Please don't let them take me," Anastasia whispered, her eyes filled with dread.

Alecia and Annie slowly closed the gap between them and their sister, careful not to startle her. Annie leaned towards Anastasia to whisper in her ear, "no one is going to ever take you away from me again. It's not like last time. I won't let them, I promise. I love you."

"Thank you, Annie," Anastasia whispered from her foetal position on the floor, heaving mighty sobs, her body trembling.

So frail her sister appeared. A mere shadow of the strong. young warrior she usually was. Annie lowered herself onto the ground to lay beside her sister, so she could stare reassuringly into her twin's eyes and began stroking Anastasia's hair in long soothing strokes.

"Anastasia," Alecia softly interrupted. "I need to stop the bleeding. Will you let me please?"

Anastasia nodded her head slightly in agreement.

Alecia lowered herself to kneel on the other side of Anastasia and with two hands, ripped the arrow from her sister's side. Anastasia released an almighty cry of pain, and the wound began oozing blood faster.

Alecia quickly discarded the arrow, placed her hands upon the now open wound and applied direct pressure. She then called upon her fire-wielding gifting and focused its power to solder the blood vessels and close the wound.

All that remained once she had completed the patch-up, was a slightly open puncture wound that would only require a simple dressing to cover, which Alecia then applied for her sister. Anastasia released a small whimper of relief after Alecia had finished tending to her wound.

Careful not to startle her sister, Alecia slowly lowered herself to the ground, bloody hands and all, to lay behind Anastasia. She then wrapped herself protectively around her. Both Alecia and Annie acted as human shields for their sister as Anastasia waited out the last of her anxiety attack. Annie all the while coaching her twin through deep breathing exercises, whilst continuing to reassuringly stroke her hair.

# Queen Annalyse of Flearia

Night had quickly rolled into morning, and the three Brandistone sisters were now sleeping blissfully together in Annie's bed. Anastasia had not wanted to be alone that night, and she was adamant she would not stay in the infirmary a minute longer. So, Annie had suggested they share a room for the night. Annie was a former healer's apprentice after all, so who better to watch over her sister through the night?

Alecia hadn't wanted to let Anastasia out her sight either, for fear that her mental health would decline if she wasn't there to watch over her, so Alecia had insisted on sleeping in Annie's room as well. Truth be told, Annie enjoyed the company. She missed the cosy nights she would spend snuggled up with Lily in front of the hearth. The physical contact brought Annie great comfort and reminded her of much simpler times.

Annie awoke to light entering the room as Lady Margarette drew open the curtains to her suite.

"Good morning, Your Majesty," Lady Margarette chimed in her cheerful singsong greeting. Walking over to Annie's bedside she warmly added, "I trust you all slept well."

Margarette had been like a mother figure to her sisters growing up, always there faithfully by their mother's side, helping her and supporting her through day-to-day life. Annie could tell that it brought Margarette great joy to see the three sisters bonding so closely. It was exactly what Queen Amealiana would have wanted.

*'It's a shame that mother couldn't see us now. I don't know what would shock her more, the fact that we are all getting along, or the fact that I am getting married in six days and I have yet to choose a King.'*

"Good morning, Lady Margarette," Annie replied pulling herself out of bed, causing her sisters to stir from their slumber.

"Good morning, Princess Anastasia and Princess Alecia," Lady Margarette greeted her other sisters as she handed Annie her fertility tonic that she had conveniently missed the night before.

Annie downed the putrid smelling mixture in one swig, gagging slightly at the horrid taste.

"I will prepare your bathing chamber, My Queen," Lady Margarette reported as she began to turn away, "breakfast with the suitors will begin shortly."

"Thank you, Margarette," Annie replied, walking over to her closet to pick out a gown for the day ahead.

*'A gown fit for a Queen looking for a husband...'* Annie released an exasperated sigh.

"Anastasia and Alecia, you better get up or we'll be late for breakfast. Tash, come and help me pick out a gown to wear will you please?"

The sisters attempted to roll over and return to sleep, but Annie threw a pillow from her chaise at each of them.

"Cut that out Annie!" Alecia exclaimed.

"We're getting up... Do I need to remind you that I almost died yesterday?" Anastasia whined, pulling herself out of bed, dragging Alecia behind her over to the cupboard.

"Annie..." Anastasia gasped, suddenly wide awake. "There is nothing in your wardrobe that will get the suitors' attention! You need to come with me!"

Before Annie could object, Anastasia looped her arm through her own and escorted her from the room. Just before Alecia closed the door behind them, she turned to Margarette who had re-entered the bedroom looking quizzical.

"Change of plans, we are going to get ready in Anastasia's room. Have the morning off Margarette, we'll look after her today," Alecia smiled wickedly.

"Very well Princess," Margarette chuckled. "But please take her crown with you," the Lady's Maid requested warmly, handing the Queen's tiara to Alecia.

"Thank you, Margarette," and with that she placed the crown upon her own head and followed her sisters over-confidently down the corridor towards Anastasia's bedroom.

"With a strong mind, wit, and impeccable grooming, a lady can achieve anything," Anastasia informed her twin. "Never underestimate the power of a stunning gown and high heels."

After combing through Anastasia's dresses, Alecia picked out the ideal dress for Annie to wear for her day ahead. The gown embodied class and beauty.

Thrusting the gown into her sister's hands, Annie objected, "I can't wear that! We're going to breakfast not out to a royal party!"

"Nonsense Annie," Anastasia backed up Alecia. "If you are going to find yourself a husband, then you need to look the part. The suitors won't be able to take their eyes off you in this gold silhouette dress," Anastasia declared confidently.

Annie sighed but conceded to wearing the dress. It was stunning after all.

After the three royals were dressed to impress, their hair styled and make-up painted, they made their way down to the family dining room for breakfast.

The Herald announced the ladies' arrival at the royal family's dining room, beginning first with Queen Annalyse, followed by her two sisters.

The suitors all stood in respect as the ladies entered the room. The Queen took her place at the head of the table, with Alecia and Anastasia electing to sit this time at the opposite end of the table, forcing the Queen to converse with her guests.

"Good morning, gentlemen," Annie greeted the suitors. "I hope you all slept well."

Confidence exuded her this morning, all thanks to her sisters' pampering.

The suitors each passed on their greetings with one noticeable suitor missing from the gathering.

"I am pleased to see you with us this morning Prince Liquire," Annie warmly offered, silently thanking the Goddess that he seemed mostly unharmed. A small bandage covered his left shoulder. "I hope your injury is healing well. I trust that our Kingdom's healers tended to you thoroughly;

they are very skilled. I sincerely thank you for your courageous actions yesterday."

"Thank you, Your Majesty. My shoulder is almost fully healed thanks to your Senior Healer's gifting," Prince Liquire nodded. "I am just thankful that you are safe. It was my pleasure to serve you. Though I do hope that yesterday's riot was a rare occurrence. I don't want to make a habit of having to save your life," The Prince teased with a wink, earning a giggle from the Queen.

"Yes, that is something we can both agree on Liquire," Annie smiled. "Please gentlemen, do eat. The cook has spared no effort with this morning's feast. It looks delicious!"

Silver platters were laid out before them, loaded with pastries, fresh bread, juices, cold meats and fruit. The cook had even prepared delicacies traditionally found in each of the five Kingdoms to make the suitors feel more comfortable.

"Queen Annalyse," Lord Andrew Amidon spoke up, "will Sir Igneous Margach be joining us this morning? I haven't seen him since the evacuation from the watch tower."

"I saw Sir Igneous leave the castle last night out the back gates in his carriage," Prince Cimmeris Davis of Shadows Peak responded before the Queen had a chance.

"That is correct," Annie confirmed. "Unfortunately, last night a messenger delivered a letter to me from Sir Igneous. The General has had a change of heart and has respectfully decided to return to his home Kingdom. I have wished him my best for a safe journey. I would encourage you, my honored guests," Annie continued, "to return to your homes and Kingdoms if you do not feel comfortable staying here. I assure you that you are safe, but I acknowledge that last night's announcement did not go as planned."

"Alearia remains a strong, mighty Kingdom," Alecia diplomatically interjected in her role as General. "Though we are going through an adjustment period as we continue to mourn the loss of Queen Amealiana and King Titian. The people will rally behind their new Queen and King. We want to reassure you that our alliances are just as important to our current Monarch as they were to our former rulers. We intend to nurture our strong diplomatic relationships," Alecia concluded.

*'For the most part, they appear reassured, though Sir Igneous' departure was a blow to our credibility. We will need to work hard to restore their confidence in our Monarchy. I must not appear weak or I will leave us wide open to scrutiny from our delegates. Our future King must believe in my Kingdom and in our people.'*

"Well said, General Brandistone," Sir Jack Thornley of Alearia agreed.

*'The wind whisperer has been quiet since his arrival at the castle this week. Jack mostly kept to himself during the coronation garden party... I am not sure what to make of him. Is he scared of the potential repercussions of his loyalty to the monarchy? Or is he just not strong enough to lead a Kingdom?*

*'An Alearian King would earn the respect of the people and help to ease their concerns, but a shy, meek ruler is not who the people need. It's not what I need. I need to choose a husband quickly and sadly; I cannot imagine Sir Jack filling that role.'*

After the meal was over, Queen Annalyse invited Lord Andrew Amidon of Quillencia for a walk through the castle rose gardens and hedge maze. She had wanted to take him for a horse ride through the forest, however, security measures had been increased following the prior evening's riots.

Annie was instructed by Alecia not to venture out of the castle grounds, or past the gardens, in case of a breach of security.

With her shimmering gold gown trailing behind her, completely inappropriate for the cool spring day, Annie walked arm in arm with Lord Andrew along the cobblestone path.

The two royals talked comfortably about Quillencia. Annie told Andrew about her upbringing in Lavender Grove, and Lord Andrew described life growing up in the Quillencian city proper.

Whilst Lord Andrew was sixth in line for the Quillencian Throne, he explained that he had never truly contemplated what it would be like to rule a Kingdom, as until recently it had seemed like such a remote possibility. Annie found she could relate to Lord Andrew more than the other Princes or Lords, though perhaps that was due to their mutual sage gifting and home country.

In many ways, Annie couldn't dream of a better match. Of all the suitors, Annie felt as though she was the most comfortable around Lord Andrew. She felt as though they could talk for hours and never run out of things to say.

*'I could imagine Lord Andrew being the close friend I have always dreamed of having. A person I could feel comfortable to share all my hopes and fears with, who I could go to for advice, to trust to stand by me. Perhaps that is what makes Andrew such a good potential match. Together we could rule Alearia with sage wisdom as our foundation.'*

"Lord Andrew," Annie said.

"Please Queen Annalyse, call me Andy, that is what all my friends call me at home," Lord Andrew requested.

"Very well, but only if you call me Annie. Just Annie," the young Queen bargained.

"Of course, Annie, it would be an honor," Andy smiled.

"Very good. Andy. I know this is very forward of me, and I do apologize but we are running out of time. I was wondering if I could ask you something?" Annie ventured, heart pounding in her chest.

"Anything Annie," Andy replied eagerly, though incongruent with his facial expression.

Annie took a seat on the edge of the fountain and motioned for Andy to join her, taking his hands in her own.

"I was wondering, Andy, could you see yourself living here? I guess what I am trying to say is... Do you think you could be happy here in Alearia, away from your family, here with me?"

Annie felt her cheeks warm as the words escaped her mouth. She found herself holding her breath slightly, awaiting his answer, butterflies fluttering around her stomach.

*'Why am I so nervous? What are these emotions I am feeling?'*

"It would be my greatest honor, Your Majesty," Lord Andrew replied, all formality. "There is no greater honor than being the ruler of a Kingdom. I would be fulfilling my duty to Quillencia by strengthening our ties. I would miss my family, my home, my friend Michaela..."

"Who is Michaela?" Annie interrupted curiously. "I haven't heard you mention her before."

"She's just a friend..." Andy began. "We grew up together. She works for my father as a stable hand. When we were younger, we used to sneak out to go on rides together in the forest around the city proper. At least we did, before father insisted I take my responsibilities more seriously. He ordered that I begin my training with the Quillencian Legion," Andy explained with a heavy heart. "I never wanted to be in the Legion. I am not one for confrontation, let alone fighting. But Quillencia hasn't been involved in a conflict for years, so the likelihood is extremely low. We are a peaceful country as you know," Andy concluded.

"Michaela was special to you, wasn't she?" Annie pushed.

"Yes. She was..." Andy admitted, "but that doesn't matter now. Family and Kingdom come before personal desires. I would care for you Annie, as my wife. It would be an honor to rule alongside you. We could become good companions," Andy concluded.

"Thank you, Andy, that means a lot to me, but I don't want to keep you apart from your friends and family, and from *Michaela*. I won't ask you to leave; the choice is yours. But if you decide you would like to stay here in Alearia, then I would be grateful for your friendship." Annie took his hands in her own.

"I cannot make you any promises either Andy," Annie explained. "I must follow my heart as well. I do believe that you and I could live a long happy life together, but I fear that you might never love me as you heart is already taken. To deprive us both of love would be a devastating tragedy."

Andy's face dropped knowingly. "A tragedy indeed Annie. You deserve to be happy; you deserve someone who can love you in the way that you deserve to be loved. I would always stand by you. I would always care for you. But I cannot offer you my whole heart. I am so sorry Annie."

"Never apologize for being who you are," Annie reassured her friend. "We cannot help who we love. Go home, be happy. Follow your heart and your own dreams. Live the life you have always wanted," Annie farewelled her friend.

# General Alecia

Alecia sat to the left of the throne at the war chamber table. Mountains of paperwork, incoming correspondence, scrolls and tactical response handbooks were spread out before her.

The importance of this room was not lost on Alecia. She was acutely aware that in this very room, over this very table, some of the Kingdom's most important diplomatic decisions had been made. And today would be no different.

Alecia quickly combed through the most recent reports from the Alearian Legion regarding the civil unrest while she waited for the other members of the council to arrive. It was Alecia who had decided to call an emergency logistics meeting of the war council. Upwards of twenty rebels had died during yesterday's attempted breech of the castle gates. Rumours had spread far and wide that such a violent means of containing the situation was evidence that their new ruler was not capable of diplomacy.

*'Goddess above, can we do nothing right? It is as though we wish to fuel the flames of gossip. The fact that the rebels were attempting to storm the gates with ill intent was all but forgotten as soon as those peasants died.'*

Beside the pile of maps, lay a parchment of notes regarding the security measures for the approaching wedding. Dealing with the regular riots, the fallout from yesterday's civil attack, all whilst planning security measures for the most important wedding of her generation, was not how Alecia imagined her introduction to life as a General would play out.

Interrupting Alecia from her thoughts, Former General Lord Ashcott entered the war chamber. He had kindly offered to stay on the war council in a supportive role until after the wedding and civil unrest were over, which Alecia was profoundly grateful for. His years of expertise were invaluable.

"Good afternoon, General Brandistone," Lord Ashcott greeted Alecia respectfully, though the title must have tasted like ash on his tongue.

"Good afternoon, Lord Ashcott. Thank you for coming. Please, take a seat," Alecia offered the former General, gesturing to the chair to her left.

"Thank you," Lord Ashcott replied, the carved wooden chair creaking as he took his place.

Alecia made a mental note to have the council chairs replaced. After years of use they were in desperate need of repair or replacement.

"I have arranged for increased Legion presence around the city proper as requested," Lord Ashcott informed the General. "An additional troop of ten Legion guards have been added to the castle gate's post. They stand positioned along the watchtower balconies on either side of the gate as a deterrent."

"Thank you, Lord Ashcott."

The chamber door opened, and the Alearian Queen, followed by Sir Tomlin, Princess Anastasia, Prince Liquire and Prince Cimmeris entered. General Brandistone and Lord Ashcott stood in respect as they entered and took their seats.

"Good afternoon Lord Ashcott," Annie greeted the former Legion leader, and nodded towards her sister in greeting.

"Good afternoon, Your Majesty," Lord Ashcott replied.

Annie nodded her head in acknowledgment. Assuming her throne at the head of the table, the Queen explained: "I invited Prince Liquire and Prince Cimmeris to join us. They were pivotal in yesterday's attempted siege on the gates and any input they could offer would be beneficial," Queen Annie declared.

"Very well, Your Majesty," General Alecia replied through gritted teeth.

*For Goddess's sake, how are we to discuss sensitive information in the presence of two foreign dignitaries without appearing weak?'* Alecia internally griped.

"Firstly, I would like to review yesterday's incident," Alecia stated now that everyone was seated. "Reports from the Legion guards suggest that public disapproval of the Monarchy is continuing to grow. The people felt a more diplomatic, peaceful solution to yesterday's attempted breach of the gates would have been more *appropriate*."

"Goddess above, this is ridiculous," Prince Liquire declared defensively. "I did what you asked me. I dealt with the mist and the attempted intruders in the most efficient means possible at the time. Those rebels were not interested in diplomacy. They were an unreasonable mob that needed to be dealt with before they could cause any further harm," Prince Liquire declared.

"I don't believe anyone is blaming you Prince Liquire," Annie reasoned, offering Liquire an apologetic smile on Alecia's behalf. "We are grateful for your service and sacrifice yesterday," Annie continued. "You acted bravely to protect us all. However, my people are grieving. A group of people died yesterday, and each member of that mob had a family. Their families are now mourning the loss of their loved ones and will look for anyone to blame. No one wants to think poorly of their loved ones, especially the dead," Annie diplomatically responded.

"Very well, Your Majesty," Prince Liquire replied curtly, still simmering from the reports.

"Thank you, Your Majesty, for that insight," Alecia responded. "As I was going to say, additional Legion troops have been stationed around the city proper and at the castle gates to discourage further rioting or other unorthodox behavior," Alecia reported.

"Very well," Annie responded. "Is there any news of the High Priestess?"

It was Lord Ashcott who spoke up this time. "Your Majesty, the High Priestess was injured during the attempted breach of the gates, but she is recovering well from what our informants told me. Unfortunately, her injuries sustained, no matter how minor, have only benefitted her cause and increased the civil unrest further," Lord Ashcott reluctantly informed the Queen. "It is my recommendation that you invite the High Priestess to the castle for another meeting and attempt to mend the Monarchy's relationship with the temple. If we can win over the High Priestess perhaps the people will follow," he suggested.

"Very wise advice Lord Ashcott," Annie responded after briefly thinking over the former General's suggestion. "Please arrange for her to attend the castle for a meeting in the throne room tomorrow after breakfast. The civil unrest needs to end."

"As you wish, Your Majesty," Lord Ashcott replied, nodding his head in agreement.

"I will remain in the shadows during the meeting if it pleases you, Your Majesty," Prince Cimmeris interjected. "Ready to wisp you away through the shadows if another security issue arises. I doubt the High Priestess will come alone and her followers cannot be trusted to remain peaceful," Prince Cimmeris added.

"Thank you, Prince Cimmeris," Alecia stated. Showing her approval of his forward thinking, but without wanting to risk her Kingdom's Legion seeming incapable, she added: "but the Legion will be enough to ensure the Queen's protection during the meeting. Your services are not required."

*'I will not have this foreign Prince believing we are incapable of protecting our own Queen. We must not appear weak.'*

"Thank you, General Alecia," Annie interjected, "but I would appreciate his presence at the meeting. Thank you for your kind offer Prince Cimmeris, we graciously accept," the Queen over-ruled.

Prince Cimmeris nodded his head in acknowledgement before sneaking a smirk towards Alecia.

*'How dare she undermine me in front of the dignitaries. That Prince is beginning to get on my nerves. I am on to you Prince of shadows.'*

"As you wish, Your Majesty," Alecia forced herself to reply graciously through gritted teeth.

"Very good," Annie responded pleasantly. "What is our next order of business General?"

Alecia shifted around the paperwork, pulling out the parchment she needed to refer to. "Security for the wedding," Alecia responded shortly.

"Have the security plans been finalised?" Annie asked.

"Almost, Your Majesty," Alicia replied uneasily. "There are still a few finer details to address that I think would be better discussed privately after the meeting if Your Majesty approves?"

"Nonsense, Alecia, everyone in this room has proved their loyalty to me. You may speak freely," Annie replied over-confidently.

*'Clearly the novelty of power is overcoming her better judgement. But as she insists...'* Alecia thought wickedly.

"As you wish," Alicia responded serenely, biting her tongue. "Our Legion numbers have decreased considerably since the former Queen and King's reign. Our numbers are limited with the increased Legion guards posted around the city. With the amount of Legion guards needed to secure the city temple and roads to and from the castle for transport, I am not sure if this event will be possible."

"I am sure you can work it out General," the Queen declared, dismissing her concern. "We have the biggest land Legion in all of the realm. I'm confident we have the numbers to cope with a few deserters."

"With all due respect, My Queen," Alecia responded cautiously, "it is true that our Legion *was* the largest in the realm, but our numbers have considerably decreased in recent times. Legion reports say that many of the lower-paid Legion warriors are dissatisfied with the Monarchy's lack of stability, and are looking to the High Priestess for leadership. If the trend continues and the civil unrest is not resolved quickly, we won't have enough loyal remaining Legion members to protect our borders and the city proper. This is the most vulnerable position we have experienced in a century and it all began with Agnes's fake *'Magical Disease'*. The Alearian people are losing their faith in the Monarchy. They are turning to the High Priestess for answers," Alecia reluctantly informed her.

The Queen remained composed but sat thoughtfully for a moment.

"Increase the lower-paid Legion warriors' wages," Annie replied. "With heavier pockets they will be less likely to defect. Offer monetary incentives for former Legion dissenters to return to our ranks."

"Very well, Your Majesty," the General replied.

"And General, one last thing," Annie began, "recall all but a small percentage of the border patrol Legionnaires. Our city needs greater protection now than our Kingdom's boundaries. Redeployment of troops to where they are most needed is the greatest way to maximise our resources," Queen Annie declared.

"As you wish, Your Majesty," Alecia replied, unable to hide the frustration from her voice.

*'Annie knows next to nothing about managing a Legion. She should leave those decisions to me. Troops are not pawns on a chess board.'*

Alecia took a deep breath after regaining her composure and set to work explaining the finer details of the preliminary security plans for the wedding day.

"Based off Lord Ashcott's prior planning and recommendations," Alecia continued, "a list of assignments has already been appointed to many of the Legionnaires possessing Goddess given giftings. But as I mentioned, our numbers are unreliable. A team of four wind whisperers will be stationed in close proximity of the Queen and her future King, maintaining a protective invisible air shield over the couple at all times. Wind whisperers are also to be stationed on the rooftops of the city proper buildings nearest to the temple, so they can monitor the surroundings. Fire-wielding Legionnaires will be stationed at regular intervals between the castle gates and city temple, maintaining a constant meter high barrier along the roads, both a symbolic gesture of the might and power of the Kingdom, but also as a protective measure. Water mages will be disguised in noble and peasant attire, hiding in plain sight amongst the crowd of spectators, on the watch for anything amiss," General Alecia finished.

"Your Majesty, I feel I must point out the flaw in our plan," Lord Ashcott began, leaning forward in his chair, resting his forearms heavily upon the war council table.

"Continue, Lord Ashcott," the Queen commanded.

"As our gifted Legionnaires form such a pivotal role in our Legion's defenses, these warriors are also quite well known amongst the ranks including those who have deserted the Legion. Unfortunately, we are unable to work around this."

"So, you are telling me that our undercover Legionnaires will not in fact be undercover? So, what is the point of dressing them as nobles and peasants in the first instance?" Queen Annie asked.

Alecia leaned forward in her chair. "The people are already concerned that we as a Monarchy are being too aggressive in our show of force. It merely reduces the Legion's perceived physical presence to the general townspeople and visiting dignitaries. It is an empty gesture where the rebels are concerned," Alecia admitted.

"Very well," Queen Annie conceded. "General Alecia, do you recommend proceeding with the event based off your security plans? "

"It is risky, Your Majesty," Alecia admitted, "but the wedding was planned with the intention of rallying the people behind the Monarchy. The potential reward at this stage may be worth the risk. The visiting dignitaries' attendance may also work in our favor," Alecia mused.

"Our defected warriors will not want to appear weak before representatives of other Kingdoms," Alecia added. "The aim of the rebellion, with all due respect, is to unseat the Monarchy and turn power over to the High Priestess. Not to undermine the Kingdom's might. Best case scenario, the rebels may not attempt to interfere in the event at all... If we are extremely lucky."

Annie reflected over Alecia's recommendations for a moment; the remaining council members looking to her for guidance.

"Thank you General, and Lord Ashcott, for all your hard work and planning. I feel confident that the day will run as smoothly as possible under your capable watch," Annie concluded.

Satisfied with the General's planning, and after weighing up the risk, Queen Annie adjourned the meeting and they all went their separate ways.

# Queen Annalyse of Alearia

Following the war council meeting, Annie invited Prince Liquire to join her for afternoon tea in one of her favourite spots in the castle. The moderately sized room overlooked the forest to the north of the castle.

The room was initially where the first Alearian royals had situated their private library. Several generations later, the royal book collection had grown exponentially, and several library rooms had sprung up around the castle. This library, she had heard from Lady Margarette, had also been Queen Amealiana's favourite room.

Comfortable, velvet, wing-backed chairs, ottomans and side tables, were arranged around each of the five fireplaces. Throw rugs were folded neatly upon a few of the armrests, in homage to the former Queen's love for curling up with a blanket and a book before the fireplace in the evenings. Annie fondly remembered doing the same in her cottage back in Lavender Grove with Lily. It warmed her heart to know that her mother had shared the same habit.

A platter of small cakes, cheese and fresh bread had been laid out for the two royals, along with a decanter of wine and two glasses. Queen Annie had insisted that Lady Margarette and the other servants allow the pair an hour's privacy while they got to know each other.

Prince Liquire was dressed in a long sleeved, button down cream shirt with light brown pants. His sandy blond hair and blue eyes shining. He was exactly how Annie had always imagined an island Prince to be.

Liquire was formal but relaxed, with a spark of unpredictability to him. His brashness caught Annie off guard at times, but his eagerness to assist during the attempted breach of the castle gates proved to Annie that she could count on him.

Annie could tell from the time they had spent together, no matter how brief, that Liquire had a loyal heart and an unmatched fearlessness to him. She felt her heart race every time she was around him, her hands often becoming clammy from giddy nerves.

In many ways Liquire was the opposite of Annie. Where Annie was usually reserved and felt most comfortable with a book and a cup of tea, Liquire was outgoing and preferred adventures on the sea. But the two shared their impeccable work ethic and both recognised the importance of strong family bonds.

With fond memories, Annie recounted to Liquire her days of assisting Lily in the Apothecary. Annie shared with the Prince how she often missed working with her hands. The Queen relayed that when she first arrived at Castle Brandistone, she would sneak down to the castle infirmary to help prepare tinctures and ointments, but since being crowned Heir and then Queen, she had very little time to partake in such activities.

Liquire shared with Annie how as a young Prince he had learned to sail his own boat, and thus his love of the sea grew. Annie asked questions about his Kingdom and the Prince described the Isle of Treseme as a tropical paradise. The castle built of white sandstone, similar to Castle Brandistone and the windows were made of colorful sea glass. Many of the archways and balconies were uncovered to maintain a moderately open plan for the cool sea breeze to filter through. Physical doors were limited to the secure parts of the castle like the dungeons, royal suites and council chambers.

"We are a small Kingdom in comparison to Alearia, but our sea Legion is the most impressive fleet the realm has ever seen," the Prince boasted. "Our people are usually Goddess blessed as water mages or wind whisperers, as I have mentioned in the past. Fire-wielders tend to avoid islands, being surrounded by the sea. Nor do they frequent Kingdoms full of water mages, so we do not often see their kind in Treseme, apart from visiting dignitaries," Liquire explained with a shameless grin.

Annie laughed in response. "I would love to see the Isle for myself one day."

"You would be most welcome, Your Majesty. King and Queen Ocea would receive you with open arms. They have always wanted a daughter. The Goddess only blessed them with sons," he said with a wink.

"Ha! That's a little forward and presumptuous of you, don't you think Prince?" Annie replied in mock shock, holding a hand in front of her mouth.

"Well I didn't travel all this way just to see the sights My Queen," Liquire joked, then took her hand in his own and pressed a light kiss upon it, his eyes gazing into her own daringly as he did so.

"You flatter me, Prince Charming," Annie chuckled, her cheeks flushing, earning herself a wicked grin from the royal in return.

Prince Liquire rose to his feet, assisting the Queen like a gentleman, to do the same. "Come with me, and we shall go on an adventure. We do not have forests and mountainous alps in the Isle as you do. I would very much like to explore them further on horseback," he exclaimed, his excitement infectious.

"We couldn't possibly, Liquire," Annie replied hesitantly. "Alecia has warned me to stay within the castle grounds."

"Annie, you are the Queen now, you make the rules" Liquire objected. "I will protect you; I promise. But from what I hear you can protect yourself with your mind conqueror gifting," the Prince flattered the Queen, once again making her blush.

"Very well..." Annie conceded defeat, rolling her eyes, causing Liquire to laugh at her sarcasm. "But we must be back before dark so I can prepare for dinner."

"As you wish, Your Majesty," Prince Liquire replied with a mock deep bow, flourishing his hands before himself as he did so, obviously pleased with himself.

Annie felt as though she floated on a cloud throughout dinner. She barely recalled any of the conversation afterwards —her thoughts were consumed by her afternoon with the Prince of the Isle.

"It was incredible Anastasia!" Annie exclaimed, feet stretched out in front of her, cosy by the fire in her suite, glass of wine in hand. The twins had been gossiping by the fire since dinner.

"You must tell me all about your afternoon with the Prince! Spare no scrumptious details," Anastasia instructed her sister wickedly, before taking a sip of her own wine. "But I must warn you, little sister, Alecia will be wanting your head after that stunt! Roaming around the forest with no one to guard you, ha! Do you have a death wish?" Anastasia teased.

Annie took another sip of her wine before biting her bottom lip.

"I am sorry if I worried you Tash," Annie apologized, and she meant it.

"You certainly did. Honestly Annie, all wisdom gets pushed aside the moment a good-looking boy shows you a good time," Anastasia laughed.

Annie expelled a sigh, putting down her glass of wine on the side table and pulling her blanket higher up her lap. "You can't really blame me; he is quite exceptional looking."

Anastasia burst out laughing, "exceptional looking? Is that the only way you can think of to describe the daredevil Prince," she chuckled.

"To be completely fair Anastasia, I have never courted anyone before, let alone several gentlemen at once! It's a miracle there are any suitors left still interested in me."

Anastasia let out another bellowing laugh. "You make a very good point sister," Anastasia teased. "But in all seriousness, you cannot run off like that again. Weeks of planning is going into making sure you live through your wedding day, and you throw all that effort in our faces the moment you disregard our warnings and show little care for your own wellbeing. I would have expected this kind of behavior from Alecia, but never from you. It's ironic that Alecia is currently the most level-headed, responsible one out of us sisters!"

Annie straightened her back. "Pardon me? I am still responsible!" She replied, hitting her sister playfully with the pillow she was previously leaning upon. "I just had a momentary lapse of judgement," Annie blushed.

Anastasia stole the pillow and threw it right back at her sister, narrowly missing the glass of wine she held.

"Ok, enough admonishment," she chuckled, "tell me all the gossip about the Isle Prince!"

The girls chattered for hours until Lady Margarette re-entered the suite just after midnight, and gently reminded the royals of their meeting after breakfast with the High Priestess.

"We'd better go to bed," Annie resigned, rolling her eyes. "I am going to need all the rest and patience I can get in order to be civil with that woman," Annie gritted her teeth, placing her fourth, or was it her fifth… glass full of wine reluctantly on the side table for Margarette to dispose of. "Goodnight Tash."

"Goodnight Annie, I hope the Goddess blesses you with sweet dreams about a certain dashing Prince," Anastasia replied with a cheeky wink, to which Annie responded by throwing another cushion at her.

The sisters burst into laughter. "I love you too, Annie," Anastasia called audaciously as she left the suite, laughter following her down the hallway.

# Queen Annie of Alearia

Annie tossed and turned; her dreams filled with every imaginable disaster occurring during her meeting with the High Priestess. Despite the crisp, spring morning air, Annie woke saturated in perspiration in her night gown. Annie beseeched the Goddess that her dreams were not prophetic.

After her tonic and a bath to freshen up, Lady Margarette assisted the Queen to dress in a regal, deep red and gold gown, topping it off with her crown: the picture of Alearian royalty.

In just four days, Annie was to be married in front of the entire Kingdom, and a new King was to be appointed. Royal guests from Alearia's neighboring Kingdoms were expected to begin arriving the day before the ceremony.

Of all their allied Kingdoms, Stanthorpe was the only Kingdom to decline their invitation to the wedding. Annie had anticipated that would likely be the case since Lord Margach, acting as their ambassador had already returned home from his brief stay in Alearia.

The coming meeting with the High Priestess would likely play a pivotal role in the current civil unrest; it could either help or harm their campaign to win back the people's support, but Annie honestly didn't know what the result would be.

Following breakfast, Annie, General Alecia, and Princess Anastasia, took their places upon the dais in the throne room, presenting a united front. The Queen sat center stage upon her throne, with her sisters sitting in smaller thrones on either side of her own.

Alecia looked every part the General, dressed in full Alearian Legion ceremony attire. Princess Anastasia opted for a golden evening gown to symbolise her allegiance to her founding house and Monarch, as well as her fire-wielding gifting. A simple topaz tiara perched elegantly atop her sandy blond hair, which was arranged in soft curls and pinned into place.

Sir Tomlin and Lord Ashcott were stationed on either side of the dais, closely guarding the royals for added protection. Sir Lawrence of the former Queen's Guard and Lord Thornley, the Alearian prospective suitor, were also invited to attend, however Lord Thornley was nowhere in sight. He hadn't attended breakfast either.

A few minutes later a knock at the door sounded, and the Herald introduced High Priestess Elizabeth, who was accompanied by five ordinary peasants, as well as none other than Lord Jack Thornley. High Priestess Elizabeth's guests took their places in the front pew of the throne room facing the Alearian royals. However, Elizabeth, escorted by Lord Thornley, walked right up the base of the dais, doing her best to appear the old weak crone.

Lord Thornley showed Annie a side to him that she had never seen before. With his back straight and overconfident smirk across his face, Annie realised she had completely misread the suitor after all.

"You summoned me, Your Majesty... Though I cannot imagine why. It is too late for peaceful democratic meetings," the High Priestess informed the Queen, her tongue as sharp as the dagger Annie imagined the crone would like to stab into her heart.

"Thank you for coming High Priestess," the Queen greeted her guest with a sweet disposition. "How lovely to see you as well, Lord Thornley. You were missed at breakfast," the Queen said, highlighting his absence earlier.

"My apologies, Your Majesty," Lord Thornley replied with an air of arrogance. "But you see, I already had plans to meet the High Priestess for breakfast, and I must say that our conversation was both enlightening and informative to say the least."

"I am pleased to hear that," Queen Annie replied, bemused.

*'That double crossing, slimy creep!'*

"Do tell, Jack, how long have you and the High Priestess been acquainted?" Annie asked sweetly.

But it was the High Priestess that interjected. "Lord Thornley has been loyal to the Goddess and her temple since he was a young boy. I helped to ensure the young Lord was raised in accordance with the Goddess's wishes and teaching. It was my privilege to do so not only as his High Priestess, but also as his family," Elizabeth added nonchalantly.

"I see," Annie replied, trying to hide her surprise though her knuckles grew white as she tightened her grip upon the arms of her throne. "How fortunate Lord Thornley was to have you as a mentor growing up," Annie ground out. "Pleasantries aside, we have matters to discuss High Priestess," the Queen declared.

"Very well, Your Majesty," Elizabeth replied, clearly pleased that she had been able to get beneath the Queen's skin.

"It has become clear," Annie began, "that you do not approve of my appointment as Queen and have lost faith in our Monarchy. My previous offer remains. Call off these protests and we can work together to restore peace to our Kingdom. We can work together to restore peace for Alearia. A new reign to reunite a dark and twisted Kingdom," Annie declared.

"What are you proposing?" Elizabeth asked suspiciously.

"Come live in the castle as my spiritual advisor," Annie offered.

Alecia choked on a surprised gasp.

*I don't think Alecia saw that offer coming,'* Annie thought to herself with amusement. *'Keep your friends close and your enemies closer, isn't that what they all say?'*

"I am a fair High Priestess. I will take your offer under consideration, *if* you can prove the value of your word," High Priestess Elizabeth smirked.

"I do believe I have proved my worth already to you and the Goddess during the Crowning rituals. But I suppose you have a suggestion in mind as to how I can prove myself further?" The Queen drawled with an edge of sass to her voice.

"As a matter of fact, I do," the High Priestess grinned like a lion sizing up her prey.

Annie pretended to yawn and allowed herself a lengthy pause for dramatic effect. "What is your suggestion, *High Priestess?* I grow tired of these games."

The High Priestess lifted her eyebrow, with a smirk that said, *'I've got you just where I want you.'* She turned around to gesture for her guests to rise from the pew.

"During the Crowning Ceremony you declared that you would reunite *all* of Agnes's mind conqueror victims with their giftings," the High

Priestess unnecessarily reminded the Queen. "Some time has passed now since you were declared Heir, and these five loyal Alearians behind me are yet to be healed," She said, gesturing towards her guests seated in the front pew. "If you are truly a Queen of your word, you would not want for your people to suffer for a moment longer. Why don't you heal them all now? Unless you have more important matters to attend to than healing *your* own people?" Elizabeth challenged.

Annie felt shame and anxiety battle it out in her stomach. A trap, that was what this meeting had become. A test to push the Queen to her limits. To gauge if she was all talk and no action.

"I apologize sincerely that you have had to wait so long for your healing," Annie stated sincerely, directing her comments to the sets of eyes looking up at her from the pew.

"What Agnes did to you was wrong," Annie empathetically acknowledged. "To sever you from your giftings was unbelievably cruel. However, healing people with my mind conqueror gifting is also taxing on my own body and mental health. Unfortunately, with my wedding only days away, now is not the best time to conduct such draining healing. I would ask that you all please wait a little longer and as soon as the festivities are over, I would be more than happy to heal you all one at a time," Annie offered her subjects.

A couple of the peasants nodded in acceptance, but the other three did not appear so satisfied with the Queen's response. The High Priestess made sure to capitalize on their unsatisfied demeanors.

"Please forgive me if I am not correct, Your Majesty," High Priestess Elizabeth began seemingly innocently, "but are you saying that your wedding is more important than these people's livelihoods? Surely a Queen would not put her own wellbeing before that of her people? Have you forgotten your coronation vows already?" Elizabeth questioned.

*'For the love of the Goddess, why does this woman have such a habit of turning everything I say against me?'*

Anastasia placed a gentle hand upon Annie's arm; a warning and comforting gesture all rolled into one. Alecia remained steel faced on the other side of Annie, ready to step in the moment Annie gave the signal that the High Priestess had overstayed her welcome. Sir Lawrence and Sir Tomlin moved their hands unsubtly within easy reach of their weapons. Annie took a calming breath, calling upon her sage gifting for guidance.

"You are entirely correct, High Priestess," Annie reluctantly accepted.

She could hear Alecia grinding her teeth to attempt to stop herself from launching across the room and tackling the old crone, who stood poised like a snake ready to attack.

"I will heal these fine citizens of our city today," Annie promised. "But I need your word High Priestess, that the protests will cease and that you will agree to work alongside me and not undermine my authority any further."

Something akin to pride shone though Alecia's eyes as a slight smirk drew across her face.

"If you fail to meet these terms," Annie continued, "I will consider your failure to comply as treason, and you will be held accountable for your past and present crimes, including inciting civil unrest which led to the death of innocents," Annie declared as she met the High Priestess in the eye.

Annie thought that her mother would be proud of the Queen she was becoming, winning one battle at a time.

The High Priestess looked down her nose at the Queen. "It appears I have no other choice. I accept your terms, but only if you heal all five of these people today. If not, the deal is off, and I will not meet with you again. I will rally the people behind me further if you do not prove yourself a worthy Queen of the Goddess," Elizabeth declared with a wicked smile, clearly convinced that Annie would fail at the task.

"We have a deal," Queen Annie declared.

Anastasia inhaled sharply in disbelief, but loyally chose to keep her objections to herself. Alecia's teeth began grinding once more.

*'Surely Alecia will come to her senses soon and see that the risk is worth the reward,'* Annie hoped.

"Sir Tomlin," the Queen beckoned.

Sir Tomlin walked around the dais to bow before his Queen. "Yes, Your Majesty. How may I be of service?"

Annie smiled at the older guard who she had grown fond of, knowing he had faithfully served her mother loyally for her entire reign.

"Could you and Sir Lawrence please take the High Priestess and our guests, to the infirmary? I will join them shortly. Please summon the Head Healer to work alongside me and cancel my appointments for the remainder of the day. Thank you," Annie requested.

"As you wish Your Majesty," Sir Tomlin responded with a bow.

Sir Lawrence followed suit, and they both escorted their five guests and the High Priestess from the room. Once they had left, Annie turned her attention back to Lord Thornley.

"Lord Thornley," Annie stated.

"Yes, *Your Majesty?*" Jack responded obnoxiously, with a smirk across his face.

The Queen rose to her feet, allowing her held-back rage to simmer to the surface as she stared the gentleman in the eye.

"You are hereby stripped of your title as Lord and banned forevermore from attending Castle Brandistone or the palace grounds," Queen Annie declared. "I do not take kindly to spies in my own home, Jack. Now leave this instance, before I exile you from the entire city proper!" Annie declared. "Lord Ashcott, please see this man out!" Annie ordered.

"It would be my pleasure Your Majesty," Lord Ashcott declared as he restrained the former Lord and led him kicking and screaming his outrage out of the throne room.

"You won't get away with this! The Goddess has my back and she will destroy you for this!" Jack yelled as he was dragged away.

Alecia turned to Annie, a little shocked — a rare moment for her sister.

"Annie, I am so proud of you right now! But honestly, did you have to invite that wretched woman to live with us?" Alecia complained, earning a laugh from the Queen.

Anastasia turned to her twin, ignoring her sassy elder sister.

"What are you doing Annie?" Anastasia asked with genuine concern. "You can't heal five people in one day. The consequences to your health will be too great. Please reconsider Annie, there must be another way," Anastasia begged her twin.

Annie turned to face Anastasia and took her by the hands, holding back tears and staying strong for her twin.

*'Anastasia is so strong yet so fragile. I pray that what I am about to do is not the end of me, but if it is, Goddess I pray that you give Anastasia the strength to live through it. She has lost so much already. I do not know if she can bear any more pain...'*

Annie took a deep breath and stared into her twin's eyes.

"The risk is worth the reward my dear sister," Annie promised her. "I would love nothing more than to run away right now, but that will solve nothing. If I can do this, the High Priestess will call off the protests and the civil unrest with dissipate. Alearia needs peace restored and if the price is my health then I will gladly pay it. I am sorry Anastasia, I wish there were another way but there is not," Annie spoke sincerely, releasing Anastasia's hands before turning to Alecia.

The General grew solemn as she realised the enormity of the task before Annie.

"Alecia," Annie began, her entire focus on her older sister, pushing aside her own feelings. "Magic always has a price; we are told this time and time again. But to know the risk and pay the price anyway, even if it means sacrificing yourself, is the right thing to do. If I become physically or mentally incapable of attending to my duties after healing these people, then I appoint you Acting Monarch of Alearia, with Anastasia as my witness. If Goddess forbid the effects prove permanent, then I command you to assume the throne as Queen of Alearia. Our people need a strong ruler and if I am incapable, I would want no one else to rule in my place. Appoint Anastasia as your General and advisor, she is wise, as you know, and offers the perfect balance to your leadership style," Annie concluded.

Alecia's eyes widened. "It would be my honor, Annie," she replied, bowing her head disbelievingly. A rare moment of understanding passed between the two sisters.

Annie smiled softly, "thank you, Alecia. For family and Kingdom," Annie whispered the ancient Alearian declaration.

"For family and Kingdom," her sisters echoed, Anastasia's voice cracking slightly as she struggled to hold back her tears.

*'Goddess, give me the strength to do what must be done to restore peace to our mighty Kingdom.'*

# 28

## *Queen Annalyse of Alearia*

Annie left the throne room and made her way back to her palace suite. There was something she needed to do before attending to her people's healing.

*'I do not know how this will play out, but I will not meet my end without hearing her final words,'* Annie thought to herself.

Annie reached into the hidden drawer in her closet, and pulled out the worn envelope. The letter Annie had been saving for a time when she most needed to hear its words of wisdom. Until this moment Annie had not felt ready to hear her mentor's final words, but Annie knew in her heart that now was the time.

Annie walked over to her favorite chair by the hearth and tucked her feet beneath her, pulling a blanket across her lap. The Queen closed her eyes and inhaled deeply, preparing for the moment she had desperately been awaiting but hesitantly been avoiding.

Pulling the letter out of the envelope, it smelled of lavender and herbs, all the comforting scents of her home back in Lavender Grove. Annie read the words that she had been waiting all this time to hear; saved for the moment she needed them most.

---

*To my dearest Annie,*

*If you are reading these words, then it means my time has finally come to meet the Goddess. Know that I do not regret one moment we spent together. I love you like my own daughter. There will never be enough time with you to satisfy my heart but alas, all good things must come to an end.*

# A Queen's Fate

We will be reunited in the beloved arms of the
Goddess one day, but until then I need you to promise
me that you will live a full life. Do not mourn those
who have gone but celebrate the time you had with them
instead. Be strong. You are braver, more resilient and
wiser than you know.

Trust in the Goddess and trust that when times get
hard, you are strong enough to live through them.

I regret that I was never able to tell you in person,
but you are even more special than you know. Your
mother was my closest friend and confidant. Find
Queen Amealiana in Flearia and she will tell you

our story. Trust her. You are more like her than you

will ever know.


Lastly Annie, I need to tell you to trust in yourself.

Many challenges will arise that you will not feel

prepared for. But trust me, you are ready. By now

you have likely discovered that you are not like

everyone else Annie, you are special. You will be the

balance that will restore peace and unity to your

Kingdom. You were born to change the realm. You

will do what needs to be done to protect those that you

love because that is who you are, and I believe in you.

# A Queen's Fate

Do not be afraid of your giftings Annie, or the costs of using them. As I have always taught you, we are blessed by the Goddess with our giftings so that we may bless others. Without great sacrifice, there cannot be transformation and restoration.

Believe in yourself Annie, as I believe in you. I love you Annie, more than you will ever know. Give my love to Amealiana, tell her that caring for you was my greatest joy and privilege. Take care my darling. I will be watching over you always.

Lily

With a renewed sense of purpose and hope, Annie dressed in her old healer's apprentice uniform, hung her mentor's family heirloom necklace carefully around her neck, and made her way down to the main infirmary wing with Lady Margarette. As they walked, Annie briefed Lady Margarette on her plans and provided her with strict instructions should anything go amiss. Loyally, the Lady's Maid gave her word that she would respect the Queen's wishes.

As the Queen and her Lady's Maid approached the infirmary wing doors, the guards by the door bowed in respect for Her Majesty before opening the door for her.

Just inside the infirmary wing, Sir Tomlin was standing, awaiting the Queen's arrival. The knight bowed in respect. "Your Majesty, may I please have a moment of your time? If we may speak frankly?"

"Of course, Sir Tomlin, is there a problem?"

Sir Tomlin took a step towards the Queen, closing the gap between them.

"Your Majesty, I would advise against proceeding with this plan," Sir Tomlin warned. "You cannot help your people if you are incapacitated. In the past you have never been able to heal more than two people at a time due to the strain it places on you. Let me reason with the people — you can heal a couple a day," Sir Tomlin suggested.

"Thank you for your concern, Sir Tomlin," Annie replied sincerely, "but I must do what is best for my Kingdom, not myself."

Sir Tomlin nodded in respect, "As you wish Your Majesty. I would expect nothing less from Queen Amealiana's daughter," the knight complimented the Queen.

"Thank you for your concern Sir Tomlin. It means a lot to me," Annie replied sincerely. "Please ask the servants to bring cheese, cold meat, fruit and bread platters, as well as jugs of fresh water up to the infirmary. It is going to be a long day and we will all need our strength."

"As you wish Your Majesty. I will always be close by if you need anything. I will keep you safe," Sir Tomlin assured her.

"Thank you, Tomlin," Annie replied. "It will be a comfort to know that I have people I can depend upon close by while I am at my most vulnerable."

Sir Tomlin nodded respectfully, a small, grim knowing smile upon his face. "May the Goddess give you strength Your Majesty."

Annie nodded in thanks before approaching the first infirmary bed where a young man no older than Annie sat. A curtain had been erected in between each of the beds to give some semblance of privacy, though Annie was acutely aware that the entire infirmary was likely listening to her every word.

"Good morning," Annie quietly greeted the gentleman, "may I ask your name sir?"

The young man bowed his head respectfully. "Good Morning, Queenie, what an honor it is to meet you. I'm Ryan Bran. I'm a farmer from the grain fields further east of the city," the young, lean muscled man replied in a thick country accent.

"A pleasure to meet you Ryan," Annie replied. "As far as I was aware, Agnes only severed the giftings of people here in the city proper. But you are not from around here, is that correct?"

"That is correct Queenie. I don't normally travel to the big city. It's far too fancy and hustle and bustle for my liking. But I needed to come here to deliver some grain from our stores," Ryan stated. "The locals in town ran out early during winter. They didn't order enough in the first place if you ask me," Ryan stated with a cheeky wink.

"The night I lost my fire I was out at the pub, having a few ales of the fancy variety you lot have here. I was talking to a pretty lady you see." He blushed sheepishly. "The next moment I went to show off my fire-wielding to her, but I couldn't even light a match to save my life. It was a disaster! She laughed at me and walked away after that she did!"

Annie smothered a giggle, "an outrage indeed."

"Sure was!"

"Well, we will have you back in full form in no time Ryan, I promise you," Annie reassured her patient warmly. "Now, can you please lie back in the bed and make yourself comfortable?" Annie requested gently with her impeccable bedside manner.

The young man followed the Queen's instructions. "These beds are soft as a cloud Queenie. I don't know why anyone would ever want to get better and leave!" Ryan declared.

Annie smiled sweetly as she pulled up a chair beside his bed.

"I am glad you are comfortable. Now, please close your eyes. I am going to lay a hand on your forehead if that is alright with you?"

"You can lay a hand on me wherever you like Queenie," he said with a mischievous wink. "A pretty lady like you need not ask."

Sir Tomlin shifted to stand beside the Queen.

"Treat the Queen with respect young man, or I will throw you out of this castle and you will never see your gifting again," Sir Tomlin warned.

Ryan held up his hands in the air. "I'm sorry Queenie. I meant no harm I swear."

Annie waved Sir Tomlin away.

"It is quite alright Sir Tomlin. No harm done. Though I have seen Sir Tomlin with a sword, so I suggest you stay on his good side," she replied with a wink of her own. "Now, close your eyes and picture your gifting. Remember how it feels, how it looks, and I will do all of the rest."

"Will it hurt, Queenie?" Ryan whispered nervously.

Suppressing a giggle, Annie replied: "certainly not for a brave young man such as yourself. Now close your eyes."

The man finally did as he was told, and Annie gently placed her left hand upon his forehead and her right hand on the bedside to steady herself. Calling forth her power, Annie pictured her gifting floating through an invisible channel connecting her mind to that of her patient's.

Annie navigated through his neurons and electrical signals, expertly examining every cell as she traversed further through his mind. Deeper she buried, until she located a series of brightly lit cells radiating red light. The cells were active, but they couldn't relay their messages to the rest of his body as the connections to his gifting had been viciously severed.

Annie worked meticulously to rebuild the connections, and as she did, she felt her strength beginning to wane. With most of the connections repaired, she carefully withdrew down the channel that connected her brain to his, releasing a sigh of relief once the connection between their two minds was once again severed.

'*Thank the Goddess for that,*' Annie thought to herself, catching her breath for a moment.

"How do you feel Ryan?" Annie asked after taking a moment to rest, gesturing for him to sit up again.

Ryan did as he was beckoned and held his hand before him, pointing it right up towards the ceiling. A mighty burst of flame erupted from his hand and burst a hole in the ceiling. Sir Tomlin protectively threw himself over the Queen to prevent debris from hitting her as it fell, but the Queen just laughed.

"I think it is safe to say your gifting has been restored Ryan," Annie chuckled. "You need not try so hard next time to use it."

The farmer flushed pink as Sir Tomlin stared daggers at him, "Sorry Queenie," he replied guiltily.

Sir Tomlin, being a water mage, quickly extinguished the remaining flames, and satisfied that the Queen was safe once more, he resumed his post behind her.

"That is quite alright, Ryan, but perhaps it is time for you to go home. We would hate to keep you from your work any longer. Sir Lawrence will show you out." She gestured to the knight standing on the opposite side of the room beside High Priestess Elizabeth, who was taking everything in.

"Yes, I think that might be for the best," his cheeks flushed pink once more. "Thank you for healing me Queenie," Ryan nodded respectfully, eagerly taking his leave.

Lady Margarette quickly walked over to the Queen's side and handed her a cup of tea before placing a small platter of savory treats on the bedside table, within easy reach.

"Please eat and drink Your Majesty, you need your strength," she kindly whispered to the Queen.

Annie thanked her Lady's Maid for the supplies. Picked at the plate for a few minutes and quickly sipped her tea, conscious of the eyes and ears that were no doubt focused on her every move.

Annie's face had paled, her strength diminishing, but onwards she pushed. She wondered what her suitors would make of her actions.

*'Will they be impressed by my gifting? Or appalled that it is so taxing on my emotional and physical strength?'*

Annie brushed aside her thoughts to focus on the task at hand. Lady Margarette attempted to help the Queen up from her chair but Annie waved her off, determined to save face and not show any sign of weakness before the High Priestess.

After rising from her chair, Annie walked around the curtain into the next makeshift infirmary room. A woman with scantily clad, well-worn blue dyed clothing, sat upon the bed with her arms wrapped around her legs.

The lady appeared as though she had seen too many horrors of the world despite her young age, and Annie empathised with the woman.

*'What circumstances led her to this life and to make the choices she has made?'* Annie caught herself wondering of the lady-of-the-night.

Annie took a seat in the chair waiting for her by the woman's bedside. Annie greeted the woman with a warm, soft tone, but the woman refused to acknowledge the Queen's existence.

"May I ask your name?" Annie asked in a further effort to engage the woman, but the young lady just stared vacantly into the distance before her. It was then that Annie noticed the woman's glazed over eyes.

Annie turned to the nearest healer and asked, "can this lady see me?"

"No, my Queen," the healer replied. "The High Priestess says she is blind and partially deaf."

*'Goddess above, the poor woman. I wonder if there is any way I can help her...'* Annie thought to herself.

Annie raised her voice to reintroduce herself and this time the woman turned her head slightly towards Annie to strain to listen to her voice. Annie placed a hand upon the woman's arm and felt the woman flinch beneath her grip, but she did not pull away.

"Do we know what her gifting was?" Annie asked the healer's apprentice.

"We believe she may have been a water mage based on the color of her gown," the healer's assistant replied. "Many of the town's establishments dress their ladies in a color reflective of their gifting."

"I see," Annie sighed, thinking of the hard life the woman must live.

Annie buried down into her gifting, having to draw deeper this time, and established a connection with the lady's mind moments later.

Annie could tell that part of her brain had been damaged from assaults of some sort. But those areas were sadly beyond repair, not a glimmer of life amongst the neurons.

Annie located a small amount of dull pulsing blue lit cells. As the neurons were not connected to any other part of the woman's mind, she guessed that they were likely the cells of her water mage gifting. The number of cells were considerably less than that of her previous patient's, so she guessed that the woman's gifting was likely not as strong when it was active. Annie re-established the gifting's connections with little effort at all due to the significantly less amount of repair needed.

Annie burrowed further into the young woman's mind, searching for the lady's inner eye. Annie had never healed anyone's sight before, and she was not sure it was possible, but she wanted to try anyway.

Annie probed around the woman's head, trying to repair the injured eye tissue as she would a severed connection, but the cells did not feel or function in the same way. Annie reattempted for what felt like hours, with no success. Annie then tried to fix the woman's hearing but was also unable to achieve a positive result.

*'A mind-conqueror I may be, but a Goddess I am not. As much as I wish I could, I cannot work miracles or heal the body of injuries unrelated to the mind. I have failed her. But if I can't heal her physical ailments, maybe there is something else I can do to help her...'*

Annie withdrew from the woman's mind and removed her hand from the woman's arm.

"Can you please try to use your gifting?" Annie asked the lady loudly.

The woman lifted her head carefully and cautiously released her arms from where they were wrapped around her legs.

The woman held out a hand before her and water poured from the girl's hand in a spiral. The girl then turned her hand back towards her and splashed herself in the face with a small spout of water, cleaning herself, and savoring the rejuvenating freshness of her gifting.

For the first time, Annie saw the girl smile. Annie thought the happy surprise on the woman's face might have been the most beautiful thing she had seen.

"Thank you," the woman cried loudly before bursting into tears, heavy sobs heaving out of her body.

Annie leant over the woman and embraced her in a hug. This time the woman did not flinch but allowed the tears to fall freely.

After the woman had calmed, Annie withdrew her embrace and offered the woman, whose name she did still not know, a job amongst the castle staff working in the gardens with her gifting. Annie arranged for the woman to receive a proper gardener's uniform and safe accommodations in the female servants' quarters.

Annie promised the woman that she would be safe in the castle forevermore.

Overjoyed with gratitude, the woman began to cry deeply once more, and finally introduced herself as Ingrid. Annie left Ingrid in the assistant healer's capable hands and excused herself from the main infirmary, walking out through the side door towards the royal infirmary suite.

On unsteady legs, Annie collapsed on the bed and cried herself to sleep.

# Princess Anastasia

Anastasia sat on the bed next to her sleeping twin, stroking her hair soothingly. Alecia had positioned herself protectively in a chair by the bedside.

The infirmary room made Anastasia feel physically unwell. The smell of ointments, the stark white sheets, the puddles of blood she could still picture on the floor. The anxiety the room incited was enough to send her heart into palpitations and make her stomach churn, but for her twin, she was determined to endure it.

"We cannot allow her to go on like this Alecia. She will burn herself out if she is not careful," Anastasia finally voiced her concerns, worry etched deep into her brow.

"The choice is not ours to make," Alecia replied, ever the General. "Our role is to support her, not to question her."

"What nonsense! You question her all the time!" Anastasia retaliated.

Alecia laughed as she shifted into a more comfortable position in her chair. "True... But I am working on it. It's hard to push nineteen years of stubbornness and sass aside overnight you know," Alecia joked, trying to lighten the mood.

Anastasia threw a pillow at her older sister. "Well right now is not the time to decide to be a good General. Now is the time to put our sister's needs first."

Annie roused from sleep, calling an abrupt end to the discussion.

"What did I miss?" Annie mumbled, still groggy from sleep.

She had been passed out for two solid hours.

"Oh, thank the Goddess, you are awake," Anastasia sighed. "Alecia has just been loyally backing your decision to let you kill yourself trying to heal a few people. Meanwhile, I'm trying to be the rebel for once, convincing her that now is not the time to be diplomatic."

Annie released a choked laugh, "gosh, I leave you two alone for a short nap and you swap roles."

A laugh escaped from Alecia this time.

"Don't worry. I'll come to my senses soon," Alecia joked.

# *Queen Annalyse of Flearia*

*'I don't know how I can possibly heal three more people today. I am exhausted as it is... Of course, that's exactly what the High Priestess is counting on. She wants me to appear weak. That was her plan all along... I doubt she intends to stick to our agreement, even if I do manage to heal all five victims without killing myself or losing my mind. I have pushed myself too far already. I don't know if I can do this, but I must try. 'I am stronger than I realise,' Lily wrote. For her, I will try.'*

Annie took a deep breath and pushed herself to sit up in bed, her head feeling unsteady from the sudden movement.

"Alecia, can you please escort me to my next patient?" Annie requested.

"You can't be serious Annie!" Anastasia exclaimed, grabbing her twins' hand to try and keep her on the bed. "It is madness to continue. You will burn yourself out!"

Annie ignored her twin and turned once more to Alecia, meeting her gaze, "remember your promise Alecia."

The General nodded and walked over to the Queen's bedside to assist her out of bed, forcing Anastasia to release her grip on her twin's hand. Then, arm-in-arm, the unlikely allied siblings walked back into the main infirmary chamber, leaving Anastasia behind.

*'It is for my twin that I must do this. I am willing to risk my life and soul to heal these people, so that she may live in a peaceful Kingdom and never fear for her safety again. It is for Tash and my people that I must make amends with the High Priestess. This is the first step towards reuniting a Kingdom, dark and twisted.'*

Annie was assisted by Alecia into a chair beside her next patient, Esmerelda. The old woman in the bed before her appeared unravelled, trembling beneath the blankets despite the warm temperature of the room. The woman's pupils were dilated, and she mumbled a chant repetitively under her breath. The exact words the woman spoke, Annie could not make sense of.

Annie laid a comforting hand upon the woman's forehead and began to work; she did not need to ask the woman what her gifting was for her sage wisdom had already told her.

Annie created a connection quickly with Esmerelda's brain, her mind a flurry of poorly discharging neurons and an overload of information. Amongst the hive of activity, Annie spotted a small collection of cells that had been maliciously separated from the rest.

Annie theorised that this was one of Agnes's earlier victims, due to the damage to the woman's brain that must have also been caused whilst her connection to her gifting was severed. Annie became short of breath as she ventured closer towards the collection of poorly lit neurons, and set to work, gradually repairing their connections.

After she had finished, Annie traced her steps back to the initial poorly firing neurons she had spotted. After some time, Annie was also able to repair those injured cells too and restore their function back to normal. As Annie withdrew back down the channel connecting their minds, Annie felt the connection suddenly unhinge and the channel snapped instantaneously back into Annie's mind, giving her a reverberating headache.

Annie slumped forward on the side of the bed, attempting to catch her breath.

Esmerelda gently pulled away the blanket that she had wrapped around her and the shaking ceased. The elderly woman sat up in the bed and peered wide-eyed around the room in awe.

"What happened?" she asked disbelievingly.

Annie forced herself to lift her head, using her arms for support against the side of the bed.

"What do you remember Esmerelda?" Annie asked gently, the occupants in the room hanging on their every word.

Esmerelda looked down upon the pale young Queen.

"I was lost," she explained apprehensively. "I couldn't remember my own name. I couldn't even remember my own family. But you helped me, didn't you? You restored my sage wisdom and repaired my mind! Thank you," the woman exclaimed, tears of happiness flowing down her face. "Thank you for helping me find myself again."

A tear trickled down Annie's own cheek as she was taken aback by the woman's words and transformation.

"The pleasure is mine Esmerelda," the Queen spoke sincerely.

*'Is that how I will feel when I lose my own mind after healing these people? I am not strong enough to keep going. The doubt is creeping in. I feel as if a part of me is broken for the first time in my life. I feel as though a piece of my own sanity has been taken in exchange for returning hers.'*

Annie became lightheaded. The light of the world began to fade into oblivion. Then all she knew was shadow and darkness.

# Princess Anastasia

"Annie wake up!" Anastasia yelled at her unconscious sister, embracing her protectively upon the infirmary bed. "Wake up! Don't you dare leave me."

Anastasia could feel someone trying to pull her away from her twin, but she would not leave her. A part of her soul had been ripped apart, fearing the worst.

"Her pulse is fading. If we do not act soon, she will leave us. General Alecia you must help us!" Anastasia heard someone yelling on the other side of her twin, but Anastasia did not look.

She would not leave her sister. They were two halves of one soul, and she could not bear to be parted from her beloved twin again.

"Come back to me Annie," Anastasia sobbed, endless tears clouding her vision.

"Tash listen to me, you must give the healers room to work," another voice insisted... Alecia, she guessed.

But she only clung harder to Annie, embracing her tighter than she thought possible.

"Come back to me Annie," Anastasia continued to sob. "Don't give up. Come back to me..."

Suddenly Anastasia felt two pairs of hands grabbing on to each of her arms, attempting to lift her away from the fallen Queen's body, but Anastasia only increased her grip.

"Please, Tash, you must let her go so the healers can try and save her!" Alecia's voice pleaded again before releasing a resigned sigh. "Sir Lawrence, do what must be done."

"I'm sorry Princess, but we do not have time for this," a male voice from behind her declared.

Suddenly, the air was sucked from the young Princess's lungs. The feeling felt like an assault on her body. She gasped but no air came. Her heart rate plummeted, and the hysterical twin collapsed unconscious beside the Queen.

# General Alecia

The war chamber was a hive of activity. The High Priestess, Prince Liquire, Prince Cimmeris, Lord Ashcott, and General Brandistone all gathered around the table in a flurry of heated debate.

"What is happening in there? Why did she only heal three and not all five of the victims?" High Priestess Elizabeth demanded to know.

Alecia took a deep breath summoning the residue of what little patience remained.

"As I have already told you High Priestess," Alecia seethed through clenched teeth, "the Queen is receiving urgent healing care from our most senior healers at this present time. Her health deterioration is a direct result of the ridiculous demands you placed upon her to earn your allegiance. We will know more regarding her condition soon, but as the healers were able to commence her treatment promptly," Alecia lied through her teeth, "Queen Annalyse is expected to make a full recovery."

"Praise the Goddess for that!" Prince Liquire exclaimed, slumping back in his chair in relief.

"How very fortunate indeed," the High Priestess drawled. "However, as the Queen was unable to complete the task, I believe I shall be leaving. Even *if* the Queen makes a full recovery, a bargain is a bargain. I have no further business here," the High Priestess declared as she rose from her seat to take her leave.

A shadow emerged before the now standing High Priestess, and Prince Cimmeris, who was previously sitting on the opposite side of the table, now stood before the representative of the Goddess, blocking her path.

"What *business?*" Prince Cimmeris demanded to know.

Elizabeth attempted to regain her authoritarian position as she stated: "this is a private Alearian matter and it does not concern the people of Shadows Peak, *Prince.*"

Prince Liquire stood from his chair and moved to stand beside the Prince of Shadows Peak.

"Sit down High Priestess," Liquire warned. "Whatever Alearian business you are referring to; I believe both of our allying Kingdoms would be very interested in hearing more."

"I believe you have some explaining to do," Prince Cimmeris stated, remaining firm in his stance until the High Priestess backed down and resumed her seat.

A proud smirk crossed Alecia's face as the High Priestess was finally put in her place. Prince Liquire resumed his seat as well, but Prince Cimmeris remained standing authoritatively behind the High Priestess's chair, swirls of shadow roaring around his feet.

"Explain," Prince Cimmeris once more prompted the High Priestess, but she refused to say word.

Alecia straightened in her chair, and with great pleasure, explained how the High Priestess had attempted to blackmail the Queen into healing five peasants in a single day — a completely impossible task — in return for the High Priestess's allegiance and agreement to call off the riots and protests.

"Forgive me if I am wrong General Alecia," Prince Cimmeris smoothly stated, "but placing conditions or demands upon a Queen is not the role of a High Priestess, is it? In fact, anyone who questions a reigning Monarch can be accused of *treason...*"

"You make a good point Prince Cimmeris," Prince Liquire confidently agreed, a smirk across his face. "In fact, through contributing to the Queen's ill health by placing such ridiculous demands upon her before you would agree to offer your allegiance, only proves your ill intentions. This is grounds for being charged with treason. As a royal representative of The Isle of Treseme and witness to your betrayal and slander, I view your actions as an attempt to incite civil war against the Monarchy. I am therefore bound by the treaty between our two allying Kingdoms to see that you are adequately held accountable for your actions."

A smug grin spread across the General's face. Satisfaction filled her soul at finally seeing the High Priestess meet her match.

"What a ridiculous accusation! I am leaving!" High Priestess Elizabeth exclaimed again, standing from her seat and attempting to push past the Shadow Prince.

"The only place you are going, is the dungeons High Priestess," Alecia declared, rising to her feet as High Priestess Elizabeth paled and stiffened in response.

"As acting Monarch whilst the Queen is temporarily incapacitated," Alecia continued, "I here-by charge you with treason and sentence you to death, for inciting civil unrest and attempting to blackmail the Queen."

"This is outrageous, you can't do that! The people will rebel!" High Priestess declared.

"I can indeed," Alecia declared with a smug look upon her face. "Sir Tomlin, please take the traitor down to the dungeons!"

"With great pleasure, General Alecia," Sir Tomlin bowed before placing restraints upon the High Priestess and forcing the old crone out of the war chamber room.

Alecia slouched back in her chair, the two Princes electing to do the same.

"I think it's time for some ale, don't you, Cimmeris and Liquire?" Alecia declared.

"I couldn't agree more," the Prince of the Isle announced, and Prince Cimmeris smirked wickedly in agreement.

# Queen Annalyse of Flearia

Annie's head felt like it had been squeezed with a vice. The Head Healer insisted on waking Annie every hour or so to assess her health and cognition. Annie felt like yelling at the woman for interrupting her precious sleep, but she barely had the energy to sit up and drink a small bowl of broth for supper, let alone reprimand the healer unnecessarily.

Annie reminded herself that if she were tending to a patient in the Apothecary, she would likely be doing the exact same thing. The former apprentice healer instantly regretted all the times she had done so unnecessarily.

The Head Healer informed Annie that it had been a full day and a half since she had lost consciousness, and Annie was mindful that time was fast running out before the scheduled wedding. Alecia had visited late the previous night and assured Annie that everything was under control. The visiting guests and dignitaries had started to arrive earlier than anticipated, but they were none the wiser about Annie's condition.

Both Prince Cimmeris and Prince Liquire had been in to visit Annie several times each since her admission to the infirmary, which she found rather sweet and considerate.

Annie's healed patients, Ryan and Esmerelda, had been permitted to leave the castle grounds to return home on the condition that they agreed to only spread positive messages regarding the Monarch in the future. Ryan and Esmerelda eagerly agreed to the terms, though they reassured Alecia that they would gladly tell the Alearian people about the Queen's kindness and compassion after all she had done for them.

Ingrid was reportedly settling in well in the staff accommodations, though according to Alecia, she was displaying some peculiar behavior, which Annie believed was to be expected given her history. The remaining two un-healed patients had requested to return to their homes, promising they would adhere to the same conditions as the healed patients. They would return to the castle in two weeks' time for their healing.

Anastasia was the biggest surprise of all to Annie. After hours of unconsciousness, fighting the battle between the living and the dead, Annie awoke briefly to find Anastasia asleep in an infirmary bed beside her.

The healers informed Annie that it had become necessary to render her twin unconscious and keep her sedated so that they could treat the Queen's critical condition. It broke Annie's heart to think of the pain she had caused her twin.

Anastasia was awake now, and after sitting by Annie's bedside diligently for many hours, she had finally agreed to go back to her own suite to freshen up and eat dinner.

A knock sounded at the door, and the awaiting guard informed the Queen that she had a visitor. Assuming the visitor was likely Anastasia returning to check on her, she permitted the guard to allow her in.

To Annie's surprise, in walked Prince Cimmeris in his signature black formal attire. The Prince flashed Annie a smile as he strolled across the room, stopping to bow before taking a seat by her bedside. Annie quickly ran a hand through her hair to try and tame what she was sure would be horrible bed hair, but conceded it was likely a losing battle and promptly gave up.

"Good evening, Your Majesty," Prince Cimmeris purred.

"Good evening," Annie awkwardly responded, her voice hoarse from her irritated throat and going so long without talking.

"I hope you are feeling better. I have terribly missed our awkward group dinner dates chaperoned by your sisters," Prince Cimmeris joked.

Annie spluttered out a laugh.

"How very inconsiderate of me to be denying you of such pleasure," Annie mocked.

The shameless flirt of a Prince offered the Queen a devious smile that made butterflies swirl around her stomach.

"What a shame indeed," the Prince replied. "Never mind, I have come up with a way that you can make it up to me," the Prince quirked his eyebrows.

*'Goddess above, I do not have the strength for anything he has in mind, especially not if he is suggesting what I think he is ...'*

"A game of cards!" Cimmeris announced.

Annie burst out a surprised laugh that made her cringe as her headache intensified. She closed her eyes for a moment and took a few slow breaths until the pain became manageable again.

"Are you alright Annie? Would you like me to summon the healer?" Prince Cimmeris asked, his eyes full of concern, the rare tender exchange warming Annie's heart.

"I will be fine, thank you. Sadly, this is not the first time my body has been through this much damage, and I doubt it will be the last," Annie attempted to joke, offering a small tense smile.

"It was very noble of you Annie, to attempt such an impossible task to try and restore peace to your Kingdom," Cimmeris complimented her.

"Thank you," Annie replied, feeling her cheeks flush and internally cursing herself for it.

The Prince chuckled quietly. "I concede playing cards against you would not be much of a challenge in your current state. So, I will let you off this once."

"How very gracious of you," Annie drawled, rolling her eyes.

"I think so!" Cimmeris replied with a wink. "I should let you rest my Queen, but before I leave, I want you to know that I have been praying to the Goddess for you. I hope you feel better soon," Cimmeris finished, not waiting to hear Annie's response before disappearing into the shadows.

Annie felt like a giddy schoolgirl.

*'Goddess above, he has been thinking of me! Perhaps there is more to Cimmeris than superficial flattery and bravado...*

*'A future with him by my side could possibly be the greatest adventure I could ever imagine. A Prince shrouded in mystery who could make me smile even on my darkest of days.'*

# Queen Annalyse of

# Quillencia

After another restless night of frequent interruptions from the healers, Annie was cleared to return to her palace suite on the condition that she did not overexert herself.

After reluctantly accepting the Head Healer's offer to replenish her strength with her healing gifting, Annie felt a great deal better. But as all magic had a cost, she knew that the energy she gained from the healer's gifting would cost the healer her own energy, which filled Annie with feelings of guilt. The healer brushed her concerns aside, reassuring her that healing others was her life calling and by helping the Queen, she was by extension helping the whole Kingdom. After that, Annie knew she had no choice but to accept the healer's kind offer.

The day after next, Annie was scheduled to be married before the entire Kingdom and neighboring allied Kingdoms' delegates. There was far too much to be done for Annie to remain on bed rest, so she had asked Lady Margarette to arrange for all her private engagements that day to be moved to her suite, no matter how unorthodox.

Despite her renewed energy, Annie felt as though she had aged another several years over the last few days. Her normally luscious locks had lost their lustre and shine despite the treatments Lady Margarette had applied to her hair that morning.

Annie was still torn in her decision as to who to ask to be her King. The fact that her choice was now down to two Princes should have made the choice easier but the more she got to know each of the suitors, the more difficult her decision became.

*'Just think of it like choosing a dessert that you get to enjoy for the rest of your life,' Anastasia had once told her. Only that it isn't nearly that simple... Whomever I chose will greatly impact the future of my Kingdom and influence the children I bear. No pressure at all...'*

A knock came at the door and Lady Margarette went to answer it. Annie continued to sip on her energy boosting, healing tea in between forcing herself to nibble on a pastry. Her appetite had still not returned.

Alecia and Anastasia entered the suite and joined Annie in her sitting room for breakfast.

"Good morning," Anastasia chimed, clearly relieved to see her twin out of the infirmary.

"Good morning," Annie smiled back at both of her sisters.

"How are you feeling?" Alecia asked, all business.

"A lot better thanks to the Head Healer, but my head is still throbbing" Annie complained.

"Well, drink your healing tonic, we have a big couple of days ahead of us," Alecia reminded Annie unnecessarily.

"Yes, yes... Tell me something I don't know," Annie mumbled.

"Is that sass I detect sister? I am so proud!" Anastasia cheered.

"Speaking of things, you don't know..." Alecia began, attracting Annie's immediate full attention, as she lounged in one of the other sitting room chairs.

Anastasia elected to do the same before helping herself to a pastry from the platter laid out before Annie.

"What did you do Alecia?" Annie moaned, resting her head in her hands.

"First of all, I did what needed to be done. Secondly, you should be thanking me for solving one of your biggest headaches," Alecia chimed over-confidently.

"What did you do?" Annie demanded to know, glaring at her sister.

"I sentenced the High Priestess to death for treason, for inciting civil unrest, for attempting to blackmail the Queen and for inadvertently attempting to cause great harm to you." Alecia quickly stated as if she were reciting from a menu rather than a list of crimes.

"You what?!" Annie bellowed, rising on unsteady feet.

"I did what needed to be done," Alecia reiterated, leaning back further in her chair, smirking at her sister in challenge. "Knowing how you would react to this news, I had her sentence carried out in private this morning at sunrise, with only the two foreign Princes as witnesses," Alecia declared, not a trace of regret in her voice.

Annie and Anastasia gasped in unison.

"How could you Alecia?" Annie fumed. "You completely abused your power. I never would have approved such a decision!"

"I did what needed to be done," Alecia repeated. "We tried the diplomatic way and all it resulted in was you being backed into a corner and nearly killing yourself in the process," Alecia fumed.

Annie slouched back in her chair and took a few calming breaths.

"How have the people reacted to news of the High Priestess's death?" Annie reluctantly asked, barely louder than a whisper.

Alecia sat upright, clearly proud of herself now that she could tell Annie was starting to come around to her way of thinking.

"I'm glad you asked," the General replied matter-of-factly. "A public announcement was made that the High Priestess died of a heart attack during her stay at the castle. Given her age, I felt it a plausible excuse," Alecia declared. "The protestors were initially reluctant to accept the announcement but as Esmerelda and Ryan have done such a good job singing your praise in the streets, the protests have stopped, though for how long I cannot be certain."

"Well praise the Goddess for small mercies... Do I want to know how she actually died?" Annie dared ask.

"Probably not... But I can promise that it was quick and *relatively* painless, despite what she deserved. Her body has been delivered back into the care of the city temple's Priestesses to bury in the cemetery," Alecia concluded.

"Very well..." Annie replied reluctantly, rubbing her temple to try and ease some of the gathered tension. "Do you have any more dramatic, potentially life altering news I should know about before I attend to my first scheduled appointment of the day?" Annie asked, though she hoped with all her might that the worst of the news was over.

It was Anastasia who responded this time.

"Regular communications with the Kingdom of Stanthorpe have gone uncharacteristically quiet," Anastasia mentioned uneasily. "We are unsure if this is due to your impending marriage, or as a result of the recent civil unrest. We will keep attempting to reopen communications with them. Maintaining alliances is one of our highest priorities."

"Thank you, Anastasia," Annie commented before pausing to consider the possible predicament. "Can you please schedule a diplomatic visit to Stanthorpe after peace has been restored to our city? I am sure the lack of communication is likely due to a misunderstanding but maintaining our diplomatic relationships as you say, is of the highest priority."

"Hopefully Sir Igneous hasn't died of an overly inflated ego by the time we arrive," Alecia teased, trying to break the tension. "I would like to see if his swordsmanship is as good as he claims," Alecia responded with a wink.

Anastasia rolled her eyes. "You would," she muttered, earning a laugh from Annie.

Another knock came at the door, and Annie nodded towards her Lady's Maid to let her guest in.

"Introducing Queen Ocea of the Isle of Treseme," Lady Margarette announced.

Annie quickly brushed her mouth to clear any remaining crumbs and checked that her hair was still acceptably arranged in the tableside mirror, before rising from her chair and crossing the room to greet her guest. Alecia and Anastasia quickly rose from their chairs to do the same.

A moment later, an elegant woman in her mid-fifties, wearing a flowing silk, turquoise gown regally entered the suite. A crown of sea pearls and delicate shells perched atop her perfectly curled sandy blond hair. Her eyes were the color of the ocean during a raging storm.

"Queen Ocea, welcome to Alearia. What a pleasant surprise this is," Queen Annie greeted her guest with a shallow bow.

Princesses Alecia and Anastasia curtsied for the guest.

"Good morning. Queen Annalyse, is it? The Alearian royals change so frequently I find it hard to keep track. I do apologize," the Isle of Treseme Queen smiled sweetly.

*'Son of a Goddess! This meeting is off to a great start...'*

"Queen Annie, if you don't mind. Queen Annalyse of Quillencia is my Grandmother. All of my close allies and family address me as Annie," Annie responded equally as sweetly.

"How… quaint," the foreign Queen responded simply. "Would you care to take a walk in the gardens? They are quite beautiful in the morning sun," Queen Ocea responded.

"It would be my pleasure," Annie replied, leaving the room and her sisters behind, feeling as though she had just fed herself to a wolf.

The two Queens walked in uncomfortable silence through the castle and out into the early morning sun shining blissfully over the hedge maze and rose gardens. Annie led the way, meandering through the rose hedges leading towards the chair beside the fountain, gesturing for the Queen to take a seat.

"Your gown is absolutely stunning, Queen Ocea," Annie complimented the Queen, attempting to break the awkward silence.

"Thank you. Our tailors use only the highest quality fabric on the Isle," Queen Ocea commented as she surveyed the Alearian Queen's plain day gown in comparison.

"I was only saying to Prince Liquire the other day that I would love to visit the Isle of Treseme one day. It sounds magical," Annie stated pleasantly.

"Yes, it is..." Queen Ocea replied, looking down her nose at the young Alearian Queen. "Let us not waste a moment more of each other's time, shall we?" the foreign Queen declared.

Annie nodded her head shallowly, unsure of how to respond to the very direct Queen.

"We have travelled a great distance to attend the wedding of our allied Kingdom," Queen Ocea relayed, "only to arrive to find out that our Prince has not yet been declared your intended..."

Annie almost gaped in shock at the Queen's bluntness, but she attempted to remain as composed as possible despite her suddenly elevated heart rate.

"Firstly, I would like to thank you," Annie began, "for traveling all this way. You honor our Kingdom with your visit. I am sure you can appreciate that after the former Alearian King and Queen passed, my coronation had to be brought forward earlier than was initially planned. Thus, my wedding has been brought forward earlier than initially planned also."

*'I don't know if honesty is the right approach in this scenario but it's the best way, I know...'*

The Isle Queen looked down her nose at the Alearian Queen: "Kingdom and duty always come first. An important part of being a Queen is learning to be adaptable. I had great respect for your parents, which is the only reason I agreed to make this visit. But may I give you some advice?" Queen Ocea offered.

Annie nodded, unsure what else to do.

"If you are going to remain Queen then you need to develop some backbone quickly. You are royalty, you do not have the luxury of time," the foreign Queen stated matter-of-factly. "Every move you make is scrutinized by not only your own people, but the entire realm. You do not have the novelty of taking time to court a prospective husband, and to waste a suitor's time is equally disrespectful. I am unsure why you were not available to greet us upon our arrival, but not to do so was equally rude and disrespectful. If we are to maintain our alliance, then you need to start acting like a Queen," Queen Ocea warned.

"Thank you, Your Majesty," Annie replied tight-lipped, "for your thoughts. However, the fact that I am taking my time in choosing a husband shows that I am taking my responsibilities seriously. I need to know that I am making the right decision for my Kingdom as well as myself. I will not be manipulated into choosing a King until I am ready. I will not justify my absence yesterday because as Queen I do not have to. But I do promise that it was unavoidable, as I am sure your son will attest to," Annie declared, straightening her back.

The Isle of Treseme Queen gave the Alearian Monarch a wicked smile, her right eyebrow raised. Her body language relaxing, clearing pleased with Annie's response though Annie didn't have the faintest idea why.

"I do believe I may have underestimated you Queen Annie," The Queen declared. "Forgive me for my rudeness earlier, but I needed to know what you were made of. My son is obviously smitten with you and I wanted to make sure you were worthy of him and our alliance. I believe we will get along just fine," Queen Ocea declared now with a warm sincere smile.

Gobsmacked, Annie attempted to hide her shock.

"Thank you, Queen Ocea," Annie replied confidently, "I believe we will too."

*'Holy Goddess, what just happened?'*

# Princess Anastasia

Queen Ocea escorted Queen Annie back to her suite, and the pair of them were conversing like old friends, much to Anastasia's shock.

*'How on earth did Annie win her over?'*

"Thank you for an enlightening walk, Queen Annie. I look forward to maintaining our alliance with Alearia, hopefully for many generations to come," Queen Ocea replied warmly as she farewelled the Alearian Queen and made her exit.

Annie collapsed into a chair by the hearth, a mixture of confusion and happiness painted across her face.

"What did the Queen of the Isle want to talk about? What was she like? Was she as intimidating as she seemed?" Anastasia asked eagerly.

Anastasia had remained in the Queen's suite the entire time that Annie was out, awaiting her return to find out all the gossip. Alecia, who assured Anastasia she had better things to do with her time than wait around, had left straight after Annie did.

A great smile spread across Annie's face as she turned to face her twin, completely speechless.

"So? Don't keep me in suspense! How did your conversation with the Queen go?" Anastasia asked excitedly.

Annie looked at her twin in awe, "she was exactly like my old mentor, Lily. I adore her!"

"What?!" Anastasia replied gobsmacked.

"Her intimidating, tyrant impression was all an act! She is an incredible Queen," Annie honestly recounted. "She was testing me. Judging from her statement regarding our continued alliance, I guess I passed." Annie relaxed back into her chair after helping herself to a pastry, her appetite having finally returned.

"Does that make your decision on selecting a husband any easier?" Anastasia asked, intrigued.

"I think it might..." Annie replied, amazed by her response.

44

# *Queen Annalyse of Alearia*

The next day following breakfast with the two suitors, Annie had her final wedding dress fitting. Annie had only permitted her grandmother, the Queen of Quillencia, and her Lady's Maid to attend the fitting, wanting to keep the dress a surprise for her sisters.

*'I can't believe that tomorrow I will be a married woman and Alearia will have a new King! Today I must choose the man I am to spend the rest of my life with. Goddess, I pray that I am making the right decision.'*

Annie stood before a full-length mirror in her suite, Lady Margarette arranging the long train delicately behind her. The ivory wedding gown with overlaid lace detail had been re-tailored to fit her like a glove. Annie stood in awe at her reflection, completely at a loss for words.

"You look so beautiful my dear," her grandmother replied warmly. "Just like your mother. Nothing would have made her happier than to see her beloved daughter wearing her own gown on the happiest day of her life."

Annie looked at her grandmother, who now stood beside her, staring back at Annie's reflection in the mirror.

"Thank you, Grandmother. I just wish she could have been here with me," Annie spoke softly, "I miss her."

Queen Annalyse of Quillencia turned to her granddaughter, Annie doing the same, so they were now facing each other.

"Your mother never left you Annie. Amealiana and Lily are with you in here, where it counts," the Queen spoke wisely, placing her hand over her granddaughter's heart.

Annie smiled warmly in return, her eyes watering. The two royals warmly embraced, silent tears of remembrance trickling down their faces.

"I love you, Grandmother," Annie whispered quietly to the Quillencian Matriarch.

"I love you too Annie, more than you could ever know."

Following the dress fitting, Lady Margarette escorted the Queen to morning tea with Prince Liquire, beside the fountain in the garden. The Queen had arranged for a picnic blanket, various pillows and a platter full of sweet and savoury delicacies to be laid out for the occasion.

Lady Margarette discretely took her leave upon the Prince's arrival.

Butterflies fluttered around Annie's stomach as the handsome Prince of the Isle, dressed in a suit the color of the deepest depths of the ocean, approached from the garden path through the hedge maze towards the rose garden. The gentle trickling of the fountain helped to soothe Annie's nerves.

Annie had chosen a stunning softly flowing, mid-length burgundy day dress for the picnic, complete with a garland of red roses atop her loosely hung, sandy blond curls.

The Prince smiled warmly, taking in the beauty of the young Queen siting upon the pile of pillows near the fountain.

Scented candles twinkled around the edge of the nearby fountain and around the edge of the picnic rug and pillows.

"Greetings Your Majesty," Prince Liquire bowed before taking a seat beside Annie. "You look as beautiful as the roses in your hair, My Lady." Liquire added, taking her hand in his own and pressing a firm kiss to the back of it.

Annie felt herself blush, "thank you Liquire, you look very handsome yourself."

The Prince smiled gently in acknowledgement and then picked up a platter of strawberries dipped in chocolate, offering the plate to the Queen before helping himself.

"Thank you, these look delicious," Annie moaned.

"Not as delicious as you look in that dress, Annie," the Prince brashly commented, causing Annie to turn away with a surprised giggle.

"That is most kind of you to say Liquire, but very cheeky of you indeed," Annie smiled as she felt her cheeks warm further, the Prince laughing in response.

"I heard that you had the privilege of meeting my darling mother," Liquire commented nonchalantly. "I do hope she didn't give you the third degree. She is such a sweetheart once you get to know her."

"I think you mother is fabulous. I must admit, she scared me initially," she replied with a laugh, "but I think I won her over," Annie commented proudly.

"I'm sure you did," Liquire replied warmly.

"Thank you," Annie blushed.

"Annie, could you close your eyes for me for a moment, I have a surprise for you," Liquire gently requested of her.

*'Goddess above...'*

Annie gently closed her eyes, and to her surprise the Prince pressed a delicate kiss to her lips. His natural scent of sea salt and tropical fruit filled Annie's core.

Annie felt herself leaning into Liquire's touch as he continued to kiss her softly but purposefully, his hands now buried into her softly fallen locks. Annie wrapped her own arms around his neck.

After their lips parted the two sat in comfortable silence for a moment, staring into each other's eyes, savouring the moment. Liquire unwound his hands from her hair and took her hands in his own.

"Annie," Liquire spoke gently, his gaze lost in her own.

Annie bit her lip in anticipation, her heart racing.

"Annie," Liquire continued sincerely, "since the first moment I laid eyes on you, I knew I wanted to marry you. You are everything I could ever want in a life partner and more. I know we haven't known each other long but even if you and I had met under different circumstances I know I would still feel the same way."

Annie felt her heart race, so many different emotions washing over her that she had never experienced before.

"You have a kind heart Annie," Liquire continued, "and I love the way that you care so very deeply for your family and your people. You never put yourself first. You are fun to be around. I enjoy the time we share together. Until now, I didn't think I could ever love anyone more than the love I share for the ocean and my family, but I was wrong. I love you Annie. Will you do me the honor of being my Queen and my wife?"

Annie was at a loss for words, and in her heart, she knew she felt the same way.

"It would be my honor Liquire, if you would be my King and my husband," Annie replied before leaning in to kiss the man of her dreams once more.

# Queen Annalyse of Flearia

After an emotional proposal from Prince Liquire, Annie couldn't wait to share the good news with her sisters, but first there was someone else she needed to talk to.

Knocking on the engraved old oak door, Annie waited anxiously, her heart fluttering with happiness whilst guilt pooled in her stomach. Annie wasn't sure how she would manage this conversation, but she knew she owed it to the Prince to offer him a proper explanation face-to-face.

Prince Cimmeris answered the door himself to Annie's surprise.

"What a pleasant surprise, Your Majesty," Cimmeris smiled handsomely.

The sight of Cimmeris was enough to send Annie speechless. She suddenly felt lightheaded, as if the air were stretched too thin.

Annie started to breathe more rapidly, and it was obvious to the Prince that something was not right. He placed an arm around the Queen, ever the gentleman, and led her into the sitting room in his suite.

After assisting Annie into one of the chairs, he knelt at her feet and took her hands in his own.

"What's wrong my dear Annie," he asked gently, genuine concern painted across his face.

Annie could feel the tears slip down her cheeks.

*'Am I making the right decision? My heart feels so conflicted. Why do I feel so upset if I love Liquire? Goddess give me strength...'*

Annie took a deep steadying breath and gazed into the Shadow Prince's deep brown eyes, seeing a world of possibilities, hopes and dreams staring back at her.

*'Trust yourself, trust your heart.'*

"I am sorry Cimmeris, but I cannot marry you. My heart belongs to someone else," Annie explained, and even as the words fell out of her mouth, seeing the Prince knelt before her, she was not absolutely certain they were the truth.

Cimmeris dropped his gaze and pulled away from Annie. He moved to stand before her but could not bear to look at her again. Instead he walked over to the darkest corner of the room and just before he disappeared into the shadows, he softly spoke his final goodbye to the Queen that he adored.

"I am sorry that I was not enough for you, but I wish you every happiness. Goodbye, Queen Annalyse," he spoke sorrowfully, tears glazing his eyes.

"I am so very sorry Cimmeris," Annie began to reply, but he was already gone.

# 46

## *Princess Anastasia*

Anastasia searched the castle grounds and then the castle, floor by floor, trying to locate her twin who had unexpectedly missed a scheduled luncheon with the delegates from the various visiting countries.

Alecia and Anastasia had smoothed over the guests with as much grace and poise as they could summon. Ever the gracious hosts, they had ensured that everyone had enjoyed themselves and passed on their apologies for the Queen's unplanned absence, stating an urgent matter had arisen and she was needed elsewhere.

Prince Liquire had seemed especially troubled by the Queen's absence but had gone along with the Princesses' excuse.

*'Ever the team player,'* Anastasia thought.

Finally reaching the top platform of the highest tower, Anastasia found Annie wrapped in a throw rug, sitting on the concrete floor. Her hair was a mess, and tracks of dried tears stained her cheeks.

Anastasia slid herself down the wall to sit beside her dear sister, pulling her into an embrace with one arm and stroking her hair gently with the other hand. The sisters sat in comfortable silence for some time, Anastasia granting Annie the time she needed to process her thoughts.

Alecia eventually located her two sisters, carrying a basket full of wine and goblets. She set the basket down before the two girls and joined them on the floor in an embrace.

"I take it your decision wasn't as easy as you thought it would be?" Anastasia asked Annie quietly, her head leaning on her twin's shoulder.

"I didn't think it was possible to care for two people so deeply in such a short period of time," Annie softly responded. "But I love Liquire and what I feel for Cimmeris… It is not the same."

"It is a strength, not a weakness, that you feel everything so deeply Annie. It is because of your kind heart," Anastasia responded. "You and Liquire will rule Alearia together with kindness and compassion. You made the right decision," Anastasia reassured her.

"For what it's worth, I completely agree with Tash," Alecia commented, surprising both Annie and Anastasia.

"Liquire will make a good King," Alecia continued, "he has the right amount of daring to balance out your sickeningly sweet demeanor," she stirred Annie, breaking the tension.

Annie elbowed Alecia in retaliation, "not all of us were born with war in our blood, sister," Annie sassily responded, causing Alecia to bark a shocked laugh.

"Well, well, well, little Annie does have some fire in her after all," Alecia elbowed her sister back, before leaning forward to pour the carafe of wine.

"I think it's about time we toast to the soon-to-be bride," Alecia announced, pouring three goblets of wine and handing them out to her sisters, Annie reluctantly accepting hers.

"To the Queen of Alearia," Alecia declared, raising her glass in the air.

A soft afternoon breeze sweeping in from the mountains crept into the tower. "May the fire in your marriage be greater than my gifting," Alecia laughed.

Annie and Anastasia burst into laughter.

Once the sisters had composed themselves, Anastasia toasted more sincerely. "To you, Annie. I hope that your marriage is full of a lifetime of happiness, and that your love grows as deep as the love our parents shared."

"Thank you," Annie replied warmly, before taking a sip of her wine. "I am so blessed to have you both in my life."

After returning to Annie's suite, the three sisters gossiped in front of the hearth for hours. Annie recounted every romantic detail of her proposal.

That night, the three sisters ate and danced at a feast beneath the stars and a thousand suspended tiny flames, celebrating Queen Annie and Prince Liquire's formal announcement of their intention to marry.

The Quillencian Queen and the Queen and King of the Isle of Treseme had been overjoyed by the news. The King and Queen of Shadows Peak respectfully passed on their well wishes to the royal couple, despite their son not being chosen as the future Alearian King. Annie spoke fondly of their son during their brief meeting, and for now their alliance appeared to remain intact.

Anastasia, who held great respect for Prince Cimmeris, offered to attend the Shadow Kingdom following the celebrations, on a diplomatic visit to restrengthen their Kingdom's ties. The idea of a visit to Shadows Peak intrigued Anastasia. The fire-wielding Princess had dreamed of seeing the Shadow Kingdom ever since she was a little girl.

According to the history books, the alps in Shadows Peak were so tall, narrow and clustered together, that a great proportion of the Kingdom was shrouded in shadows at any one time, hence the name Shadows Peak. This allowed the shadow walkers to transport almost anywhere and transport any item instantaneously.

The Princess hoped that she would get the chance to travel by shadow walking during her journey.

# Queen Annalyse of Alearia

Just like the day Annie was born, the sky was dreary and overcast. The thick, dark clouds threatened to break at any moment. An unfavorable wind swept across the mountains. Alearian superstition would declare this a bad sign for the day ahead, but Annie was determined not to let superstition ruin the happiest day of her life.

As the new day dawned, the three Alearian Royals were already busy being preened and pampered in Queen Annie's royal suite. Lady Margarette seemed like she was floating on air, overjoyed to be playing her part in preparing the young Queen for her wedding day.

The castle was all hustle and bustle as guests and servants were all busy preparing for the day's events. Stunning arrangements of white roses had been hung all around the castle and the Alearian city proper's main Goddess Temple, in celebration of the royal wedding.

As was agreed upon at prior war council meetings, security was in place leading from the castle to the Alearian city proper's main Goddess Temple. Fire-wielders, as planned, created a ribbon of fire stretching the entire length of the journey from the castle to the temple as a symbol of Alearia's power. Its beautiful aesthetic and protective qualities were an additional benefit of the flames.

Tens of thousands of Alearians had gathered in the streets along the fire-wielding barriers to catch a glimpse of the happy royal couple.

According to the whispers in the street, many of the townspeople were looking forward to the wedding, though rebels still moved, hidden amongst the masses. General Alecia waited on bated breath to see if and how they would choose to act during the celebrations.

The Alearia Legion, on high alert, monitored all aspects of the city and stood ready to eliminate any sign of dissent before it could develop any further.

Senior Priestess Lavinia, who had conducted Annie's coronation, had been selected by the Queen herself to officiate today's royal wedding and coronation of the King. Disregarding the objections of the Goddess temple sisters. However, as a new High Priestess had yet to be agreed upon by the Sisterhood, there was little they could do to alter the matter.

Back in Annie's suite, each of the three royal sisters were seated before mirrors in the sitting room, having the final touches added to their hair and makeup. Alecia had opted to have her honey blond hair styled in an intricate braid; her favourite ruby encrusted tiara placed upon her head. As General Alecia planned to be on the lookout for any signs of trouble throughout the day, being stationed near the Queen during the celebrations also meant that she was in the perfect position to protect Her Majesty if needed.

Due to her role, Alecia had opted for a layered, burgundy, flowing gown that she could easily conceal weapons beneath. The hem length falling just short of full-length, allowing for easier movement. Alecia was no stranger to elegant shoes and felt confident that she could fight and run in high heels if need be. Therefore, she wore matching burgundy high-heeled shoes encrusted with shimmering jewels. Alecia was a vision of a warrior Princess.

Anastasia's role as Maid of Honor afforded her the freedom to concentrate on her twin and enjoy the day. Anastasia wore a pale blue, luxurious ball gown with loose off-the-shoulder, elegantly billowing chiffon sleeves. Her dress was the perfect fairy-tale dress, featuring embroidered lace detailing, full skirt, and a short train flowing behind her. Anastasia had a diamond encrusted tiara placed upon her head; her sandy blond curls pinned up simply to not detract from the mesmerizing opulence of her gown.

After Anastasia and Alecia were fitted into their gowns, Annie withdrew to her bedroom to be assisted into her wedding gown by Lady Margarette. Annie's sandy blond hair hung in lovely flowing curls, with the late Queen Amealiana's crown placed upon her head. As the doors to Annie's bedroom were opened to reveal her gown to her sisters, Anastasia released a surprised cry.

"You look absolutely beautiful Annie, mother would be so proud to see you in her gown," Anastasia smiled warmly, tearing up.

Annie looked a vision in her mother's billowing ivory wedding gown. The lace detailing added a romantic touch to the dress, a long train delicately flowing behind her. The bodice fit the young Queen like a glove. Annie wore her mother's crown and the heart-shaped sapphire earrings gifted to her, and Lily's family heirloom necklace.

Alecia walked over to her sister with a look that Annie could not quite pick.

"You look just like mother did on her wedding day," Alecia spoke in awe, standing before her sister. "I have admired the portrait of mother on her wedding day regularly since her passing. It is as though you have brought her painting to life. Seeing you standing before me is like seeing a glimpse into our mother's life before we were born."

Annie choked up, and she could feel the tears in her eyes welling.

"Thank you, Alecia. Thank you, Tash. I am so glad you love it. I was so excited to show you but also terrified that you would hate me for wearing it," Annie confessed nervously.

Anastasia walked over to her sister and held her in a warm embrace, Alecia joining her.

"Never apologize," Anastasia reassured her, "for wanting to include our mother in your special day. Our mother's light shines brightly through you and I never want you to feel afraid to let that light shine."

The tears she had been trying to hold back now spilled over entirely as Annie embraced her two sisters. The three siblings stood hugging for a moment longer before a knock came from the door and in walked Queen Annalyse of Quillencia, adorned in an exquisite gown of Quillencian emerald green and gold.

"My dear Annie," the Quillencian Queen exclaimed, embracing her granddaughter in greeting, "you look a vision!"

"Thank you, Grandmother," Annie replied fondly.

The Quillencian Queen took a step back to appraise her two other granddaughters' dresses. "I see you have both showed some restraint ladies. How gracious of you to not want to outshine the bride on her wedding day."

Anastasia beamed whilst Alecia smiled wickedly with delight.

"I assure you Grandmother," Alecia drawled, "that this drab gown is purely for practicality's sake," she teased, patting the concealed daggers strapped to her thighs.

"I must say," the elderly Queen replied, "that I am surprised even you would sacrifice fashion for practicality," the Queen teased in return, earning a wicked grin from the General.

"What can I say, I am full of surprises."

In front of the stables, Annie and the Quillencian Queen were assisted into a carriage to make their way to the temple. Annie's sisters rode confidently on horseback, with Alecia in front, and Anastasia behind her carriage.

The fire-wielding sisters suspended opulent flames above the procession, morphing from a crown, then into the image of the royal family's crest before morphing back into a crown. Whilst Annie had originally wanted to travel on horseback, she did not want to risk damaging her mother's dress, so she agreed to ride in the carriage.

The crowd cheered with excitement as the people caught their first glimpse of the procession approaching the now open castle gates. Queen Annie waved regally to the townspeople as they weaved their way through the city proper from the castle to the temple seamlessly; the barrier of fire provided by the Alearian Legion helping to control the crowd and achieving its goal in protecting the Queen. The townspeople waved flowers and applauded the royal procession as they passed.

Rounding the final corner before the temple, beholding the elegant colosseum-like structure, Annie felt her nerves suddenly rushing back. Her palms began sweating as her impending marriage suddenly felt real. Annie felt her heart rate quicken, and attempted to remain composed, though she was sure that the people would see right through her fake smiles and seemingly confident demeanor.

*"Oh my Goddess, what am I doing? I feel like a country girl playing dress up. I do not feel worthy to be a Queen, how can I possibly crown a new King?"* Annie's heart rate quickened further, and she turned to her grandmother for reassurance.

Queen Annalyse of Quillencia took her granddaughter's hand and gave it a gentle reassuring squeeze.

"You can do this Annie," she whispered so that only Annie and the wind whisperers could hear. "You are about to marry the man you love — a love that is rare amongst royals. You must treasure this love and trust in it with all your soul. You and Liquire will rule this Kingdom with kind hearts and compassion. Nothing could make me prouder of you."

Annie swallowed down the sob she felt catching in her throat and squeezed her grandmother's hand in return.

"Thank you," was her only reply.

As the carriage pulled up in front of the packed temple, Anastasia and Alecia let their flames dissipate as they unsaddled from their horses. With a quick bow to the Queens, Alecia made her way up the temple aisle to resume her place in the front pew by the temple alter.

Thousands of white rose petals had been scattered along the aisle to guide the Queen's way to her destiny. A choir of children began singing the hymns of the Goddess in perfect harmony. Anastasia led the way down the aisle, thousands of eyes upon her, the audience not wanting to miss a moment of the historic event.

Annie and her grandmother were assisted to climb down from the carriage, and the two Queens began to elegantly walk up the temple stairs and then arm-in-arm down the center aisle, guided by the harmonious music.

The main city temple was like nothing the young Queen had ever seen. The walls stood thirty feet tall with images of the Goddess in her various forms, painted intricately upon the ceiling. Inside the colosseum-like temple, a thousand nobles and royal visiting dignitaries stood from their seats in the pews to watch the Alearian Queen make her entrance, escorted by her grandmother. At the end of each of the center aisle pews, chains of white roses hung, guiding the way for the Queens.

Walking down the aisle, Annie felt the weight of the Kingdom upon her shoulders, but raising her head, she caught her first glimpse of the Prince waiting for her at the altar. Prince Liquire was dressed in a silk suit, the color once more resembling the deepest depths of the ocean, a royal sash hung across his chest. His medals of valor pinned upon his breast pocket.

Annie felt her anxiety wash away as she blocked out the site of the overwhelming number of guests and focused on the man before her that had stolen her heart in such a short period of time. Annie knew in that moment, that she was following her Goddess given destiny.

A Queen's fate, to marry the man she loved. Together they would thrive forevermore. A new reign to reunite a kingdom, dark and twisted.

*'As a healer and a gifted Sage, I feel things more strongly than most. But I am also able to see the rhyme and reason for everything that happens. Everyone assumes I can cope with anything. But the truth is, I feel as though my heart cannot take much more stress.*

*'I feel as though I am not fit to be Queen, but then I look upon Liquire and I see hope. I see the future we will build together. Together with Liquire, I feel as though anything is possible.'*

Approaching the alter, Annie's grandmother took the young Queen's right hand and joined it with Liquire's left. Then, taking a ribbon she was handed from Anastasia, the Quillencian Queen gently tied the royal couple's hands together as a symbol of the Goddess given bond they would always share.

Senior Priestess Lavinia, who led the ceremony, raised her hands toward the Goddess in praise, and the temple guests resumed their seats in the pews. Annie felt herself trembling from the adrenaline pulsing through her veins, but Liquire squeezed her hand reassuringly, drawing her back to the present and calming her final nerves.

"Greetings esteemed guests and royal dignitaries," the Senior Priestess began to announce. "We are gathered here before our mighty Goddess, to witness the blessed union of Queen Annalyse Brandistone of Alearia and Prince Liquire Ocea of the Isle of Treseme. After the union is conducted, Prince Liquire Ocea will declare his vows to serve our Queen and country faithfully as King of Alearia. For family and Kingdom," the Priestess declared.

"For family and Kingdom," the assembly echoed as one voice.

"Holy Goddess, we ask your blessing upon this royal union. We pray that together, Annalyse and Liquire, will become one soul, one heart, and one mind, reflective of your teachings and values. May they be a continual strength to each other throughout their long life together. We pray that the royal couple are a continued blessing to each other and to our mighty Kingdom." The Priestess unwound the couple's ribbon and directed them to face each other.

"The rings, please?" The Priestess asked Anastasia, who passed the Priestess a gold box with matching wedding bands inside.

Prince Liquire then took his bride's ring in his fingers, and as he slipped Annie's wedding band gently upon her ring finger, he recited his vows.

"Queen Annalyse, I vow to you and Alearia that we will be one soul, one mind, one heart. I promise to love you unconditionally and to support you always, in sickness and in health. I will not fail you Annie, for I love you and I always will. I vow to be the husband that you deserve," Liquire promised his bride.

Annie felt her heart melt, and her tears resurface.

*'I had always dreamed of falling in love and finding my perfect partner, and here he is. Standing before me, this perfect gentleman is declaring his love for me before a crowd of strangers.'*

Annie mirrored Liquire's actions, slipping the remaining wedding band upon Liquire's ring finger and reciting her vows.

"Prince Liquire, I promise to love you and our Kingdom with all that I am. As your wife, I will give you my whole heart and soul. I will stand by you through triumphs and heartache. I vow to be honest with you always, and I place my eternal trust in you. I promise to love you unconditionally. I will not fail you Liquire, for I love you too," Annie sincerely vowed.

The guests applauded the happy couple and as the applause began to soften, the Priestess continued.

"Prince Liquire Ocea," Senior Priestess Lavinia instructed, "please kneel before your people and declare your coronation vows."

Anastasia carefully passed the Priestess former King Titian Brandistone's ceremonial crown, and the Priestess moved to stand alongside the Prince. Prince Liquire had dropped to one knee upon the altar and projected his voice clearly to the crowd.

"I, Liquire Ocea, wholly declare my loyalty to the Kingdom of Alearia. Through this union, our Kingdoms are now bound in an everlasting alliance. I vow to serve the people of Alearia with all my heart and soul. I vow to rule alongside Queen Annalyse of Alearia with kindness and compassion. I vow to uphold the values of this mighty Kingdom and of the Goddess who rules over the entire realm. I pledge my loyalty to the Alearian Queen, and I vow to uphold her commands and support her through every decision as your new King. For family and Kingdom," Liquire strongly declared.

"For family and Kingdom," the crowd echoed.

The Senior Priestess lifted the crown and gently placed it atop Liquire's brow. "By the power granted to me by our almighty Goddess," Senior Priestess Lavinia announced, "I now declare you, King Liquire Ocea Brandistone of the Kingdom of Alearia."

The Senior Priestess gestured for King Liquire to rise and once more bound the happy couple's hands together with the ribbon.

"By the power bestowed upon me by the almighty Goddess, I now declare you husband and wife," the Senior Priestess declared. "All rise, as I present our new rulers, Queen Annalyse Brandistone and her husband, King Liquire Ocea Brandistone."

Annie felt jubilation flow through her as the crowd rose to their feet to bow before their Queen and King, declaring: "all hail Queen Annalyse! All hail King Liquire!"

Liquire and Annalyse turned to face each other and without waiting to be directed, they kissed each other blissfully as their heart and souls intertwined as one.

# Epilogue

# General Alecia

The royal celebrations continued long into the night. Music and dancing filled the streets; all whispers of dissent seemingly overshadowed by the joy the people felt as they celebrated their new King and Queen's wedding day. However, Alecia ordered the Legion guards to remain on high alert as the celebrations continued in the streets.

Queen and King Brandistone were dancing arm-in-arm beneath a thousand glittering stars in the palace garden, having briefly escaped the castle ballroom reception to savor the final moments of the evening alone in private celebration.

Alecia watched on from the shadows as the two royals were lost in each other's gaze, treasuring their newfound love, the most sacred of gifts a person could give and receive.

The sky had cleared, and the clouds threatening to burst earlier in the day were a long-forgotten memory.

Alecia allowed herself a moment's reprieve from her security duties as she turned to walk back into the ballroom, but was intercepted by Sir Tomlin, a tight grim look upon his face.

"I have just received disturbing correspondence via a raven. We need to talk."

Taking in his appearance and tone, Alecia redirected Sir Tomlin away from the party and out of ear shot of the guests and newlyweds.

Once safely within the confines of the war council chamber, where not even the wind whisperers could overhear, Alecia perched upon the edge of the council table, her attention squarely upon the knight.

"What's happened?" Alecia demanded.

Her heart in her chest, Alecia feared the worst.

She waited anxiously to hear the number of casualties she was sure to be delivered in his report.

"General, there has been an attack," Tomlin informed her, suddenly pale, his expression grave.

"Where?" Alecia asked impatiently.

"The southern watchtower along the border between Stanthorpe and Alearia. We received word via raven. One of the Legion Captains sent it before the battle..."

"Give it to me," Alecia declared, snatching the note anxiously from Tomlin's right hand.

The note read:

### *HIGHLY CLASSIFIED INFORMATION*

*Prepare the city for siege.*
*The entire land Legion of Stanthorpe is approaching our Kingdom's border. Their battle flags are flying.*
*Our entire watchtower Legion will be dead within the hour.*
*Tell my wife and children that I love them,*
*Captain L. Reynolds, Southern Watchtower*

*A Queen's Fate*

# Acknowledgements

To the readers and my fellow creatives, thank you for taking this journey with me, I couldn't do this without you. Thank you for supporting me as an Indie author.

To my husband Joel and my daughter Lily, thank you for believing in me. Thank you for your patience through all the highs and lows of getting this book finished. Thank you for valuing my dreams and pushing me to fulfil them. I could not have finished this book without your support. I love you.

Thank you to my family. Clare, Josh, Marie, Mum, and Dad, thank you for your continuous support and encouragement.

Thank you to my friends new and old, who have encouraged me along the way.

Thank you to the amazing Chloe Hodge, my friend and copy editor. I appreciate all your help in transforming this book into a little slice of magic.

To the amazing bookstagram community and my remarkable Perth squad of book loving friends, thank you for supporting me through every stage of the writing process. Thank you for being my cheerleaders. I am so lucky to have you all as friends. Thank you to my beta readers, without your feedback, this book would not be what it is.

To my fellow Authors, particularly Bec, Helen, Chloe and Tenielle, thank you for your friendship and the supportive role you have all played in helping me along my author journey.

Thank you to the bookstores, markets, pop-up shops, home businesses, candle makers, book merch creators and book lovers, for taking a chance on me. Your support means the world to me.

Thank you to Beth Gilbert for designing the new incredible covers for this series.

Thank you to Jess, for adding the proofreading sprinkles to this amazing cupcake of a book.

I encourage anyone out there who has a dream on their hearts that has yet to be fulfilled, get out there! Dream big! You and your dreams are worth it. Do what makes you happy and live your best life.

# About the Author

Nattie Kate Mason is an independent self-published author from Australia. Mum to the gorgeous Lily and wife to supportive husband Joel. Nattie works as a nurse in her day job, but her passions are reading and writing. Nattie has traveled around Australia with her little family of three and their pets, living in various towns and cities for various periods at a time. Life is never dull for Nattie and her unique little family. Nature, life and reading help to inspire Nattie's creative side. You will often find her reading a good book outdoors, enjoying the peace and quiet, drinking an endless amount of exotic tea.

Nattie's books can be found in many independent bookstores throughout the Perth region, through most online retailers or via her website.

# *Titles by Nattie Kate Mason*

The Crowning young adult fantasy series:

The Crowning

A Queen's Fate

Heart of a Crown

Chapter Books by Nattie Kate:

Lily Rose and the Pearl Crown

Lily Rose and the Enchanted Fairy Garden

Visit nattiekatemason.com to stay up to date on the latest new releases from this author.

Follow Nattie on social media

IG/FB: @nattie.kate.mason.writer